Tribute

C.S. Kading & Tony Fuentes

SandDancer Publications

Copyright © 2026 by C.S. Kading & Tony Fuentes

All rights reserved.

No part of this publication may be reproduced, distributed, or transmitted in any form or by any means, including photocopying, recording, or other electronic or mechanical methods, without the prior written permission of the publisher, except as permitted by U.S. copyright law. For permission requests, contact info@sanddancer.pub

The story, all names, characters, and incidents portrayed in this production are fictitious. No identification with actual persons (living or deceased), places, buildings, and products is intended or should be inferred.

Book Cover by StoryGraphixPlus

Editor Finley Hislop

Digital ISBN: 979-8-9879820-6-8

Paperback ISBN: 979-8-9879820-5-1

First edition 2026

To Julie and Sheri and the rest of the Spicy Test Kitchen.

As I am on the subject of thunderstorms, I may as well here mention the Scholomance, or school supposed to exist somewhere in the heart of the mountains, and where all the secrets of nature, the language of animals, and all imaginable magic spells and charms are taught by the devil in person. Only ten scholars are admitted at a time, and when the course of learning has expired and nine of them are released to return to their homes, the tenth scholar is detained by the devil as payment, and mounted upon an Ismeju (dragon) he becomes henceforward the devil's aide-de-camp, and assists him in 'making the weather,' that is to say, preparing the thunderbolts.

Gerard, E. (Emily). "Transylvanian Superstitions." *The Nineteenth Century*, vol. 18, July–December 1885, pp. 130–150

Contents

		IX
1.	Ilena	1
2.	Smoke and Mirrors	13
3.	Pretty Liars	29
4.	Arrival	39
5.	Vino	51
6.	Sunshine	61
7.	Dragons	73
8.	Compulsion	83
9.	Until You Burn	97
10.	The Stacks	107
11.	Ozone and Bad Decisions	121
12.	Silver and Shame	139
13.	Blood and Fire	153
14.	Fall of Gods	169

15.	Witness	179
16.	Into the Dark	191
17.	The Gallery	205
18.	Dragon Seed	215
19.	Midnight Approaches	227
20.	The Binding	239
21.	Blood and Ash	251
22.	Fugitives	267
23.	The Choice	281
24.	Reckoning	291
25.	What Remains	303
Epilogue		313
Acknowledgements		321
About the authors		323
Also by		325

Ilena

THE RAIN WAS SUPPOSED to be gentle.

Instead, I was killing a man's crops and trying not to panic.

"Fräulein, bitte..." Herr Müller's voice cracked as he watched ice crystals form on his cabbage leaves. "You said you could..."

"I know what I said." I bit the words out, hands extended toward the sky, sweat running down my back despite the cold I'd accidentally conjured. The clouds above his farm roiled, dark and pregnant with sleet instead of the soft spring rain he'd paid for.

Well, was *supposed* to pay for.

Eighteen-hundred Deutschmarks for a simple rain job. Enough to cover this week's rent and maybe—*maybe*—a meal that wasn't day-old bread and whatever I could shoplift from the corner market. Easy money. I'd done this a hundred times.

Except my hands were shaking, and the magic tasted wrong in my mouth—metallic, sharp, like the moment before that awful event at The Wall...

No. Don't think about The Wall.

I gritted my teeth and reached deeper, trying to warm the system and to gentle the precipitation. The pressure in my skull built, that familiar ache behind my eyes that meant I was pushing too hard, reaching too far. The vodka I'd had for breakfast wasn't helping.

"Please," Müller whispered.

Please. Like I was doing this on purpose. Like I hadn't spent the last year terrified of my own gods-damned power.

I closed my eyes. Breathed. Found the thread of the storm—*my* storm, the one I'd called—and pulled. Gently. Like coaxing a scared animal. Like I gave a shit about cabbage.

The temperature rose. Slowly. The ice on the leaves began to melt.

The rain that followed was hardly gentle, but at least it wouldn't destroy his crop. Probably.

I lowered my hands and opened my eyes. The world tilted slightly—magic hangover mixing with the regular kind. I bent my knees and braced to keep from swaying.

Müller stared at his field, rain soaking through his jacket. He was maybe sixty, weathered and bent, the kind of man who'd worked this land his whole life and would die on it. The kind of man who'd scraped together eighteen hundred marks because his crops were dying and weather-workers didn't come cheap.

The kind of man who'd now seen exactly how unreliable I was.

"It's raining," he said finally.

"That's generally what happens when you pay for rain." My voice came out harsher than I meant. I softened it. "Your cabbages will be fine, Herr Müller."

He looked at me then, really looked, and I saw the moment he decided I wasn't worth the full price. I'd seen that look before. Lately, I'd been seeing it a lot.

"Twelve hundred," he said.

I should have argued. Should have pointed out that his crops were getting the water they needed, that the contract said eighteen hundred, that I'd *done the job*.

But I'd fucked it up again.

I sighed and held out my hand.

He counted out the marks slowly, each bill a small judgment. When he reached twelve hundred, he stopped and closed his weathered fingers around the rest.

"For the... trouble," he said.

The trouble of almost killing your livelihood, you mean.

"Generous," I said flatly, and pocketed the money.

He nodded once and turned back toward his farmhouse, shoulders hunched against the rain. My rain. The rain that should have been easy and wasn't, because nothing was easy anymore.

I stood there like an idiot, getting soaked, watching him go. Twelve hundred marks. Not enough for rent. Not enough for groceries. Just enough to keep me one week ahead of eviction instead of two.

The rain picked up, matching my mood.

"La naiba," I muttered, and turned toward the road where I'd left my bicycle. A bicycle. In 1984. Because my car had been repossessed three months ago, along with everything else I'd been stupid enough to think I owned.

I was halfway across the field when I felt it.

A pressure change. Not weather something old and deliberate, pushing against the natural patterns I could always sense. The rain faltered, confused.

I stopped walking.

A raven landed on the fence post ahead of me.

Not unusual. Germany had plenty of ravens. Except this one was too large, too black, and it was staring directly at me with eyes that reflected light like polished glass.

"Oh, you've got to be fucking kidding me," I said.

The raven tilted its head. In its beak, it held a small scroll, sealed with red wax.

I knew that seal. Everyone who'd ever attended the Scholomance knew that seal.

My stomach dropped.

"No." I didn't move. "Absolutely not."

The raven hopped closer along the fence. Water beaded off its feathers in a way that water shouldn't—too perfect, too deliberate. It set the scroll down on the post and stepped back, waiting.

I stared at it. At the seal. At the past I'd tried so hard to outrun.

Eight years. I'd had eight years of freedom after graduation. Eight years to make something of myself, to prove that the outsider from Bucharest could thrive without the Scholomance's shadow hanging over her.

Eight years, and I'd spectacularly fucked it all up.

The summons. It had to be. The Convocation... the gathering where all graduates returned to the Scholomance during the Black Moon, where ten would be chosen by lottery to provide the next year's candidates. Where I'd have to face everyone who remembered me as promising and see what I'd become.

Where I'd have to face *him*.

My hands were shaking again. Not from the magic this time.

I'd known this was coming. The Convocation happened during the Black Moon...the second darkness... the month with two new moons. It was rare. Graduates were summoned back when the Black Moon fell closest to their seven-year mark. Eight years since graduation. Eight years since the trial. Eight years since he looked at me with such hatred that it felt like lightning burning through my chest.

The final trial.

Every graduate's last test before The Devil judged them worthy... or not. Partners sent into the caverns beneath the lake, separated by ancient magic, each forced to navigate their own path through darkness and danger. The trial fed on fear, amplified every weakness, turned the mountain itself against you. You either emerged with your magic intact and your sanity holding, or you didn't emerge at all. The partnership was supposed to be a safeguard. Two magics, two minds, two chances at survival. We'd planned for it, trained together, knew each other's strengths and weaknesses better than we knew our own.

I'd made it through my path in under two hours. Clean. Controlled. Perfect.

Alexi had taken six. When he finally staggered out, he was barely conscious, covered in burns and blood, his magic so raw and chaotic it had taken three faculty members to stabilize him.

And the way he'd looked at me... not relief or gratitude or love. Pure, incandescent hatred. Like I'd been the one who'd nearly killed him.

Eight years, and I still didn't know why.

The raven cawed. Once. Sharp and impatient.

"Yeah, yeah." I walked forward, my boots squelching in the mud. The scroll was dry despite the rain. Of course it was. Magic didn't give a shit about convenience.

I picked it up. The wax seal was warm under my fingers, embossed with the coiled dragon that marked all official Scholomance correspondence. For a moment, I considered not opening it. Considered throwing it in the mud and walking away.

Except you couldn't walk away from the Scholomance. Everyone knew the stories. Miss one summons, you get a second chance. Miss the second, and the Vânători came for you.

The Vânători... *the Hunters.*

I wondered if he was one of them now. If he'd be the one dragging me back if I ran. That seemed like exactly the kind of cruel poetry the universe specialized in.

I broke the seal.

The scroll unrolled itself in my hands—because normal paper was apparently too mundane—and the words appeared in precise, archaic script:

> *Ilena Firan*
>
> *Graduate of the Scholomance, Class of 1976*
>
> *You are hereby summoned to return to the Scholomance beneath Lake Cincis on the night of the Black Moon, the second darkness of May, Year of Our Lord 1984, to fulfill your obligations as a graduate and participate in the Convocation and selection of candidates for the coming year.*
>
> *Failure to appear will result in enforcement measures as outlined in your graduation oath.*
>
> *You have three days.*
>
> *—Stăpânul*

Three days.

I read it again, looking for some loophole, some escape clause. There wasn't one. There never was.

Behind me, Herr Müller's farmhouse door closed with a distant thud. The rain continued to fall, steady now, gentle enough. The job was done. The money was in my pocket. And in three days, I'd be standing in the place I never wanted to return to, surrounded by people who'd known me when I was someone else.

Someone better.

Someone who hadn't killed five people at The Wall because she got greedy and stupid.

The raven cawed again and took flight, its wings cutting through the rain with unnatural silence. I watched it disappear into the gray sky.

"Du-te dracului," I told the empty air, the absent raven, the Scholomance itself.

Go to hell.

But hell, apparently, was going to Lake Cincis. And I had three days to figure out how to face the wreckage of everything I used to be.

I folded the summons and shoved it in my jacket pocket, next to the twelve hundred marks that wouldn't be enough, next to the flask that was already empty, next to all the other failures I carried around like stones.

Then I turned back toward the road, toward my ridiculous bicycle, toward the shitty West Berlin apartment that I'd have to abandon for this.

Three days.

I'd need more vodka.

The apartment was exactly as depressing as I'd left it.

One room. Peeling wallpaper. A mattress on the floor because I'd sold the frame three months ago. A hotplate that worked half the time. A sink full of dishes I'd been meaning to wash for a week.

The window looked out onto a brick wall. Barely functional as a living space.

Home Sweet Home.

A cracked mirror hung by the door—I'd stopped looking at it weeks ago. When I did catch my reflection, I barely recognized the girl staring back: dark hair falling in damp waves around my face, pale skin made more so by exhaustion, eyes rimmed with yesterday's smudged eyeliner that I hadn't bothered to wash off.

I looked like a drowned witch. Appropriate.

I dropped my bag on the floor and pulled out the summons again, smoothing it against the chipped counter as if the words would have changed. They hadn't.

Three days.

I had no money for the train to Romania. I had no car. I had twelve hundred marks, a bicycle, and a rapidly approaching deadline.

I also had no choice.

The vodka bottle in the cupboard was half-full. I poured two fingers into a cracked mug and drank it standing up, looking at the summons.

Eight years ago, I'd left the Scholomance as one of the best graduates they'd produced in decades. The outsider who'd proven she belonged. The weather-worker who could hold three storm systems at once without breaking a sweat. The girl who'd won the heart of...

Don't.

I poured another two fingers.

Eight years ago, he'd looked at me like I'd killed him. And then they took him away, and I never saw him again. Never got to ask what I'd done. Never got to explain—except I didn't know what I'd be explaining, because I didn't *do* anything.

I'd spent the first year trying to find him. Asking other graduates if they'd seen him. Following rumors. Getting nowhere.

I'd spent the second year telling myself I didn't care.

I'd spent the next five proving it by making a name for myself in Germany, taking jobs that paid well and asked few questions, building a reputation as someone you called when you needed weather magic and couldn't afford to fail.

Then came The Wall.

Then came the investigation, the blame, the blacklist. He'd been there then. Wearing the black uniform of an Enforcer, and then I *knew* what he had been doing all that time. Hunting rogue magicians. Enforcing order. Dealing with fuckups who got their clients, and four innocent mortals slain.

Dealing with magicians like me.

I drained the mug and caught my reflection in the window glass. Dark eyes staring back... my grandmother used to say I had witch eyes. *Ochi de vrăjitoare.* She meant it as a compliment. Back when I thought being a witch meant power, not poverty.

If he was at the Convocation, and he would be, everyone came back, or paid a high price for that absence, I'd have to see him. Face whatever hatred was still burning in those storm-gray eyes. Pretend it didn't gut me every time I thought about the way he used to say my name.

Leni.

Soft. Like a prayer. Like I was something precious.

I didn't feel precious anymore. I felt like a girl who'd lost everything and couldn't remember where she'd put it down.

The summons sat on the counter, accusing.

Three days to get to Romania. Three days to figure out what I'd say if I saw him. Three days to prepare for the lottery, for the possibility that I'd be chosen to provide a candidate next year, except how the hell would I do that? I could barely take care of myself.

Three days.

I looked at the vodka bottle. At the empty apartment. Out the window, with its view of nothing.

My fingers found the silver rings I hadn't pawned yet: three thin bands on my right hand, one with a small moonstone. I twisted them, a nervous habit I'd developed after The Wall.

"Fuck it," I said to no one.

If I was going back to the Scholomance, back to the place where everything started and then fell apart, I wasn't going sober.

I picked up the bottle and the summons. I had a train to catch. Eventually. Once I figured out how to pay for it.

But first, I had a bottle to finish.

Smoke and Mirrors

THE BASS WAS SO loud I felt it in my teeth.

SO36 on a Wednesday night, half-empty but still too crowded, too loud, reeking of cigarettes, spilled beer, and desperation. The kind of place where everyone was trying to forget something. I fit right in.

When you go to whorehouses, they always use colored lights to hide imperfections and unsightly diseases. The entire nightclub scene (legal or otherwise) held to the same aesthetics. Hanging lights emitted shades of deep red or shadowy blue. In some clubs, there would be no rhyme or reason to it. The nameless people who ran SO36 knew otherwise. Color was essential for setting the mood. The bar was set alight in red, as if trying to warn patrons who would never listen. The makeshift booths against the walls hid in deep blues to hide deals, drugs, and the occasional sex act. Yet it was the dance floor that drew the most attention. Rapidly changing lights from yellow to green to white lit up the sweaty, writhing bodies as they moved in time to the music.

I pushed through the bodies near the bar, past couples grinding against walls and past the girl crying in the corner while her friend held her hair back. A standard Wednesday in West Berlin. The Wall loomed somewhere beyond these concrete walls, cutting through the city like a jagged scar that wouldn't heal.

Klaus would be upstairs in the DJ booth. He was always upstairs in the DJ booth, assuming he'd shown up at all.

The stairs were sticky. I tried not to think about what with.

A bouncer blocked the landing; shaved head, leather vest, arms like tree trunks. He looked me up and down, unimpressed by my thrift-store aesthetic.

"Closed," he said in accented German.

"I'm looking for Smoke."

"He's working." His tone tried to remain neutral, but I could see that the name set him on edge. He needed a slight push.

"Tell him Frost is here."

The bouncer's expression shifted slightly; everyone in the underground knew those names. Smoke and Frost, the Scholomance failures who'd ended up in Berlin's gutters. He looked at the sixty-mark notes I held up, money I absolutely couldn't spare, and took it with a meaty hand.

"Five minutes."

The booth was cramped, dark except for the glow of equipment I didn't understand. Klaus stood behind the decks, headphones around his neck, a cigarette dangling precariously from his lips. His brown hair was artfully disheveled, which meant he'd spent thirty minutes on it. Dark circles under storm-gray eyes. Leather jacket over a torn Bauhaus shirt. Designer jeans that probably cost more than my rent.

He looked like a beautiful corpse with expensive tastes.

"Lena, *Liebling*," he said without looking up, adjusting something on the mixer. "To what do I owe the pleasure of your lovely presence in this cathedral of sonic desperation?"

"You know why I'm here."

"Do I?" He cued up the next track, fingers moving with the accuracy he only had when he was high. "Perhaps you've come to finally admit that industrial music is the perfect soundtrack to our collective existential crisis. Or maybe..." He looked at me then, pupils like pinpricks. "...you got your summons and came crawling to see if misery still loves company."

The words hit exactly where he'd aimed them. This was Klaus, always knowing exactly where to press.

"Three days," I said flatly.

"I know, darling. We all got summonses. Everyone in our year." He reached for a bottle of something expensive-looking and took a long drink. "The Devil requires our presence. How delightfully ominous."

His smile was wide as he looked at me, his expression playful. If he was worried or afraid, it was hard to say. Smiles... seductive, angry, fearful... were just his way.

"How much do you have saved?"

He laughed, sharp and bitter. "Oh, Lena. Sweet, naïve Lena. What makes you think I have anything saved?"

"Klaus..."

"Four hundred and twenty marks." His voice dropped the performance for a moment. "And I owe my dealer six hundred."

I leaned against the wall, watching him work the decks with muscle memory while his mind was somewhere else entirely. "I have eleven forty."

"Not enough. Not even close." He lit another cigarette with the dying embers of the first. "Berlin to Bucharest is at least twenty-five hundred each. More if we can't get the cheap seats."

"So we need thirty-five hundred thirty marks in three days."

"We need a miracle." He cranked the bass. The booth vibrated. "Or we need to make some terrible decisions quickly."

Through the booth's window, I watched the crowd below moving to his beats. Lost, desperate and beautiful in their surrender to the sound, just like us.

"There is one option," he said, not looking at me.

"What?"

"I know someone. Someone with money. Someone who might..." He stopped. "Never mind."

"Klaus." I reached out to touch his elbow.

He stopped, glanced down at my hand, and offered a reassuring smile.

"I said never mind." He pulled off the headphones completely, letting them hang around his neck like a millstone. "Meet me tomorrow. Noon. Café Kranzler. We'll figure something out."

I knew that look, the one that said he was about to do something spectacularly self-destructive to solve our problem. "What are you planning?"

"Nothing you need to worry about." He turned back to the decks, but his hands were shaking now. "Go home, Lena. You look like death warmed over."

"Charming as always."

"We can't all be pretty." But his smile was sad, broken.

"Please don't do anything dangerous."

He turned back to look at me, holding up his hands in mock defense, and gestured to his face, "And ruin this money-maker? Never!"

I rolled my eyes at him.

The bouncer pounded on the door, "Five minutes are up!"

"Alright, alright!" I yelled back and headed for the door.

"And Lena? When you see him... Alexi... and it destroys you the way we both know it will?" He said as he pulled his headphones back on, "Remember that you're not the only one who got broken by that place. Some of us just wear it better."

I left him there in his red-lit booth, laying down beats for people too drunk to care.

The walk home took an hour. Five kilometers through West Berlin at 2 AM, all shadows and sirens, neon bleeding into puddles of last night's rain. I couldn't afford the U-Bahn, so I walked and thought about Klaus's warning, about someone with money, about what prices we'd pay before we even got to Romania.

By the time I reached Kreuzberg, the district where I lived, my feet hurt and my head was spinning with exhaustion. My building squatted on its corner like it always did, five stories of water-stained concrete and broken dreams. The front door's lock had been broken for three months. This close to The Wall, half the tenants were squatters, anyway.

I climbed four flights that reeked of piss and cumin spice. My door, 3B, had new graffiti. Something about capitalism in angry red letters; at least they were politically aware vandals.

I closed the door behind me and stared at the dank dump that was my domain. Across from the door, a hot plate was balanced on a board across two cinder blocks. The summons sat next to it, where I'd left it, patient as death.

I sat on the mattress and poured vodka into my cracked mug. Three days until the Black Moon. Three days until the Scholomance. Three days until I'd see Alexi again.

Smoke and Frost... and *Storm*.

We'd done this dance before, the three of us. Back when we thought we were invincible, when magic was a possibility instead of a curse, when love was simple and betrayal was unimaginable.

I drank deep and tried not to think about storm-gray eyes—two sets of them now. Klaus and Alexi. My disasters, past and present.

Morning came too soon.

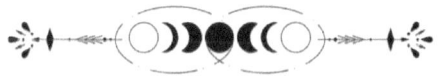

Noon - Café Kranzler

The place tried too hard to be elegant. White tablecloths, gold fixtures, servers in bow ties. An establishment where West Berliners pretended the Wall didn't exist, that we weren't all trapped on an island in the middle of East Germany.

I'd been nursing the same three-mark coffee for thirty minutes. Klaus was late. Around me, the morning crowd went about their lives... business types with newspapers, old women with small dogs, teenagers skipping school. None of them counting down to disaster.

Lucky bastards.

12:27

He came in like a hurricane trying to pretend it was a breeze... oversized coat that cost more than my rent, sunglasses despite the gray day, moving too fast, talking too loud to himself. Or maybe to the ghosts only addicts could see.

"Sorry, sorry, sorry." He collapsed into the chair across from me and didn't take off the sunglasses. "Long night. Longer morning."

"You look worse than yesterday."

"Impossible. I looked magnificent yesterday." He flagged the server. "Coffee. Black. Triple espresso. Actually, make that two."

The server fled. Klaus turned to me, and I could see myself reflected twice in his dark lenses. "I have good news and bad news."

"Bad first. Always."

"The bad news is I couldn't get all of it." He pulled out a roll of bills... all different denominations, some crumpled, some pristine. "Eighteen hundred. That's all I could manage on short notice without selling organs."

I stared at the money. "Klaus, what did you... "

"Good news!" He cut me off as his espressos arrived. He downed the first in one shot. "There's a poker game tonight. High stakes. Buy-in's eighteen hundred." The second espresso followed the first. "If I win... "

"If you lose, we have nothing."

"Then I won't lose." He finally took off the sunglasses. His pupils were pinpoints; the whites bloodshot. Whatever he'd taken to get through the morning was changing, shifting. "I'm good at cards, Lena. You know this."

"You're high."

"Functionally high. There's a difference." He was already standing, throwing too many bills on the table. "Come on. You need to look the part if you're coming with me tonight."

"Klaus... "

"What? We're facing doom in three days. Might as well look good doing it." He held out his hand. It was steady now; the drugs doing their work. "Trust me, *Liebling*. When have I ever let you down?"

"The Wall," I said immediately, scooping up the extra cash on the table.

His face went still. "That wasn't... I couldn't have stopped that."

"I know." I took his hand. "But you tried."

It was a low blow, and I hated myself for saying it. Yet he laughed and smiled as he put his sunglasses back on. Can't see pain if they can't see you, right?

"I always try." His grip was too tight, desperate. "Even when trying just makes it worse."

We spent money we didn't have on a dress I'd never wear again—black, simple, the kind that looked more expensive than it was. Klaus knew all the right places: the Turkish tailors who could work miracles with hemlines and the back-alley shops where designer knockoffs looked real if you didn't examine them too closely.

"You clean up nice," he said, watching me stumble in heels that hurt everywhere.

"I look like a kid who raided her mother's closet."

"Perfect. Rich men love that wounded bird aesthetic. Makes them feel powerful."

By evening, I looked like someone else entirely... someone who belonged at illegal poker games instead of scrubbing floors for rent money.

Midnight - Schöneberg

The factory squatted in the industrial district like something that had given up on decay and settled for ruin. Broken windows reflected nothing. Graffiti in six languages decorated the walls... promises, threats, and the occasional philosophical musing about the nature of existence.

Despite his occasional sniffle, Klaus looked immaculate. The coat from earlier had been dumped for something white, fur-based, and warm. I had done my makeup before we got there, but he had done his with a steady artistic hand... which meant he was manic and high. The positive side of this combination was that he was walking with confidence and ego. Both of which would either kill us or make us legends.

Klaus knew the password. Klaus knew the doorman. Klaus knew exactly which corridors to take through the maze of rust and industrial decay.

The game was on what used to be the factory floor. Someone had strung lights, hauled in tables, and created a temporary oasis of organized crime. Large men (either in muscle or fat) stuffed in suits worth more than cars. Women in dresses that could pay my rent for a year. Everyone pretending this was Monte Carlo instead of a dead factory in divided Berlin.

"Stay close," Klaus murmured. "Look bored. Look like you belong."

"What if someone talks to me?"

"Be French. No one wants to talk to the French."

"Manger de la merde." *Eat shit.*

"See, I already don't feel like talking to you–perfect!"

He bought in with our eighteen hundred marks—all the money we had in the world—and took his seat at a table with five other players. I stood behind him, one hand on his shoulder, playing the part of... what? Girlfriend? Sister? Lucky charm?

Did it matter?

The cards were dealt.

I knew nothing about poker, but I knew Klaus. Knew his tells when he was sober—the eye twitch when he bluffed, the finger tap when he had something good. But tonight he was unreadable, even to me.

In the first hour, he lost half our money.

In the second hour, he won it back.

By 2 AM, we were up two hundred marks. Not enough. Not nearly enough.

"All in," Klaus said, pushing everything to the center.

The table went quiet.

The man across from him—older, scarred, Russian accent thick as winter... smiled. "You sure, boy?"

"Never been more sure of anything in my life."

The Russian matched the bet. Then raised it. More than we had. More than we could cover.

"I'm short," Klaus said.

"Then you fold."

"Or," Klaus pulled off his watch... a Rolex I'd never asked about... and set it on the table. "This covers it."

The Russian examined the watch with an expert's eye. "Stolen?"

"Does it matter?"

A laugh. "I suppose not."

The cards were revealed.

Klaus had a full house. The Russian had four of a kind.

We'd lost everything.

The silence stretched like a held breath. Then Klaus smiled... that dangerous smile I'd seen before, right before he did something spectacular or catastrophic.

"Double or nothing," he said. "One hand. Your deal."

The Russian leaned back, amused. "You have nothing left to bet."

Klaus stood and shrugged off his jacket. Under it, strapped to his side in a holster I hadn't noticed, was a gun. He pulled it out slowly, checked the chamber with practiced ease, and set it on the table.

"Walther P38," he said conversationally. "Wehrmacht issue, 1943. Still fires like it just came off the line. Worth at least five thousand marks to the right collector."

The room had gone silent. Everyone was watching now.

Wehrmacht. World War Two German army issue. There was some heavy history on that gun.

"And if you lose?" the Russian asked.

Klaus's smile widened. "Then you get the gun and a story to tell your friends."

I wanted to grab him, drag him away, and find another plan. But there was no other plan. This was it.

The Russian dealt the cards.

Klaus didn't look at them immediately. Instead, he pulled out his cigarettes, lit one with steady hands, and took a long drag. The smoke curled up toward the industrial ceiling, and for a moment, he looked exactly like what he was... a beautiful disaster making one last desperate play.

He picked up his cards.

His face gave away nothing.

The Russian smiled, sure of victory.

Klaus laid down his hand.

Straight flush.

The Russian stared. Then laughed... deep and genuine. "You lucky little shit."

He pushed the money across the table. All of it. More than enough for two tickets to Bucharest.

Klaus pocketed the gun, the money, and the watch. "Pleasure doing business with you."

We left quickly, before anyone could change their mind or decide we needed to pay a different kind of price for winning.

Outside, in the pre-dawn darkness, Klaus lit another cigarette with shaking hands.

"You had a gun," I said.

"Always do."

"Wehrmacht issue?"

He paused for a moment, thinking. Then, "My grandfather's. He had... questionable... allegiances during the war." He looked at me. "You're judging me."

"I'm wondering what else you're hiding."

"Oh, *Liebling*." He flicked ash into the gutter. "If I told you all my secrets, you'd never sleep again."

We walked through empty streets, two broken people with four thousand marks and matching summons. We'd done it. We'd found a way.

"Klaus?"

"Yeah?"

"Thank you."

"For what?"

"Being broken with me."

He smiled... real this time, no sharp edges. "Anytime, Frost. Anytime."

The sun was rising over Berlin, gray and reluctant, as if it knew what was coming. In two days, we'd be in Romania. Back to the Scholomance. To whatever the Devil wanted with his wayward graduates.

To Alexi.

I thought about Klaus's words: *Some of us just wear it better.*

But at least we wouldn't face what came next alone.

Smoke and Frost, returning to the scene of the crime.

What could go wrong?

Everything.

Absolutely everything.

Pretty Liars

THE TRAIN TO BUCHAREST left Zoo Station at 6:47 AM, which meant we were on the platform at 6:30, and that meant neither of us had slept.

Klaus looked like death trying to pass for merely hungover. Oversized coat and sunglasses, despite the gray morning, cigarette dangling from his lips. He'd stolen the sunglasses from someone at the poker game. The coat was genuinely his; Yves Saint Laurent, bought back when the Bergmann name still opened doors instead of closing them.

"Romantic, isn't it?" He gestured at the departures board with his cigarette. "Two broken souls, fleeing toward their inevitable doom. Very *Casablanca*."

"We're going to Romania, not Morocco."

"Details, *Liebling*, details." He took a long drag. "The point is, we're running toward something instead of away from it. That's character growth, Frost."

"That's stupidity."

"Also character growth."

Our tickets were for third class... hard benches, no heat, the smell of too many bodies in too small a space. We found our compartment wedged between a woman with three crying children and two men who looked like they'd been awake for several days. Klaus surveyed the peeling vinyl seats, the window that wouldn't close properly, and graffiti in four languages carved into the walls.

"Home sweet home," he said and collapsed onto the bench.

I took the seat across from him and watched Germany slide past... gray sky, grayer buildings, everything the color of old dishwater. West Berlin was fading behind us like a bad memory we were trying to outrun. Could you really call a place home when you fucked it up so badly?

Neither of us said what we were both thinking: that in two days we'd be standing in the place we'd been dreading for eight years, surrounded by people who knew us when we were someone else.

Someone better.

An hour in, Klaus went for coffee. He returned with two paper cups that smelled like burned rubber and regret. His sunglasses were pulled down. The smeared eyeliner offset his dark circles. However, his eyes were filled with a mixture of exhaustion and annoyance.

"Good news: Stefan Kovács is also on this train." Klaus handed me a cup. "Bad news: he's already placing bets on who gets chosen for the lottery. We're not the favorites."

"Shocking."

"I know, right? You'd think Berlin would give you better odds."

I sipped the coffee. It tasted exactly as bad as it smelled. "What are our odds?"

"Yours? Ten to one against. Mine?" He settled back onto his bench. "Let's just say Stefan laughed."

"Fuck Stefan Kovács."

"Many have. Few enjoyed it." Klaus pulled out his cigarettes and offered me one. I took it. "The Németh sisters are in second class. Gábor Horváth is somewhere in first, probably drinking champagne and practicing his acceptance speech."

"Is anyone else from our year here?"

Something flickered across his face. "Didn't see anyone."

Which meant he'd looked. Which meant he'd been hoping, same as me, that maybe we wouldn't be the only disasters from the Class of '76.

We smoked in silence. The train rocked. Germany soon became Austria, and Austria became Hungary. The borders were just lines on a map. It was land that knew no master. Before the incident, I swore that I could hear the hum of power in the earth... but now it was all silence and mist.

Klaus finished his cigarette and immediately lit another. His hands were steady... for now.

"I need to use the toilet," he said, standing.

He left. I knew what he was doing. He knew I knew. We'd done this dance before—him pretending, me pretending to believe him.

Fifteen minutes later, Klaus came back brighter. Pupils tight. Movements loose and easy.

"Better?" I asked.

"Much." He pulled out his cigarettes. "That toilet is horrifying, by the way. I've seen Berlin clubs at 4 AM. Same thing."

"We should make a plan," he said. "Strategy. Who we talk to, who we avoid... "

"Klaus."

"What?" he looked at me. Sunglasses still on, even inside the dim compartment. He sniffed.

I pursed my lips and nodded, "You out?"

"Yup." He leaned his head back and stared at the ceiling. "What are you going to say to him?" he asked quietly, changing the subject.

I'd been expecting this question. Dreading it.

"Nothing," I said. "There's nothing to say."

"Eight years of nothing? That's a lot of nothing."

"He made his feelings clear. I'm just the idiot who keeps forgetting."

Klaus turned to look at me. His eyes were starting to lose focus; the immediate high already wearing off.

"You're not an idiot. You're stubborn, self-destructive, and have terrible taste in men, but you're not an idiot."

"Your pep talks need work."

"My everything needs work, *Liebling*." He smiled, thin and tired.

The train pulled away. Ahead, somewhere in the darkness, was Romania. The Scholomance. Everything we'd been dreading.

Klaus leaned his head against the window. Not sleeping, just resting.

I closed my eyes and let the rhythm of the rails usher me along.

It was too fucking cold to be outside.

The ruined tower behind me offered no heat, no shelter—just a view of the night sky and the illusion of privacy. This was one of three spots we'd found, hidden from the prying eyes of legacy students and their gossip. I could have given a fuck what any of them thought. But the Scholomance had rules about fraternization, and breaking them came with consequences neither of us could afford.

So we took every chance to ignore them.

I crushed the empty pack of Carpați cigarettes and watched the final ember of my last one die, leaving me alone with the stars and the cold. Looking up, I took a deep breath of freezing air, trying to stay awake and not to think about Vogel's exam tomorrow.

Trying not to think about life after graduation...

The night sky was beautiful. A thousand diamonds scattered across dark velvet.

There was talk—rumors, really—that I might be one of the lucky few chosen to bond with a dragon. A beast of legend. Something that would let me ride the night skies like a nightmare that made men's souls quake.

Part of me wanted to race far into that sky, away from all of this. Away from rules and legacy families and the constant weight of proving I belonged.

But mostly, I wanted a different kind of heat. Rough hands running along my skin. Storm-gray eyes looking at me like I was the only thing that mattered.

A strong arm wrapped around my waist, trapping my arms. A hand clamped over my mouth, stifling any chance to scream or draw a word of power.

I started to fight—thrashing, trying to slam my head back—but his grip was iron. I was about to bite down when a whisper crept into my ear.

"What if I were a bad man?"

His voice was low, trying to play the sinister villain. My heart was still racing, but I stopped fighting.

He let go of my mouth.

"If you were a bad man," I said, "you wouldn't smell like that cheap Troynoy cologne. Real villains wear something more expensive, like Drakkar Noir or Obsession."

"I could be a villain on a student budget." His hand slipped under my shirt, fingers running across my stomach.

"Fuck, your hands are freezing!"

As if it were an invitation, his hand crept lower, toward the waistline of my jeans.

"Don't you dare..."

I spun, shoving him against the crumbling stone wall. Reached down and grabbed the growing bulge in his pants.

"How would you like it if I took this icy hand and grabbed you? Would he shrivel up and hide?"

He didn't answer. Just leaned down and kissed me.

His hands gripped both sides of my head, fingernails running along my scalp, tongue playing with mine. His lips tasted like caramel—his perpetual sweet tooth always made him taste better.

Four days. It had been four fucking days since we'd had any time alone. We'd see each other in lessons and pass in the corridors. Always so close, never close enough. Always someone watching, always somewhere else we had to be.

But right now, I had him to myself.

I squeezed gently, and he moaned against my mouth, body tensing, kiss turning desperate.

"How much time do we have?" I breathed.

He smiled, wicked and hungry. "Enough."

"Enough for you, or will I get mine too?"

His eyes met mine. Storm-gray, serious, beautiful. Seeing right through me. Wanting me. Needing me.

Like I was the last meal of a dying man.

His hands found the front of my jeans. With practiced ease, he undid the button, pulled the zipper down. When he dropped to his knees and looked up at me—hunger real and growing—I forgot about the cold entirely.

"You'll get your satisfaction," he murmured.

And then his mouth was on me, and the stars overhead burned brighter than they had any right to, and I understood why they called us Storm and Frost—because together we were something wild and untamed and completely unstoppable.

I buried my fingers in his dark hair and let him prove his promise true.

I woke with tears on my face, the dream already fading, but the ache staying sharp and real.

The train was still moving. Klaus was awake now, watching me with tired eyes. The high had burned off completely. He looked hollow, but not destroyed. Not yet.

He didn't say anything. Just pulled a handkerchief from his pocket and handed it to me.

I wiped my face. "Thanks."

"Anytime, *Liebling*."

Outside, the landscape had changed. We were in Romania now. Getting closer.

Klaus shifted on his bench, restless. Starting to feel it now... that itch under his skin that said the drugs were leaving and reality was coming back.

"How much longer?" he asked.

"Few more hours. We'll reach Bucharest by morning."

The old man with the chicken got off at the next stop. A young couple took his place, clearly in love.

I envied them.

Klaus closed his eyes. His leg started bouncing... barely noticeable, but there.

"Klaus?"

"Hmm?"

"We're going to be okay."

He opened his eyes. Looked at me. The mask dropped for just a moment.

"Liar," he said softly. "You always were a terrible liar, Frost."

Arrival

THE VILLAGE DIDN'T HAVE a name.

Or it did, but no one who mattered used it. On the maps... the ones civilians saw... this was just another mountain village near Lake Cincis. Except Lake Cincis on those maps was ten kilometers northeast, a perfectly nice tourist destination with boat rentals and overpriced cafés.

This lake didn't exist. Neither did this village, technically.

The mortals had their legends, of course. Bram Stoker had heard the stories when he was researching his vampire novel—even mentioned in Dracula that the count himself had attended the Scholomance. The legends said it was under Lake Hermannstadt. Or Lake Văcărești. Or some unnamed alpine lake that moved locations, that could never be found by those who weren't meant to find it.

All intentional misdirection. The real Scholomance had been here for centuries, hidden in plain sight, while the stories and maps sent curious fools chasing ghosts across Romania.

Our taxi driver dropped us at the edge of town as the sun broke over the mountains. He took our money and drove away like his ass was on fire.

Klaus lit a cigarette. His hands shook enough that it took three tries.

The village looked like a postcard. Stone houses, red tile roofs, a church steeple against green mountains. Picture-perfect. Completely normal.

That was the point.

A Mercedes passed us heading out... German plates, the family arguing about directions. Lost tourists. They wouldn't find what they were looking for.

An old woman swept her front steps. She glanced up, her eyes sliding over Klaus and catching on me for half a second before looking away.

She knew.

Klaus tried asking for directions in Romanian. She told him Lake Cincis was ten kilometers northeast without stopping her sweeping. Very popular this time of year.

We kept walking.

Half a block later, a man emerged from a café. Gray beard, ageless clothes. Our eyes met. He nodded once and tilted his head toward a side street angling up into the mountains. "That way," he said quietly in Latin.

I thanked him in the same tongue. He was already gone.

The side street became a trail, and my legs remembered even though it had been eight years. Through a forest that made you feel watched, up slopes that stole your breath. Klaus was breathing hard beside me, working on his fourth cigarette since we started climbing. We weren't alone... ahead, two figures climbed in expensive clothes gone shabby, and behind us, younger voices with bright laughter that didn't belong here.

The forest thinned, and there it was... Lake Cincis spreading below us. Black water, too still. No birds. No boats. Just that mirror-smooth darkness reflecting mountains and sky.

I stopped walking. Klaus stopped beside me.

"Fuck," he said.

Yeah. Eight years ago we'd climbed out of this place knowing we'd have to return, knowing when we came back our names would go into the hat. We'd just thought we'd have our shit together by then. Thought we'd be successful, connected, ready. Wrong on all counts.

Around the lake, stone buildings emerged from the forest... ancient, solid. The Scholomance's surface campus, where ceremonies happened, where the Devil took attendance. The real school was below, under the lake. But I wasn't thinking about that.

Not yet.

The compound was already busy when we arrived, people converging from multiple paths, settling in before the ceremonies started. The air felt thick... too many magicians in too small a space. The pressure made my teeth ache; magic pressed against magic, everyone holding tight to their control because one slip could level the compound.

I stopped just inside the gates. My chest tightened, ice gathering under my skin without permission. The last time I'd stood here, I'd been twenty-one years old and convinced I understood how the world worked. Convinced I had a future. Convinced someone loved me.

Eight years. The compound looked exactly the same. Stone walls, ancient archways, the courtyard fountain with its carved dragons. Nothing had changed.

Everything had changed.

"Lena?" Klaus touched my arm. "You good?"

I forced the ice back down, made myself breathe. "Yeah. Let's get this over with."

A young man sat at a desk near the entrance, a massive ledger in hand. Village staff, probably... one of the bound servants. He took our names without looking up. "Class of '76. East wing, second floor. Names on the doors. Schedule posts tomorrow. Dinner's at seven if you want it."

Klaus opened his mouth, but I touched his arm. We took our room assignments and left.

The courtyard was bigger than I remembered. And full. A woman in her sixties held court near the fountain, laughing with men in tailored suits. Expensive jewelry caught the light. Near the dormitory, someone demonstrated fire magic for an appreciative crowd. Applause. Laughter.

Other clusters spoke in lower voices. Cheaper clothes. Tighter faces. A man my age kept checking over his shoulder.

And there, near the eastern colonnade...

A figure in dark clothes, standing apart from the groups. Tall. Shoulders I'd know anywhere. He was talking to someone in enforcer grays, his back to me, but I felt it anyway. That pull. That recognition that went deeper than sight.

I looked away before he could turn. Before I could do something stupid like stare. Like hope he'd look back.

"Coming?" Klaus had already started toward the dormitory.

I followed, keeping my eyes down, my magic locked tight.

We found the east wing. Second floor. Long hallway, identical doors. My name was on one: ILENA FIRAN - CLASS OF '76. Klaus's was three doors down.

My room was exactly like every room I'd inhabited during the three years underground... single bed, desk, chair, window overlooking the courtyard. Clean but impersonal. Someone had left a towel on the bed, soap on the desk, and fresh flowers in a cheap vase on the windowsill. The Devil's hospitality, making sure we were comfortable before he fucked us over.

A knock. Klaus stood in my doorway, gray-faced and sweat-soaked despite the cool mountain air, shaking.

"I'm going to lie down," he said, voice thin. "Before I fall on my face."

"You need food. Water. Something."

"Can't." He swallowed hard. "Can't keep anything down. Just... just need to sleep."

He disappeared down the hall, and his door opened and closed. I sat on my bed and stared at the closed door between us.

By late afternoon, Klaus still hadn't emerged.

I knocked. No answer.

Knocked harder. "Klaus?"

Nothing.

I tried the handle. Locked.

"Klaus, I'm coming in." I pulled a hairpin from my pocket... old habits... and worked the lock. Thirty seconds.

The room was dark, curtains drawn against the afternoon light. It smelled like sweat and something sour... bile, maybe, or the chemical tang of whatever he'd been using finally leaving his system.

Klaus was curled on his side on the bed, back to the door. Not moving.

My heart stopped.

"Klaus?"

He jerked at the sound of my voice. Rolled over slowly, as if his body weighed twice what it should. Eyes unfocused, pupils blown wide despite the darkness. "Leibling?"

"Yeah, it's me." I crossed to him, navigating around discarded clothes, and his bag spilled across the floor. Pressed my hand to his forehead. Cold and clammy despite the sweat soaking through his shirt, darkening the collar and armpits. "Christ, Klaus."

"'M fine." He tried to sit, got halfway up before his arms gave out. Fell back against the pillow with a sound that was half-laugh, half-sob. "Just... just need..."

His hands were shaking. Not the usual tremor—this was his whole body trying to come apart.

"You need something to take the edge off." I pulled back, wiping my damp palm on my jeans. "I'm getting you help."

"No staff." His hand shot out, grabbed my wrist with surprising strength. His skin was cold, fingers like ice. "They'll report it. Can't... can't give them reason..."

He was right. The Devil's staff reported everything. A graduate showing up sick, weak, vulnerable? That got noted. Filed. Used.

"Then I'm getting you something." I pulled free. "Stay here."

"Where else would I go?" he laughed. It came out broken.

Dinner was being served in the courtyard when I came back down. Long tables, simple food. Graduates clustered in groups—some animated, some quiet. The division was obvious. The successful ones treating this like a reunion. The desperate ones just trying to survive until May 30th.

I needed to find someone. Someone who knew things. Someone who'd help for the right price.

Stefan Kovács was already holding court at a center table, halfway through what sounded like a filthy story judging by the laughter. Expensive watch. Custom suit. Wine glass in hand. A loud voice carrying across the courtyard.

Kovács traded on the London Exchange. His specialization was rumored to be basic numerology, which he'd turned into an art form. Add that talent to three years of infernal education, and he was the man all bookies feared. At the same time, possessing the Devil's Luck meant you were always on the precipice of making it big, but just a number or deal off. It was ironic that his lot scrambled the hardest to accumulate wealth beyond their means. I'd seen Kovács types before... French Champagne one year, refilling the empty bottles with discount swill the next when the floor fell out. 1984 seemed to be a good year for him. A rise before another inevitable fall.

Perfect.

I grabbed a bowl of stew and made my way over, waiting for a break in his story.

"...and then I said, 'No darling, that wasn't my cock!'"

The table erupted in laughter. Kovács grinned, basking in it.

"Stefan," I cut in before he could start another. "I need a word."

He looked up, registered me with wine-glossed eyes. "Ilena Firan! Sweet Stefan remembers a classmate." He gestured to a seat. "Join us..."

"I can't stay." I leaned in close, lowering my voice. "I need information. Fast."

The surrounding crowd was already losing interest, turning to their own conversations. Kovács's smile dimmed slightly... this wasn't the audience he wanted.

"Klaus got hold of something bad on the train ride up," I whispered. "He's turning inside out in his room. I need someone who can help. A cleanser. Something to take the edge off."

Kovács studied me, calculating even through the wine haze. "Information like that... expensive."

"A favor," I said. "I don't want Klaus's bad decision ruining this reunion. Being under the influence... that's disrespectful to everyone here."

The words tasted like ash, but I needed this. Now.

He motioned me closer. "Lisowska. Krystyna Lisowska. Late sixties graduate. Tell her the business between us from the Dschungel is square if she provides a Sunshine draught." He held out his hand. "In return, Ilena Firan, you owe me a favor. Deal?"

I grabbed his hand. Shook. "Where is she?"

He pointed toward a group near the fountain. An older woman with a cane, talking animatedly despite the late hour.

"Thank you." I was already standing, bowl of stew in hand.

I didn't wait for his response. Just headed toward the serving table, eating the stew as I walked. My body was screaming for food, but I couldn't sit. Grabbed bread and cheese, shoved them in my pockets along with two wine bottles someone had abandoned.

Klaus needed help. Now.

Krystyna Lisowska was exactly where Kovács had pointed—near the fountain, holding court with a small group despite the late hour and the cane she leaned on. She had to be in her sixties, maybe older, but her eyes were sharp when they landed on me.

I waited for a break in the conversation. Didn't get one.

"Excuse me," I said, stepping closer. "Krystyna Lisowska?"

She looked me over... quick, assessing. "Yes?"

"Stefan Kovács sent me. He said to tell you the business between you and the Dschungel is square if you can provide a Sunshine draught."

Her eyebrows went up. The others in her group had gone quiet, watching.

"Did he now?" She smiled slightly. Turned to her companions. "Excuse me, darlings. Business calls."

She gestured for me to follow, leading me away from the fountain toward a quieter corner of the courtyard. Her cane tapped against the stone with each step.

"The Dschungel," she said, voice dry. "That man still owes me for Berlin, but I suppose this will do." She pulled a small vial from her pocket—amber liquid that glowed faintly even in the darkness. "Sunshine draught. Make sure your friend drinks it all at once. Preferably with food, if he can keep it down."

I took it. The glass was warm against my palm. "What does it do?"

"Takes the edge off. Helps him sleep without the nightmares." Her sharp eyes found mine. "It won't fix everything. Won't make him clean. But it'll get him through tonight."

"Thank you."

"Don't thank me. Thank Kovács." She paused. "And be careful what you owe that man. The Devil's Luck runs both ways."

She was already turning back to her group, conversation resuming as if I'd never interrupted.

I tucked the vial into my jacket pocket alongside the wine bottles and bread. The glass clinked softly against the bottle. Everything Klaus needed to get through the night—draught, food, something to take the edge off.

I headed back toward the dormitory. The courtyard was quieter now, past midnight. Most graduates had retreated to their rooms or were still drinking in the great hall. A few shadows moved near the colonnade. Voices low and indistinct.

My stomach was finally full... the first real meal I'd had in days. The stew had been simple but good, reminding me of home back when home was something other than a shitty Frankfurt apartment.

I should have gone straight upstairs. Should have given Klaus the draught and collapsed.

Instead, I paused near the fountain.

The night air was cool. Clean. Mountain air, nothing like Frankfurt's industrial haze. Stars overhead, brilliant without city lights. The water ran steady—that constant sound that had been the soundtrack to three years of my life.

I closed my eyes. Just for a moment.

Breathed.

Then I heard his voice.

Vino

MY BODY KNEW BEFORE my brain caught up. That particular timbre, the cadence of his Romanian—not the formal classroom version but the real thing, the language he'd spoken as a child, the one he used when he was comfortable or angry or making love. Eight years, and it still cut through me like a blade.

My feet stopped. My breath caught.

I told myself to keep walking, that I'd known I'd run into him, eventually. This was a closed compound. Two hundred people. Of course our paths would cross.

My legs wouldn't move.

He was standing near the fountain with an older man... late sixties, in traditional Romanian clothing, an embroidered vest over a white shirt. Silver hair pulled back, deeply tanned face, the bearing of someone who'd never questioned his authority because no one had ever dared.

The Master. Stăpânul.

I'd seen him three times during my student years... entrance ceremony, graduation, once in the library. He didn't involve himself in daily operations. Didn't teach. Barely spoke to the students.

But here he was, talking to Alexi as if they were colleagues.

I stepped into the shadow of a pillar. Listened.

"...Inge's passing was peaceful," the Master was saying. His voice carried in the quiet courtyard. "Seventy years is a long life, even for one bonded."

"And Govirrod accepts the bond's end?" Alexi's voice. Deeper than I remembered. Rougher.

"Dragons understand mortality, even if they don't share it. He arrives tonight to choose again." A pause. "The candidates will be... eager."

"That's one word for it."

I frowned. Govirrod. A dragon's name. Someone named Inge had died, and now a dragon was coming to... choose? Choose what?

My history lessons surfaced through the shock. Dragons and their riders were the apex of our world... the legends that kept the Scholomance feared and respected. Weather-workers were common enough. Storm-callers, rare. But dragon riders? They commanded the weather itself. Hurricanes. Blizzards. Droughts that lasted for years. Power that toppled kingdoms, which mortals attributed to gods.

The old stories said the Devil kept dragons, though no one knew how many or where they came from. That only the most powerful graduates... or the most ruthless... ever bonded with them. That the bond granted power beyond measure, the ability to reshape the world.

The stories also said that most who tried to bond died screaming.

But for those who succeeded? They became legends. They became the reason mortals feared the Scholomance, why kings and presidents sent their children to us, why our graduates commanded respect and terror in equal measure.

An unbonded dragon arriving at Convocation wasn't just news. It was an event.

"The bonding must happen before the lottery," the Master continued. "We need to know who survives. Can't have names drawn for graduates who are already dead."

Cold spread through my chest. *Who survives.*

"And the candidates? For Govirrod?" Alexi asked.

"Will be chosen from those who prove... worthy. Or foolish enough to try." The Master's voice held dark amusement. "You understand what's required?"

"I understand."

Alexi's head turned. Sharply. Like he'd sensed something.

Our eyes met across twenty feet of darkening courtyard.

The world narrowed. Sound faded.

He looked different. Harder. The boy I'd known... all sharp intelligence and careful control... had been replaced by something darker. His face had lost its softness, all angles now, cheekbones sharp enough to cut. Black hair pushed back from his forehead, longer than he used to wear it, touching his collar. Stubble shadowed his jaw... deliberate, not accidental.

Scars I didn't recognize cut through his left eyebrow, another along his jawline disappearing into that dark stubble. His mouth... the one that used to smile at me like I was his whole world... was a hard line.

He wore all black. Leather jacket over dark shirt, expensive but worn in that way that said he actually lived in his clothes. Oddly, the shirt was unbuttoned, almost daring the cold to approach his pale skin. His posture made him look taller, his body more fit than I remembered. Despite the cold, the jacket he wore struggled to keep a much more muscular build contained. Jeans that fit perfectly. Boots that had seen actual use. The outfit that would've gotten him stopped at the Wall... too Western, too rebellious, too dangerous.

Storm-gray eyes locked on mine. No surprise in them. Like he'd sensed me there.

Then his face went stiff. Not angry... that would have been something. Just... blank. Empty. Like looking at a stranger.

I couldn't move. Couldn't breathe. The vial in my pocket pressed against my ribs, a sharp reminder that Klaus was upstairs dying and I was standing here frozen, staring at someone who'd stopped looking at me like I mattered years ago.

A woman stepped between us.

She appeared from somewhere to Alexi's left... I hadn't noticed her before. Mid-forties, maybe, though something about her made age feel irrelevant. Tall, dark hair in an elegant twist, wearing clothes that cost more than my last six months' rent. Beautiful in a way that felt almost unnatural. Too perfect. Too still.

She moved with liquid grace, placing herself in front of Alexi. Her hand touched his arm... familiar, comfortable, possessive.

She said something to him in Romanian. Low. Intimate. I caught only fragments: "...not now..." "...she doesn't matter..."

The words hit like a fist to the gut. My throat tightened. Heat flushed up my neck, my face... humiliation burning under my skin.

Of course he'd moved on. Found someone successful and beautiful and powerful enough to stand with the Master like she belonged there.

The woman glanced at me. Her eyes were strange... too dark, reflecting the lamplight wrong. The look lasted only a second, but I felt assessed. Measured. Found wanting.

Then she turned back to Alexi, her hand still on his arm, her body language clear: Mine. Back off.

The Master was watching the entire exchange with something that might have been amusement.

"Alexi," he said mildly. "Perhaps we should continue this conversation elsewhere."

The woman leaned in, said something else to Alexi. He nodded. They turned away as if I wasn't there. Like I'd never been there.

The couple near the dormitory had stopped talking, watching now. Great. Witnesses.

Move. The word cut through the fog. I forced my legs to work. Not back to my room... I wouldn't retreat. Forward. Toward the dormitory entrance. Like that had been my destination all along.

I walked past them with my head up, hands steady even though my pulse hammered in my throat, face blank even though my eyes burned.

Didn't look at him. Didn't look at her. Didn't acknowledge the Master's calculating gaze.

Made it to the dormitory entrance. Inside. Stairs. Door. Lock.

The wine bottles clinked as I set them on the desk. The vial of Sunshine next to them, amber liquid catching the lamplight.

I sat on the bed.

She doesn't matter.

That's what the woman had said. Even through the Romanian, even from twenty feet away, I'd heard it clearly enough.

She doesn't matter.

I opened one of the wine bottles without bothering to find a glass. Took a long drink to steady myself. Then grabbed the vial of Sunshine and the bottle, and headed back out into the hallway.

Klaus's door was still locked. I knocked. "Klaus, it's me. I have something for you."

Silence.

"Klaus, open the door or I'm picking the lock again."

A shuffle. A thump. The lock clicked.

The door opened a crack. Klaus looked worse than before... if that was possible. His pupils were still blown, skin gray and clammy, but at least he was upright.

"Got you something," I said, holding up the vial. "Sunshine draught. Supposed to take the edge off."

He stared at it. "What'd it cost you?"

"A favor to Kovács. Don't worry about it."

"Lena..."

"Drink it. All at once. And try to eat some of this." I shoved the bread and cheese from my pockets at him.

He took the vial with shaking hands. Uncorked it. The amber liquid glowed faintly in the dim hallway. He downed it in one swallow, grimaced, then grabbed the bread and tore into it like he was starving.

"Stay in your room," I said. "Lock the door. Sleep if you can."

"Where are you going?"

"My room. To drink and try not to think."

He caught my wrist as I turned. His grip was weak but insistent. "You saw him."

Not a question.

"Yeah."

"And?"

"And he's moved on. Has someone. Looked at me like I was nothing." I pulled free gently. "The wine's calling."

Klaus's expression softened with something that looked like pity. "Lena..."

"Good night, Klaus."

I left before he could say anything else. Back to my room. Locked the door. Sat on the bed with the wine bottle.

And drank.

The wine was good. Too good for someone like me. I drank anyway.

Mortals had their legends about the Scholomance. Most of them were wrong. Some were close enough to be dangerous. They said the Devil kept a school beneath a lake in Romania where he taught black magic to ten students at a time. They said nine students graduated and went into the world, and the tenth became the Devil's servant—the zmeu—the dragon who carried out his will.

Most of it was bullshit.

Three years of training, not seven. Three years of hell. Three years of learning things that would drive mortals mad. Three years of surviving challenges that killed candidates before they even reached graduation.

All ten students had the potential to graduate... provided the tests didn't kill you in the process.

But one of them... one chosen by the Devil himself... stayed behind. Became his... Tribute. Payment for the knowledge, the power, the magic we'd all learned. There was no freedom from that servitude. Not ever.

One soul, in exchange for nine mortals made into magicians.

Not a bad deal, if you were the Devil. A fucking nightmare, if you were the one chosen.

And then the rest graduated. Made your oath. Got your freedom... if you weren't the one chosen. Seven to eight years in the world. Do what you want. Build your life. Use your power. Get rich, get powerful, or... in my case... get fucked.

Then the summons came.

You returned for the Convocation. Every graduate was expected. The Devil took attendance. The lottery happened. Ten names drawn from everyone present... from forty, fifty, sixty years of graduating classes. Ten were chosen to provide candidates for the next class.

Find someone. Bring them to the school. Watch them go through what you went through.

And if your name wasn't drawn? You went home. Lived your life. Came back at the next Convocation. Again and again, until you died or failed to answer the summons.

Miss once, you got a warning. Miss twice, the enforcers came.

I'd heard stories about the enforcers. None of those stories ended well.

I took another drink, letting the wine burn down my throat.

Tributes were different, the stories said. Harder. Haunted. Changed in ways that went deeper than scars. They never spoke about their service. Never talked about what the Devil asked of them, what they did in his name. They just... existed. In his shadow. Forever.

I'd seen Alexi tonight. Talking to the Master like an equal. Standing in that courtyard like he belonged there, like he had authority.

He'd been there. He looked human. Scarred and cold and looking at me like I was nothing.

What had those years of service bought him?
What had he been doing for the past eight years?

Sunshine

I MADE IT THROUGH half the bottle before the guilt got too heavy.

Klaus was detoxing alone. I'd been there for the Sunshine handoff, watched him down it with shaking hands, told him to lock the door and try to sleep. Then I'd left him to face the next four hours by himself. Because I was too wrapped up in my own shit... in storm-gray eyes going cold, in a woman's possessive hand on his arm, in *she doesn't matter* echoing through my skull... to be the friend he needed.

The wine wasn't helping. Neither was the silence. Every time I closed my eyes, I saw Alexi standing in that courtyard. Harder. Scarred. Looking at me like I was nothing.

I'd spent years trying to outrun that moment. Trying to become someone who didn't need him, who didn't wake up reaching for someone who wasn't there, who could hear his name without flinching.

Eight years, and one look undid all of it.

She doesn't matter.

I took another drink. The wine burned going down but didn't touch the ache in my chest.

Klaus was alone. Going through hell. And I was sitting here drowning in self-pity over a man who'd moved on.

Fuck that.

I grabbed the second wine bottle and headed back down the hallway.

The corridor was quiet when I arrived. No screaming... the Sunshine worked that way, turning everything inward, chemical fire burning through your veins without giving you the mercy of voicing it. But when I pressed my ear to his door, I could hear harsh breathing. The occasional thump of him hitting the wall or floor. The wet sound of retching.

Alone.

I picked the lock. Again.

The room was dark except for the predawn light creeping through the window. Klaus lay curled on his side on the narrow bed, fully dressed, trembling. A basin on the floor beside him. The smell hit me immediately... bile, sweat, the sour-sweet stench of poison leaving a body.

He didn't react when I came in. Maybe didn't even know I was there.

I closed the door softly, sat down on the floor with my back against the stone wall, and opened the wine.

And waited.

Four hours later, I still sat on the floor of Klaus's borrowed room, back against the stone wall, watching him not die.

The Sunshine draught had done its work. Ten minutes of silent hell... convulsions, vomiting, every muscle locked in agony while he bit down on a rolled-up shirt to keep from screaming... followed by sudden, eerie stillness. Now he lay on the narrow bed, chest rising and falling in steady rhythm, looking almost peaceful. Almost normal.

Except for the way his hands still trembled slightly. And the hollow look in his eyes.

"Feel like death?" I asked.

"Feel like nothing." His voice was rough, scraped raw from the inside. "Which is... almost worse."

He looked it too. The eyeliner he'd worn on the train had smeared into bruise-like shadows under his eyes. His skin had that grayish cast that came from purging poison. When he lifted his hands to rub his face, they were pale and shaking, the silver rings he always wore suddenly too big on fingers that had lost weight.

Someone had left clothes folded on the chair, basic toiletries on the table. Everything necessary, nothing welcoming.

The room reeked of withdrawal... stale alcohol sweating through pores, bile, and underneath it all, that sour-sweet smell that lingered no matter how many times you cleaned.

"You should eat something," I said.

"Can't."

"Klaus..."

"I said I can't." He turned his head away, staring at the wall. "Stomach feels like broken glass. Just... give me a minute."

I gave him ten.

The dawn light strengthened. Somewhere in the building, bells chimed... six AM. May 28th. Two days until the lottery. Tomorrow the Class of 1984 would graduate. Tomorrow night would be their tribute ceremony... one of them chosen to stay with the Devil forever.

And the night after that, under the Black Moon, ten of us would be chosen to provide the next generation of candidates.

My stomach twisted.

"Lena?"

"Yeah?"

"What time is it?"

I glanced at the window. "Little after six."

"Feels like I've been dead for a week." He shifted on the bed, wincing. "Everything hurts."

"That's the Sunshine. Your body remembering what normal feels like."

"Normal feels like shit."

"Welcome back to reality."

He was quiet for a moment. The trembling in his hands was lessening, but not gone. "Two days until the lottery."

"Yeah."

"Think we'll get chosen?"

"Hope not. Can't afford to be."

"None of us can." His voice was flat. "That's the point, isn't it? The Devil doesn't care what we can afford."

He was right. The lottery didn't care about your circumstances, your finances, your ability to actually provide a candidate. You got chosen; you figured it out, or you faced the consequences.

And the consequences were never good.

A knock on the door. Bright. Peppy. Aggressively cheerful at six in the morning.

We both froze.

The knock came again. "Klaus? Klaus, honey, are you up? It's Linda!"

Klaus's eyes met mine. Horror and resignation mixing equally.

"Fuck," he breathed.

"Maybe she'll go away," I whispered.

"You don't know Linda."

He was right. The door opened... because of course she had a key, or picked the lock, or talked her way past whatever enchantments were supposed to keep out uninvited visitors.

Linda Appleton swept in like a force of nature, dressed in country club armor.

She wore white linen pants with a knife-edge crease, a silk blouse, blazer with gold buttons. Pearls at her throat and ears. Hair perfectly coiffed in blonde waves. Makeup flawless despite the early hour. She carried a wicker basket covered with a gingham cloth and radiated aggressive optimism that made you want to either hug her or throw something.

"Oh good, you're both awake!" She beamed at us. "I brought muffins. And coffee. Well, terrible Romanian coffee, but I added sugar, and it's really not so bad once you get past the... oh Klaus, sweetheart, you look awful."

And smell worse, probably. The window was cracked open, but it wasn't enough to clear the air.

Klaus hadn't moved from the bed. Couldn't, probably. Just stared at her like a deer watching a freight train approach.

"Hi, Linda," he managed.

"Don't you 'Hi Linda' me, young man." She set the basket on the small table, then really looked at him. Her smile faltered. "Oh, honey. Oh no."

She crossed to the bed in three quick steps. Up close, I could see the concern cracking through her cheerful veneer.

"How bad?" she asked quietly.

Klaus's jaw worked. "I'm fine now."

"That's not what I asked."

Silence. Linda's gaze flicked to me, then back to Klaus. Understanding dawned in her eyes... she'd always been sharper than her country club persona suggested.

"You took something," she said. Not a question.

"Sunshine draught," I said. "Few hours ago."

Linda's eyes closed briefly. When she opened them, they were bright with unshed tears. "Oh, Klaus."

She sat on the edge of his bed, reaching out to smooth his hair back from his forehead in a gesture so motherly it made my chest hurt. He didn't pull away. Didn't say anything. Just let her touch him like he was still someone worth caring about.

"How long?" she asked softly.

"Does it matter?"

"No. I suppose it doesn't." Her hand stilled, then withdrew. She straightened, smoothing her blazer in a gesture that seemed to reset her entire demeanor. The tears didn't fall. The concern remained but got wrapped in efficient determination. "What matters is you're clean now. And the Bergmanns would love nothing more than to see you fail publicly. We're not giving them the satisfaction."

She turned to me. "Ilena. You look terrible, too. When did you last sleep?"

"Define sleep."

"That's what I thought." She retrieved the basket, pulling off the gingham cloth to reveal muffins, rolls, butter, jam, even a thermos of coffee and two cups. "You're both going to eat. Then Klaus is going to shower and rest. And we're going to get through today without anyone realizing you spent last night detoxing."

"Linda..." Klaus started.

"Not negotiable." She poured coffee with the precision of a woman who'd hosted a thousand charity brunches. "Today is relatively quiet. More graduates arriving throughout the day. Informal meals. People catching up, forming alliances, spreading gossip. Tomorrow is the graduation ceremony for Class of '84. Tomorrow night is their tribute ceremony... poor bastards."

She handed me a cup of coffee. It was terrible and over-sugared and exactly what I needed.

"And the night after that is the lottery," I said.

"Under the Black Moon. Yes." Linda's voice lost some of its brightness. "Two days. That's what we have to prepare for. Which means today you rest and recover, Klaus. And you, Ilena, need to start rebuilding your reputation because right now you're the cautionary tale everyone's using to scare their apprentices."

"That's comforting," I muttered.

"It's fixable." She said it with such confidence I almost believed her. "You're both survivors. You clawed your way here despite everything. That counts for something."

"Does it?" Klaus's voice was hollow.

"It does to the people who matter." She smiled. "And I've been working on who matters for eight years now. I know exactly who to introduce you to, who to avoid, and how to make sure the narrative shifts from 'tragic failures' to 'overcame adversity.' "

"Christ, Linda," I said. "You sound like a PR manager."

"Darling, I married one. PR firms, political consultants, image rehabilitation... that's the family business." Her smile turned sharp. "The Appletons didn't stay powerful by being nice. We stayed powerful by being strategic. And right now, you two need strategy."

Klaus managed to sit up, accepting a muffin with shaking hands. "Why are you helping us?"

Linda's expression softened. "Because we're Class of '76, honey. All ten of us graduated alive. Do you know how rare that is? Most classes lose two, three or more students before the end. We survived together. That means something." She paused. "And because I heard he's here. Alexi. I haven't seen him yet, but people are talking."

The cup was warm in my hands. Too warm. Everything felt too warm, too close, like my skin didn't fit right anymore.

"They say he looks different," Linda continued quietly. "Harder. That eight years as the Devil's servant changes people." She stopped. "I'm sorry, Ilena. I know you two were..."

"We were nothing." The words came out sharp, practiced. Like if I said them enough times without feeling, they'd stop hurting. "That was a long time ago."

"Eight years is a long time," she said gently. "People change. Sometimes they have to."

"Or sometimes they just show you who they always were." The bitterness in my voice surprised even me.

Linda studied me for a long moment. "Did you see him? Last night?"

I nodded.

"And?"

"And he's different. Harder. There was someone with him... beautiful, possessive, unnatural." I swallowed. My throat felt tight. "She said I don't matter."

Klaus made a small sound. Sympathy or pain, I couldn't tell.

"He looked at me like she was right." I stood before anyone could say anything else, before the understanding in their eyes could undo me completely. "He looked right through me. Like I was nothing."

"Oh, honey." Linda's voice was soft. "I'm sorry."

"Don't be. I should be over it by now."

"Should doesn't mean much when it comes to the heart." She stood, smoothing her blazer. "But dwelling on it won't help either. What will help is getting through the next two days with your dignity intact."

She moved to the door, then paused. "So here's the plan. Klaus bathes, and you both rest until this afternoon. I'll come back with appropriate clothes for tonight's dinner. Nothing fancy. Just... presentable. Like you belong here."

"Linda..." I started.

"Not negotiable, dear." She opened the door. "Tonight there's dinner in the Great Hall... everyone who's arrived so far. Nothing formal, but appearances matter. Tomorrow is graduation day." She glanced to Klaus, "The Bergmanns are hosting afternoon drinks before the ceremony. Klaus, your mother didn't invite you."

"Shocking," Klaus muttered.

"Which is why we're going, anyway. All of us. Class of '76 solidarity." Linda's smile was pure steel wrapped in pearls. "Besides, Thomas will be there. He should be arriving within the hour."

Images of a massive wall of flesh with a sheepish smile. Thomas Pedersen would have been a monster if the Devil had chosen him.

Instead, he was Nature's equalizer. Hell forbid if you hurt an animal in his presence.

Linda paused in the doorway, and something in her posture shifted. Less country club mom, more the strategic political operative her family had raised. "One more thing."

I waited.

"Whatever happened between you and Alexi eight years ago? People are already talking. And the Devil doesn't put his hunters on people he considers irrelevant."

The air left my lungs. "His hunters?"

"That's what he is now." Linda's voice was gentle but unflinching. "The Devil's hunter. His enforcer. The one who tracks down oath-breakers deals with... problems. Graduates who miss Convocations. People who violate their oaths. Anyone who becomes a liability. He's very good at his job, Ilena. Very thorough. And from what I've heard, very... cold about it."

Cold. Like those storm-gray eyes meeting mine across the courtyard.

"If you're planning to run," Linda continued quietly, "you should know... he's the one they'll send after you. Both of you."

She left before I could respond. Before I could process that the boy who used to look at me like I was his whole world had spent eight years hunting people like us.

The door clicked shut.

Klaus bit into his muffin, chewing slowly. His hand had stopped shaking. "She's terrifying."

"Yeah," my voice sounded distant.

"Also probably right about everything."

"Yeah."

We sat in silence. The sun was fully up now, golden light streaming across Lake Cincis through the narrow window. Beautiful. Deceptive.

Two days until the lottery. Two days of social warfare and political maneuvering. Two days until ten names would be drawn and ten lives would get exponentially more complicated.

And somewhere in this compound, Alexi was waiting. The Devil's hunter. The enforcer. The weapon.

Looking for problems to solve.

I took another drink of terrible coffee and tried not to think about what it meant that he'd looked at me at all.

Dragons

BY LATE AFTERNOON, LINDA had transformed us into something resembling functional adults.

I wore borrowed burgundy silk and clean boots. Klaus looked almost like himself again... eyeliner perfect, silver rings catching light, the mask of charm firmly back in place. We stood in Linda's room while she performed last inspections like a general reviewing troops.

"Remember," she said, adjusting Klaus's collar, "tonight is about being seen. Showing you're not hiding." She turned to me, straightened an invisible wrinkle. "We're walking in together. All of us. Class of '76 presenting a united front."

"All of us?" Klaus asked.

"I've already rounded up the others. Maria and Andrei are waiting downstairs. Thomas said he'd meet us at the entrance. Cristina's coming from the east wing. Of course, Stefan... provided he isn't too...full of himself." Linda checked her watch. "That's eight of us. Not bad."

Eight out of ten. Two missing from our graduating class.

Alexi made nine, but it was for our tenth that I had a bit of concern. I didn't want to know if they were dead, all things considered.

"United front," Linda repeated. "We all survived together. We walk in together. No one picks us off one by one." She looked between Klaus and me. "And tomorrow, Klaus, the Bergmann family event is non-negotiable. Lena will be with you."

"Mother will hate that," Klaus said.

"Good." Linda smiled sharply. "Now come on. The others are waiting."

We met them in the main corridor. Maria pulled me into a brief hug. "Ilena. Good to see you still breathing."

"Barely."

"Same." She gestured to a tall, weathered man. "You remember Andrei?"

He nodded. Drought magic specialist. Last I'd heard, he was working in North Africa.

Cristina joined us... sharp features, sharper eyes. "Prague's keeping me busy. Weather consulting for the Party."

Thomas arrived, stocky and bearded. "Sorry. Got cornered by legacy families."

Then Stefan Kovács strolled up, expensive suit, too much cologne, that salesman smile. "Class of '76! All together again." He spread his arms. "Just like old times, except older and more desperate."

"Stefan," Linda said coolly.

"Already placed my bets on the lottery. Klaus, you're at fifteen to one. Ilena's at ten to one." He winked. "Berlin really improved your odds."

"Fuck off, Kovács," Klaus muttered.

"Now, now." Stefan straightened his tie. "Eight of us. Not bad for a survival rate. Though I heard Mihai's in the infirmary... fifty-fifty on whether he makes it."

"That's enough." Linda's voice went sharp. "We're presenting a united front tonight. You keep your odds-making to yourself. Understood?"

Stefan held up his hands. "Message received."

Linda clapped her hands softly. "Eight of us. We walk in together; we sit together. No one gets to whisper about how we've fallen apart." She paused. "All ten of us graduated alive. That's rare. Most classes lose three or more students. And we're the youngest class here... '78 and '81 won't return until their seven-year marks. Right now, we're the newest blood in a room full of people who've been doing this longer." Her eyes swept over us. "So we show them we belong. Maria, you're on my right. Andrei left. Ilena and Klaus in the center... you're the ones people will be watching. Cristina, Thomas, take the flanks. Stefan... " She fixed Kovács with a look.

"You walk with us and keep your mouth shut unless it's helpful. Clear?"

"Crystal, darling."

"Good." Linda's smile softened. "I'm proud of us. Now let's show them why."

The great hall at sunset looked like something out of a fever dream.

Massive stone space, vaulted ceiling disappearing into shadow. Long tables in a U-shape, with candles and oil lamps providing the only light. Bare stone walls carved with symbols that hurt to look at directly. High windows showed the lake and mountains beyond, the sky turning gold and pink.

It should have been beautiful.

Instead, it felt like walking into a tomb.

Graduates filled the space... over a hundred and fifty of them, spanning decades. Every living Solomonari from the past eighty years. The oldest looked barely mobile, magic the only thing keeping them upright. Classes from the seventies, sixties, and fifties. Gray-haired survivors from the forties. A few ancient ones from even earlier.

We were the youngest. The newest blood to return. The babies in a room full of veterans who'd survived decades.

At the center head table sat the Master. Stăpânul. Ancient and powerful and patient as stone. Two figures flanked him, perfectly positioned like pieces on a chessboard... bishops or knights protecting their king.

On his left, the woman from the courtyard. Elegant in deep crimson. Unnaturally still.

On his right, Alexi.

All in black. Sitting with the calm confidence of someone who belonged at that table. Who'd earned his place in service.

I'd spent years scraping by in Berlin, taking whatever jobs I could get, wondering what I'd done wrong. Wondering why he'd looked at me like that on graduation day... like I'd destroyed something precious. Wondering if our love had ever been real or if I'd imagined the whole thing.

He'd spent them here, at the Master's right hand. Trusted. Powerful. Important.

The boy who used to laugh at my terrible jokes was gone. The one who'd trace patterns on my skin while we lay tangled together in stolen moments, whispering plans for our future... vanished.

In his place sat a stranger in expensive black. Someone who looked like they'd forgotten I ever existed.

The matched set. The Devil's enforcers. The Master's weapons.

And I was just another failed graduate in borrowed silk, trying not to drown.

My chest tightened.

Klaus's hand found mine. Squeezed once.

"Breathe," he murmured. "Just breathe."

We found seats midway down the left table. Close enough to show we weren't hiding. Far enough from the head table that I could pretend not to feel the weight of his presence.

The Master stood. Conversations died.

"Să trăiești," he said. The ancient greeting.

"Să trăim," the hall responded as one.

May you live. May we live.

The ritual phrases we'd learned as students, repeated at every Convocation. A reminder that our oaths weren't temporary. That we'd sworn ourselves to this... to the Scholomance, to the Devil, to the magic that marked us as different from mortals... for life.

Some oaths you kept until they killed you.

The formal words. Everyone here knew them.

"Tonight we dine together. Tomorrow, the Class of 1984 will join our ranks. Tomorrow night, one will be chosen to serve." His eyes swept the room. "And the night after, the lottery will call ten more to provide for our future."

One hundred fifty-six living graduates. Ten names drawn. I did the math automatically... a six percent chance. Could be worse. At least it wasn't fifty-fifty like the tribute lottery for the Class of '84. Poor bastards.

Tomorrow. It was all happening tomorrow.

"But tonight," the Master continued, "we celebrate survival. Those who remain. Those who answered the summons." A pause. "Eat. Drink. Remember why we endure."

He sat. The hall erupted into noise... louder now, an edge of desperation underneath. We were all thinking about tomorrow. The lottery. Which ten names would be drawn.

Food appeared. Elaborate spreads. Roasted meats, fresh vegetables, bread that tasted fresh and real out of the oven. Wine that kept flowing. I ate mechanically. Tasted nothing.

The head table was impossible to avoid. The Master at the center. The woman in crimson speaking to him occasionally. Alexi was mostly silent, watchful. The inner circle. The ones who truly held power. Everyone else just subjects. Oath-bound and expendable.

I tried not to look. Failed.

His head turned. Just slightly.

Those storm-gray eyes found mine across the hall.

For a moment... just a heartbeat... an emotion flickered across his expression. I couldn't name it. Recognition, certainly. But underneath that, something rawer. Something that made my chest tighten and my breath catch.

Pain? Longing?

It was gone before I could be sure, shutters slamming down so fast I might have imagined it.

For one heartbeat, he'd looked like the boy I'd loved.

Then his face went blank. Carefully, deliberately blank. Like he was hiding something. Like seeing me cost him something.

He looked away first. Back to the Master. Back to whatever secrets they were discussing.

My chest ached.

I'd expected hatred. The same look he'd given me on graduation day... rage, betrayal, contempt. I'd braced for that. Rehearsed how I wouldn't flinch, wouldn't show him it still hurt.

This was different. Complicated.

Like looking at me hurt him too.

Or maybe I was reading too much into a moment. Maybe the time away was long enough for him to stop caring. Maybe I meant nothing to him now... not worth hating, not worth remembering. Just another graduate in a room full of them.

That should hurt less than hatred.

It didn't.

Klaus nudged my foot under the table. "Stop staring," he murmured.

"I'm not..."

"You are." His voice was gentle. Knowing. "And he knows it."

I tore my eyes away. Focused on my wine. My hands weren't quite steady.

"What did you see?" Klaus asked quietly.

I didn't know how to answer. What had I seen? A flicker of something I couldn't name. A carefully constructed mask. The space between us humming with silence and questions I'd never gotten to ask.

"I don't know," I said finally. "That's the problem. I don't know what any of it meant."

"Whatever's between you two," Klaus said, watching me with those too-perceptive eyes, "it's not dead. Everyone's noticing."

"There's nothing between us."

"Lena," he said it softly. "You can lie to them. Don't lie to yourself."

Before I could respond, the temperature dropped. Not gradually. All at once.

Conversations died. Everyone felt it.

I looked up. The sky beyond the windows had gone dark. Wrong dark. The kind that meant something unnatural.

Thunder rolled. Distant but coming closer.

"Mein Gott," Klaus breathed.

The great hall doors burst open.

Wind howled in... cold, violent, carrying the smell of ozone and something older. Ancient. The candles guttered but didn't go out, flames bending sideways.

And then we heard it. Wings. Massive wings beating the air, each stroke like thunder, like mountains moving, like the world remembering what fear meant.

Everyone was standing. Chairs scraping. People moving toward the doors, toward the windows, drawn by something primal and terrifying.

I knew what this was. I'd overheard the Master and Alexi in the courtyard.

Knowing and experiencing were two very different things.

I followed.

We poured out into the courtyard. The sky had gone full dark despite the sunset, clouds roiling like something was stirring them from above. Lightning flickered... not natural lightning, too controlled. It illuminated shapes in the clouds.

Massive shapes.

"Holy mother of God," someone whispered.

The dragon descended.

Govirrod.

Compulsion

WATER CASCADED FROM WINGS the size of sails, each beat sending spray across the courtyard. He was massive... bigger than anything alive had a right to be. Storm-cloud scales caught the lightning still flickering through the air. Eyes like molten silver swept across us, ancient and predatory and hungry.

Then the compulsion hit.

Not gradually. All at once. Like being doused in ice water and set on fire simultaneously.

Need.

It slammed into me, physical as a fist to the gut. My magic surged without permission, crackling under my skin, desperate to reach out, to connect, to *bond*. Every nerve ending screamed.

My pulse hammered in my throat. Heat flooded through me... inappropriate, overwhelming, impossible to ignore.

I wanted. God, I wanted with an intensity that bordered on pain.

Around me, others gasped. Stumbled. Someone whimpered. The sound was raw, almost sexual. It should have been embarrassing. Instead, it just made the need worse.

Because we ALL felt it. Every Solomonari in the courtyard was caught in the same terrible pull. The same desperate hunger.

My feet moved without my consent. One step. Two. Toward the lake. Toward the dragon. My magic was screaming *yes yes closer must get closer...*

The dragon's head swung toward us. Intelligence burned in those silver eyes. He knew exactly what he was doing to us.

Then his voice filled my skull.

Not words. Not sound. *Meaning*, pressed directly into my consciousness like a brand. Thunder and inevitability and grief so deep it had weight. It reverberated through my bones, my blood, the magic humming desperately under my skin.

I SEEK A WORTHY BOND.

The force of it drove me to my knees. Pain and pleasure mixed until I couldn't tell the difference. My hands hit the wet stone, palms stinging. Around me, half the courtyard was down—some on their knees like me, others collapsed entirely, gasping.

MY RIDER HAS RETURNED TO DUST.

Grief. Ancient, bottomless grief. It rolled through the mental connection, and I *felt* it, felt seventy years of bonded partnership severed by death, felt the dragon's loneliness like a physical wound.

And underneath it—that terrible, magnetic pull. *Choose me. Choose me. I could fill that emptiness. I could be everything you need.*

WHO AMONG YOU DARES STAND BEFORE ME?

Yes. The word formed without thought. *ME. I DARE. CHOOSE ME. NEED ME.*

I was trying to stand. Legs shaking, magic wild, every cell in my body demanding I get *closer*. The dragon's presence was intoxicating—raw power and primal danger and something that felt horrifyingly like desire.

This wasn't rational. Wasn't safe. Was probably going to kill me. I didn't care.

TWO NIGHTS HENCE, WHEN DARKNESS IS COMPLETE, THOSE WHO WOULD BOND SHALL PROVE THEIR WORTH.

Two nights. May 29th. I could do it. I could prove myself. I could...

My magic surged higher, responding to the promise. Lightning crackled between my fingers. The surrounding air dropped ten degrees without my conscious command. I was half-standing now, swaying, every instinct screaming to throw myself into the lake if that's what it took.

MANY WILL COME.

The dragon's massive head swiveled, scanning the crowd with those silver eyes. Evaluating. Judging. I felt the weight of that gaze like a physical touch.

ONE WILL SUFFICE.

The compulsion tripled. My vision narrowed. The world was just me and the dragon and this overwhelming, all-consuming *need* that felt like it was tearing me apart from the inside.

I took another step forward. Then another.

Around me, others moved too. Klaus was on his feet, swaying but moving toward the shore. Linda had one hand pressed to her chest like she was trying to hold her heart in. Even the ancient ones from the forties were standing, eyes glazed, pulled by the same irresistible force.

We were moths to a flame. And we knew it would burn us alive.

THE REST...

The dragon paused. Heavy. Ominous.

The unspoken ending hung in the air: *will die.*

My heart hammered. Sweat slicked my palms despite the cold. I was still moving forward, magic wild, barely conscious of anything except the dragon's presence and the desperate, clawing need to get *closer...*

Someone stepped beside me.

"Magnificent, isn't he?"

Alexi's voice. Low. Conversational.

The compulsion shattered.

Not gradually... violently, like a cord snapping. The dragon's pull vanished, replaced by something equally overwhelming but far more dangerous.

Him.

I gasped, stumbling. My magic didn't settle... it redirected, coiling hot and confused under my skin. Every nerve ending that had been screaming for the dragon was suddenly screaming for the man standing inches away.

The absence of the compulsion was worse than the compulsion itself.

Because now I could think. Could process what had just happened. How close I'd come to throwing myself at the dragon like I was in heat. How I'd been *this close* to volunteering for something that would probably kill me, all because the pull felt like...

I couldn't finish that thought. Especially not with him standing this close.

I was acutely, viscerally aware of him. The heat radiating from his body despite the icy wind. The way he smelled... leather and sweat and a darkness that made my pulse spike. How close he was standing. Close enough that if I swayed forward...

My magic reached for him instinctively, and I felt the moment it connected. Just a brush, a whisper of contact, but it sent lightning up my spine.

He went still.

The dragon's massive form turned, wings beating once... a sound like mountains colliding... before it dove into Lake Cincis.

Black water exploded upward, then swallowed Govirrod whole. The crushing pressure on my chest vanished with it. Around us, a hundred and fifty magicians drew breath at once, the collective gasp ricocheting off obsidian walls as bodies dropped and stumbled.

The courtyard was chaos. People struggling to stand, helping each other up. Eyes wide with shock and residual desire and dawning horror as they realized what they'd almost done.

"Fuck." Klaus's voice, rough and shaking. "Fuck. I need... " He didn't finish. Just fumbled for his cigarettes with hands that wouldn't cooperate.

But I barely registered it. Because Alexi was looking at me now, and whatever careful blankness he'd worn at dinner was gone. His eyes were dark, pupils blown wide, tracking my face and cataloging my responses. His jaw was tight. A muscle jumped in his cheek.

He was feeling it too.

The realization sent heat flooding through me that had nothing to do with magic and everything to do with the way his gaze dropped to my mouth for a fraction of a second before snapping back up.

The silence between us felt louder than the dragon's mental roar.

I should say something. Should ask why his presence worked when I couldn't break free myself. Should demand to know what the hell just happened.

Instead, I stood there, heart still racing, magic still humming with residual need, acutely aware of every inch of space between his body and mine. I knew this body. Had memorized it eight years ago. Every scar, every angle, every sound he made when...

Stop.

"You felt it," I said finally. My voice came out rougher than intended.

"Everyone felt it." His tone was carefully neutral, but his voice had that wrecked quality underneath. Storm-gray eyes still tracking the water where the dragon had disappeared.

"That's not what I mean." I turned to face him fully. "You *broke* it. Whatever that was, you..."

"I didn't do anything." He finally met my gaze fully. Those eyes were darker up close, storm clouds before lightning strikes. "Just made an observation."

Liar.

The air between us felt charged. Dangerous. Like standing too close to a cliff edge.

His hand came up... stopping himself or reaching for me, I couldn't tell. It hovered in the air between us, close enough that I could feel the heat of his palm.

"Ilena." My name on his voice. Rough. Almost a warning. "Don't."

"Don't what?" The words came out breathy. "You're the one who..."

"I know what I did."

Then Linda's voice cut through: "Is everyone alright? Klaus, sit down before you fall down. Maria, check on..."

Alexi stepped back. Away from me. The sudden absence of his presence left me cold.

The careful blankness slammed back over his features, though I could see the effort it took. His shoulders were rigid. His hands had curled into fists at his sides.

"Two nights," he breathed. Just to me. Voice under control now but still rough at the edges. "Some of them will try. Most of them will die."

A pause. His eyes held mine, and for just a moment I saw everything he was trying to hide.

"Don't be one of them."

Then he walked away, black coat disappearing into the chaos of shaken graduates, leaving me standing alone with my pulse still hammering and my magic still reaching for him instead of the dragon, and that terrified me more than anything.

Klaus found me ten minutes later.

I was still standing in roughly the same spot, trying to convince my legs to move. Around us, the courtyard settled, slowly regaining some fragments of composure. Small groups clustered together, voices rising and falling, everyone talking about the dragon. About who would try. About who would die.

He pressed a lit cigarette into my hand without a word.

I took it gratefully. The smoke burned going down, grounding me back in my body. My hands had finally stopped shaking.

"You good?" he asked.

"Define good."

"Fair." He lit his own cigarette, inhaled deeply. His color was better than this morning... the Sunshine had done its work. But his eyes were sharp, watching me with that unsettling perceptiveness he got sometimes. "Never thought I'd want to fuck an ancient mythological beast, but here we are."

Despite everything, I laughed. Just a short bark of sound, but real. "Jesus, Klaus."

"Just saying what everyone's thinking." He took another drag. "That was intense."

Understatement of the year.

"The dragon?" I asked, knowing that wasn't what he meant.

"Sure. The dragon." He took another drag. "Also the part where Alexi broke whatever spell you were under and you two proceeded to have an entire conversation without saying a word."

My stomach dropped. "We didn't... "

"Lena." Klaus's voice was gentle. "Everyone saw."

"Saw what? There was nothing to see."

"Right. That's why half the courtyard is now speculating about what happened between you two." He flicked ash. "Linda's already doing damage control. Spreading the narrative that you're both professionals, past is past, nothing to see here."

"There *is* nothing to see."

"Then why did his presence break the compulsion when nothing else could?" Klaus turned to face me fully. "I felt that pull, Lena. We all did. It was..." He stopped, searching for words. "It was like every cell in my body was screaming to get closer. And then he stepped next to you and it just... stopped. For you."

I didn't have an answer for that.

"Not for the rest of us," Klaus continued quietly. "Linda was still swaying. Maria was on her knees. Even the ancient ones from the forties were trying to stand. But you? The second he spoke, you were free."

"I don't know why."

"Don't you?" His eyes were too knowing. "Or do you just not want to admit it?"

I took a long drag from the cigarette, buying time. Around us, the speculation was getting louder. I caught fragments...

"...dragon bonding in two nights..."

"...who's powerful enough..."

"...did you see how many collapsed..."

"...most won't survive..."

"How many do you think will try?" I asked, deflecting.

Klaus let me change the subject. "For Govirrod? Maybe twenty? Thirty?" He shook his head. "Legacy families will push their best candidates forward. The desperate will volunteer. Anyone who thinks they can handle it."

"Plus the entire Class of '84," I added quietly. "They graduate tomorrow. Ten fresh graduates with nothing to lose and everything to prove."

Klaus's expression darkened. "Fuck. I hadn't thought about that. They'll be the most eager... graduation high, full of power, convinced they're invincible." He took a long drag. "They're going to die in droves."

"The dragon said one will suffice."

"And the rest will die." Klaus's voice was flat. He paused. "Are you thinking about trying?"

"No," the answer came too quickly.

"Lena..."

"I said no." I dropped the cigarette, crushed it under my boot. "I can't afford to die. Can barely afford to be here."

"That's not why you won't try."

I looked at him.

"You won't try," Klaus said quietly, "because he told you not to."

My chest tightened. "That's not..."

"It's okay." He smiled, sad and knowing. "Whatever this is between you two, it's not over. Eight years, and it's still not over."

I didn't respond. Couldn't.

Movement caught my eye: Stefan Kovács hurrying past, his jacket held awkwardly in front of his expensive trousers. His face was flushed, avoiding eye contact with everyone.

Klaus's eyes tracked Stefan's movements. His eyebrows rose. "Did Kovács just...?"

"Looks like it."

"Christ." Klaus's laugh was sharp and slightly hysterical. "The dragon call really did a number on everyone, didn't it?"

"Apparently some more than others."

"At least he's going to clean up before..." Klaus stopped, shook his head. "You know what? I don't want to think about it. I really, really don't."

Linda appeared from the crowd, pearls gleaming in the lamplight. She'd somehow maintained her composure despite everything... hair still perfect, smile still bright, but her eyes were sharp and assessing.

"There you are." She linked her arm through mine, through Klaus's, pulling us both close. "We're doing a strategic retreat. Class of '76 is gathering in Maria's room. Wine, debriefing, and making sure no one does anything stupid tonight."

"Like volunteering for dragon bonding?" Klaus asked.

"Exactly like that." Linda's voice went steel-edged. "I'm not losing anyone to ambition or desperation."

She looked between us. "Tomorrow's going to be brutal enough. Graduation, your family's event, Klaus... the lottery." Her grip tightened. "But tonight, we rest. We survive. Understood?"

"Yes, ma'am," Klaus muttered.

"Good." She squeezed both our arms. "Now come on. The others are waiting, and Maria has actual Romanian wine, not this terrible local vintage."

The three of us stood there, linked together in the chaos. Around us, graduates scattered—some to their rooms, some to continue speculating, some already planning their attempts at bonding.

Two nights until the bonding.

Two nights until some of them died.

And three nights until the lottery drew ten names and made our lives exponentially more complicated.

"Come on," Linda said gently. "Let's get you both inside. Tomorrow's going to be brutal."

She wasn't wrong.

Until You Burn

"Wait, Kovács... he came in his trousers?!"

Maria giggled into the wine bottle before taking a long drink.

Andrei chuckled. "It's one thing to piss yourself in fear. Admittedly, I may have done so. But to experience full arousal? I mean, not to shame anyone, but..."

Thomas's massive frame gave a slight 'humph' of amusement. He took another pull from the bottle and handed it to me, completely bypassing Klaus.

"Rude!" Klaus said indignantly.

Thomas shrugged. "Blame the den mother."

Linda gave that diplomatic, steely smile. "Klaus, my lovely dove. Detox, just a few days. I love you to the stars above, but I need you focused. At least for tomorrow."

Klaus's face went dark for a moment. Then he reached into his pocket and pulled out a fresh pack of Davidoff cigarettes.

I shot him a look of surprise.

"Let's say it wasn't just his load that Kovács lost from his trousers." Klaus smiled as he tapped the pack against his palm. "Can I interest you in fine western tobacco?"

I smiled for the first time since we got here. I took the pilfered cigarette and lit up, inhaling deeply.

"Fucking Klaus."

Thomas and Andrei weren't smokers, but they still gave familiar smiles of approval. For a moment, I felt a decade recede as we sat in the small room... smoking, laughing, drinking.

The years faded with each drag of imported Western tobacco. The flavor reminded me of wheat bran, which somehow made it more intoxicating. For a brief moment, I let my fears leave and invited the ghosts of the past to intermix with the faces around me.

Maria's room was small, meant for one. We'd crammed ourselves in any way... Thomas taking up half the floor space by the window, Linda perched on the desk like she was holding court, Cristina sprawled across the bed with the languid confidence of someone who knew exactly when she'd die and it wasn't tonight. The rest of us found space where we could. Klaus sat beside me on the floor, back against the wall, close enough that our shoulders touched.

All of us paying a price for power. A price just to fucking live.

The room smelled like smoke and wine and something else... us. Eight years of distance couldn't erase the familiarity of being together. The way Thomas took up space without apology. How Linda's laugh, rare as it was, could fill a room. Maria's habit of touching things when she talked... the rim of her glass, her necklace, reassuring herself the physical world was still solid.

We'd survived the Scholomance together. Survived the Devil's binding. Some of us had thrived in the years since. Others... I looked at Klaus, the tremor in his hands... were barely holding on. But we were here. Still breathing. Still bound by something deeper than magic or obligation.

"Remember Stefan's attempt at cooking?" Maria said suddenly, refilling glasses. "That night he tried to make us goulash?"

Thomas's rumble was almost a laugh. "Burned the bottom. Raw in the middle. We ate it anyway."

"Because we were too drunk to care," Andrei added.

"Because we were family," Linda corrected softly.

The word hung in the air. Family. Not by blood. By survival.

Outside, the wind picked up. I could hear it whistling through the corridors, rattling the old windows. The sound of water lapping against stone drifted up from somewhere below—rhythmic, patient, like breathing.

Maria's hands were steadier than mine as she poured. Steadier than Klaus's, who was holding his cigarette too tight. The wine was good... too good for people like us... but tonight, no one was counting costs.

"So," Maria said, "who had money on the dragon showing up during dinner?"

"I thought we'd at least get through the first night." Andrei had loosened his collar, looking less like a saint and more like the rest of us—tired, wary.

Thomas rumbled from his corner. "Govirrod. Inge's dragon. Seventy years bonded. He'll be selective."

"Selective... meaning most people who try will die horribly." Linda lit her own cigarette. Even now she maintained that perfect posture, but I could see the tension in her shoulders.

The wind picked up again. Stronger this time. Something creaked deep in the building's bones.

Maria exhaled smoke, watching it curl toward the ceiling. "Twenty-seven will attempt. Twenty-six will fail."

The room went still.

Klaus's face paled. "You saw that?"

Maria shrugged. "I see what might be. But yes. Many deaths tomorrow night." She took another drag, rings catching the lamplight. "Some will drown. Some will burn. Some will simply break."

No one moved. Outside, the wind howled. I could hear water now—not just lapping, but moving. Like something large displacing it in the depths.

"Jesus," Cristina whispered.

"Unlikely," Klaus quipped.

We all felt it...that pull, that need. Hours later and I could still feel the echo in my chest. The wanting.

"Can you ward against it?" Klaus asked Cristina. "The compulsion?"

She shook her head. "I can protect others from curses, dark magic, even death itself if I'm fast enough. But I can't protect myself. That's the cost." She paused, listening to the wind. "Besides, Govirrod's not something you ward against. He's not an attack. He's... permission."

"Permission to want something badly enough to die for it," Andrei said quietly.

Maria tilted the wine bottle. Empty. "Shit."

"There's more downstairs," Linda said. "Common room had cases."

"I'll go." Thomas pushed himself up, the floorboards groaning under his weight. He had to duck through the doorway.

The silence after he left felt heavier. Colder. The wind was constant now, moaning through cracks in the stone. And beneath it, something else. A sound I couldn't quite identify. Deep. Resonant. Coming from the lake.

The dragon.

Klaus's leg bounced against mine. His hands trembled as he lit another cigarette. Withdrawal and fear tangled together.

"What do we actually know about dragons?" Andrei asked. "Actual knowledge, not stories."

"They're rare." Maria wrapped her arms around herself. "The Devil keeps maybe a dozen. No one knows for certain."

"They bond for life," Linda added. "Once bonded, the connection is permanent. Rider and dragon until one of them dies."

"The bonding itself," Andrei said slowly. "What does it actually do?"

"Shares magic. Amplifies it." Cristina's voice was distant. "Dragon and rider become extensions of each other. The rider gains power, endurance, lifespan."

"How long?" Maria asked.

"Centuries. Maybe more." Cristina paused. "It changes you. Makes you something between human and... not."

A sharp crack echoed through the building. We all jumped.

Klaus was on his feet instantly, body coiled. Thomas had stopped in the doorway, one hand on the frame. Linda's cigarette had frozen halfway to her lips.

Silence.

Then another crack. Settling. Just the old building adjusting to the cold and wind.

"Fuck," Klaus breathed, sitting back down. His shoulder pressed against mine, solid and shivering.

"We're all on edge," Linda said, but her voice wasn't quite steady.

Thomas returned with two bottles, water droplets beading on the glass. "It's colder. Temperature dropped at least ten degrees since dinner."

He wasn't wrong. I could see my breath now, a faint mist in the lamplight.

I looked toward the window. Beyond the glass, the lake was invisible in the dark. But I could feel it. Feel him. Govirrod, somewhere in those black depths, waiting.

Maria poured fresh wine, the bottle clinking against the glass. "Linda, you worked with Inge. What was she like?"

Linda took a long drag before answering. "Different. Powerful, yes. But there was something... not quite human about her. She could sense storms forming three days out. Could feel pressure systems like you or I feel temperature. She said the dragon's thoughts mixed with hers. Said sometimes she couldn't tell where she ended and Govirrod began."

"That doesn't sound like power," Klaus said. "That sounds like losing yourself."

"Maybe it's both," Cristina said.

The wind rattled the windows. Water splashed against stone somewhere below—harder than before, like waves were building.

"That compulsion though." Maria's voice was quiet. "I've felt nothing like it."

"The Devil's timing was perfect." Linda's voice took on that sharp, analytical edge. "Maximum audience. Immediate announcement. No time to think."

"Just react," Andrei said.

"Population control," I said. "Kill off the ones who might challenge him."

Maria's eyes went distant, unfocused. Seeing something.

"Lena." Linda's voice was careful. "You seemed to shake it off faster than most. By the end."

I felt everyone's attention shift.

Klaus's shoulder pressed harder against mine. "Alexi was standing next to you. That's when you stopped swaying."

The room went quiet. Even the wind seemed to pause.

"We all noticed," Cristina said softly.

"The pull stopped for you." Linda leaned forward. "The rest of us were still feeling it."

"I don't know why."

Maria blinked, coming back to herself. "Your magic recognized his. Storm and ice. You've always been mirrors."

My chest tightened. The truth of it sat heavy between us.

"You two were different at school," Maria said. Her voice had gone soft, remembering. "I mean, everyone knew you were together, but it was more than that. You moved like you were connected. Like you shared the same heartbeat."

"He balanced her," Linda added quietly. "She could call storms, but he could direct them. When they worked together..." She trailed off.

"It was beautiful," Andrei finished. "Terrifying, but beautiful."

I remembered. God, I remembered. The way our magic had woven together. Lightning and ice, storm and frost. We'd created blizzards that could level forests. Hailstorms that sang. He'd been my anchor, and I'd been his wildness, and together we'd been something neither of us could be alone.

My magic stirred at the memory, reaching for something that wasn't there anymore. Ice crystallized on my fingertips before I forced it back down. Even now, my power remembered his, wanted his...was incomplete without him. The pull was almost as strong as the dragon's compulsion; that desperate, aching need for connection.

I'd loved him. Completely. Stupidly. Love that burns everything else away until there's nothing left but two people and the magic they make together. We'd talked about after... after graduation, after whatever the Devil demanded. We'd had plans. Foolish, impossible plans that felt real when he held me.

And then graduation night, when it all shattered. When The Devil chose him, he'd looked at me like I was poison. Like every touch, every whispered promise, every moment of our magic singing together had been a lie.

I didn't know which hurt more... losing him, or never knowing why.

"What happened?" Andrei asked. "Between you two?"

"Aside from him becoming the Tribute... I don't honestly know." The confession of my feelings stung.

"Seeing him tonight... in uniform... " Linda trailed off.

"He's not Alek anymore," Klaus said quietly. "He's Alexius. The Storm."

"I've heard stories," Maria said. "Oath-breakers who run. He finds them."

Andrei's voice dropped. "And what's left of them isn't pretty."

A silence fell. Different from before... heavier. I knew what Maria and Andrei said was true. He'd been sent with others to investigate the incident at The Wall. I tried to talk to him then, but it was impossible. It was like he was a completely different person.

Maybe that's what happened when you became the Tribute.

"Did anyone else notice the woman with him?" Maria asked finally. "During the compulsion?"

"Luminița." The way Linda said the name made it sound like a curse.

"I saw her too." Maria's voice was quiet. "Rumor has it she's been with the Master for decades. Maybe longer. Never ages. Never changes."

Thomas rumbled from the window. "Doesn't feel human. Something else wearing a woman's shape."

"Demon," Cristina said flatly. "The Devil's eyes. His advisor. The one who whispers in his ear."

"She looked at Lena like she wanted her dead," Klaus said.

Maria's gaze slid to me. "Because she knows what's coming."

Everyone looked at her.

"What's coming?" I asked.

"I don't know exactly," Maria said. "The futures split. But you and Alexius... your threads are tangled. Have been since graduation. Will be until... " She stopped.

"Until what?" Cristina pressed.

Maria met my eyes. Her gaze was distant, seeing something none of us could.

"Until one of you breaks free," she said quietly. "Or both of you burn."

The Stacks

THE COMPOUND WAS QUIET at two in the morning.

I couldn't sleep. Couldn't stop my mind from circling back to the courtyard, to Govirrod's massive form descending from the clouds, to the compulsion that had locked every muscle in my body until Alexi's presence shattered it. For me. Only for me.

I needed answers. About what dragon bonding actually meant. What I was facing in two nights when graduates would throw themselves at a creature that could kill them with a thought.

The only solution was to do something I'd disliked even when I actually attended... study.

The library door was unlocked. Inside, the air smelled exactly as I remembered: old paper and older magic, dust and secrets and knowledge that had outlived the people who wrote it down.

Moonlight filtered through high windows, painting everything silver and shadow.

Empty.

My footsteps echoed on stone as I headed for the back stacks. The restricted section, where they kept the dangerous texts. Where we used to meet when we didn't want anyone to find us. Where he'd pressed me against these same shelves and kissed me until I forgot my own name.

I shoved the memory down.

My fingers trailed along leather spines as I walked, reading titles embossed in gold leaf. Romanian. Latin. Languages I didn't recognize. I found the section on dragons tucked between weather manipulation and necromancy, and pulled a heavy tome from the shelf.

Draconis Vinculum: On the Nature of Bonds.

The leather binding was cracked with age, pages yellowed and brittle. I settled onto the floor with it, conjuring a soft ice-glow for light. The magic came easily... small, controlled, just enough to read by. Blue-white luminescence that didn't flicker.

The text was dense. Academic. Whoever wrote this had studied dragon bonds the way others studied anatomy... clinical, detailed, occasionally gruesome.

The dragon bond requires perfect magical compatibility between rider and beast. Complementary elements that stabilize rather than destroy. Ice and rain. Lightning and water. Storm and frost...

My chest tightened. Storm and frost. Lightning and ice.

I kept reading.

Historical records show the most powerful bonds occur between mages whose magic naturally grounds the other. The dragon's raw elemental force requires a rider who can channel, direct, and contain that power without being consumed by it. Conversely, the rider's magic must be wild enough to match the dragon's nature while maintaining enough control to...

I turned the page.

A note in the margin. Fresh ink, recent enough I could smell it. Handwriting I didn't recognize... sharp, precise, authoritative.

By order of the Master: No ice-worker or lightning-worker shall attempt the bond this convocation. Violation will result in immediate termination of both parties.

I read it again.

And again.

The Devil had specifically forbidden ice and lightning mages from trying. Why? The book made it clear we were ideal candidates for dragon bonding... complementary elements that could stabilize Govirrod's raw power.

Unless that was exactly the problem.

My hands were shaking. I set the book down carefully, pressing my palms flat against the cold stone floor. Breathing slowly. Thinking.

If ice and lightning together could bond with Govirrod...

If Alexi and I both tried...

"You always did hide in the stacks when you couldn't sleep."

I jerked so hard the book nearly flew from my hands.

Alexi stood at the end of the row, backlit by moonlight streaming through the window behind him. Still in his enforcer blacks, sleeves rolled to his elbows, showing the scars that crawled up his forearms. Arms crossed. Expression unreadable.

My heart was trying to punch through my ribs.

"What are you doing here?" My voice came out steady. Good.

"Making rounds. Saw the light." His eyes flicked to the book in my lap, the ice-glow still hovering above my palm. "Dragon lore."

"Is that against the rules?"

"Depends on what you're planning to do with it."

I stood slowly, keeping the book between us like a shield. The ice-glow brightened involuntarily, responding to my pulse. "That's none of your business."

"It is if you're stupid enough to try for Govirrod."

The casual certainty in his voice made my teeth clench. "And if I am?"

"Then you'll die." Flat. Matter-of-fact. Like he was discussing the weather. "Along with however many other idiots think they can survive the choosing."

"Worried about the body count?"

"Worried about the paperwork." He moved closer. One step. Deliberate. "Dead graduates create complications."

The temperature dropped. Not from me... from him. His magic responded to proximity, to whatever tension was building between us like pressure before a storm.

"How considerate of you," I said.

"I'm a considerate person." Another step. The ice-glow flickered. "When people don't make my job harder."

Three feet between us now. Close enough, I could see the exhaustion shadowing his eyes, the tension in his jaw. Close enough to smell leather and ozone and something underneath that made my magic reach before I could stop it.

He felt it. I watched his pupils dilate, watched him force his expression back to neutral.

"You should leave," I said.

"You should put the book back and go to bed."

"I'm not taking orders from you."

"Then we have a problem." Another step. Two feet now. "Because that book's restricted for a reason."

"I'm allowed to be here."

"At two in the morning? Reading about dragon bonding when everyone knows you're desperate enough to try?" His voice dropped. "That's not research, Ilena. That's suicide planning."

"So what if it is?" I lifted my chin, meeting his eyes. "What's it to you?"

Something flickered across his face. Too fast to read. But I felt his magic spike... lightning crackling just beneath his skin, responding to mine.

"Nothing," he said. "Not a damn thing."

But he didn't move away.

Neither did I.

The air between us felt electric. Literally... I could feel the charge building, raising the hair on my arms. My ice-glow had gone from soft blue to brilliant white, pulsing with my heartbeat.

"Then why are you still here?" I asked.

"Making sure you don't steal anything."

"Fuck you."

"Already done that." The words came out sharp, cutting. "Didn't end well, as I recall."

I threw the book at him.

He caught it one-handed without looking, set it carefully on the shelf beside him. Then he was in my space... not touching, but close enough that I felt the heat radiating off him, close enough that our magic was screaming at each other.

Temperature fluctuated wildly. Cold. Hot. Cold again. Frost spread across the shelf behind me while sparks danced between his fingers.

"You want to die that badly?" His voice was low. Dangerous.

"Better than whatever the hell you've been doing for eight years."

"You don't know anything about what I've been doing."

"No. You made sure of that." I met his eyes. Refused to back down even though my legs were shaking. "One look on graduation night and then nothing. Eight years of nothing. So forgive me if I don't give a shit about your concern for my safety now."

His jaw tightened. Lightning crawled up his forearms, visible through his skin. "You think I wanted..."

"I don't care what you wanted." Ice spread from my hands, coating the shelf beside us in crystalline patterns. "I stopped caring about what you wanted the night you looked at me like I was nothing and let them take you without a word."

"There were things I couldn't say."

"There's always an excuse with you."

"Not an excuse. A fact." His hand slammed into the shelf beside my head. Wood cracked under the impact. Not threatening—frustrated. But caging me anyway, his arm bracketing my shoulder, his body close enough I could feel the electricity dancing across his skin. "You think I had a choice? You think any of this was... "

He stopped. Breathing hard. Too close now. I could see every detail... the muscle jumping in his jaw, his pupils blown so wide his eyes looked black, the lightning crackling between his fingers where they gripped splintered wood.

Our magic was fighting. Pulling. Trying to merge.

"Was what?" I demanded. My voice shook. "Was what, Alexi?"

"Doesn't matter." He fought for control. I watched him wrestle his magic back down, force his voice flat again. "None of it matters now."

"Then why are you here?"

"I told you. Making rounds."

"Bullshit."

"Fine." His eyes locked on mine. Storm-gray and burning. "I'm here because you were stupid enough to wander the library alone at two in the morning and someone needs to make sure you don't do something idiotic."

"Like, try for the dragon?"

"Like try for the dragon."

"And if I do it anyway?"

"Then you'll die." He said it simply. Certainly. But his hand tightened on the shelf, wood creaking under the pressure. "And I'll file the report and move on with my life."

It should have sounded cold. Dismissive.

But there was something in his eyes that didn't match the words. Something raw and bleeding that he was trying to hide behind careful neutrality.

"You're lying," I said.

"About what?"

"About not caring."

His hand tightened until wood splintered. "You don't know what you're talking about."

"Don't I?" I leaned forward. Testing. The space between us crackled with displaced energy. "Because I felt what happened in the courtyard. When the dragon's compulsion hit. You broke it for me. Only for me."

"That was... "

"What? Coincidence? Your magic just ground mine while everyone else was losing their minds?"

"Proximity."

"It was specific." I took a risk. Reached up, slow enough that he could stop me. My fingers found the scars on his forearm... raised tissue in deliberate patterns. The moment I touched him, our magic connected. Hard. My ice racing up his arm, his lightning sinking into my hand. Neither of us pulled away. "Ice and lightning. Complementary elements. The book says they ground each other. Stabilize the chaos."

He caught my wrist. Fast. His grip was careful but firm, stopping me from tracing the patterns any further. His skin was hot under my fingers.

"The book says a lot of things."

"Does it say why the Devil would specifically forbid ice-workers and lightning-workers from attempting the bond this year?"

I watched the color drain from his face.

"What?"

"There was a note. Fresh ink. Margin of page forty-seven." I pulled my wrist free, but didn't step back. Our magic was still tangled, still pulling. "By order of the Master. No ice or lightning mages allowed to try. Care to explain that?"

"Where did you see that?"

"In the book you just confiscated."

His eyes cut to the tome on the shelf. Back to me. Something dangerous flickered across his expression. "Show me."

"No."

"Ilena..."

"You want to see it, you can look yourself." I crossed my arms, trying to ignore the way my whole body was vibrating from the magical contact we'd just broken. "After you tell me why the Devil cares if I try."

"I don't know."

"Try again."

"I said I don't know." But there was something in his voice. A hesitation. A crack in the armor.

"You're lying again."

He grabbed the book. Flipped through pages with controlled violence. Found the section. Read the margin note.

His expression went very still.

"Fuck."

"Care to share?"

"No." He closed the book. Set it down with deliberate care. "And you're not trying for the dragon."

"You don't get to tell me what to do."

"Someone needs to before you get yourself killed."

"Why do you care?" The question burst out before I could stop it. "Why does it matter to you what I do?"

He stared at me. Something burning behind those storm-gray eyes. Something he was fighting desperately to keep locked down.

The temperature plummeted. Then spiked. Our magic was spiraling, feeding off each other.

"It doesn't," he said finally.

"Liar."

"Ilena..."

"Prove it." I stepped into his space. Close enough, our chests almost touched. Close enough that our magic started reaching for each other again, ice and lightning trying to merge. "Prove you don't care. Look me in the eye and tell me it wouldn't matter if I died trying to bond with Govirrod."

"That's not—"

"Say it."

His hand came up—tangled in my hair before I could process the movement. Not gentle. Not rough. Just desperate, fingers threading through the strands, tilting my head back.

"You don't know what you're asking for."

"Then show me."

He kissed me.

Hard. Angry. Eight years of whatever-this-was compressed into contact.

His mouth on mine, hand fisted in my hair, the other at my waist pulling me against him. Not sweet. Not tender. This was frustration and loss and things neither of us could say turned physical.

I bit his lip. Tasted copper.

He made a sound that went straight through me.

Our magic exploded.

Lightning and ice, fighting and grounding simultaneously. Books flew from shelves as if they'd been hit by a blast wave. Frost spread in fractal patterns across every surface, while electricity crackled through the air in visible arcs. The temperature plummeted, spiked, plummeted again.

My back hit the shelves, and he pressed against me. One hand still tangled in my hair, the other sliding up my ribs. Magic bled between us in ways that should hurt but didn't.

This was what complementary elements meant.

Ice and lightning recognized each other. My frost racing up his arms, cooling the fever-burn of his skin. His electricity sinking into me, making every nerve ending sing. We were grounding each other, stabilizing the chaos, creating a circuit that fed back and amplified.

His mouth moved to my throat. I gasped, fingers digging into his shoulders. Ice spread everywhere I touched... his shirt crystallizing under my palms, frost creeping across his collarbones. But he was burning up beneath it, running so hot my ice melted on contact with his bare skin.

The contrast was making me dizzy.

"This is a mistake," he said against my skin. His voice was wrecked.

"I know."

"Changes nothing."

"I know."

His laugh was broken. Hurt. "Then why..."

I pulled his mouth back to mine. Didn't have an answer. Didn't want to think about answers. Just wanted this... his weight against me, his magic tangling with mine, silence replaced by the undeniable fact of connection.

We stood there in the wreckage, kissing like we could rewrite history through contact alone. His magic was wild... barely controlled lightning that should have stopped my heart. But my ice was grounding it, channeling it, making it safe. Making *us* safe.

His hands slid under my shirt. I arched into the touch, into the burning-cold contrast of his palms on my skin. Lightning danced across my ribs. Ice bloomed under his fingers. Neither of us could control it anymore.

The restricted section looked like a war zone. Books scattered everywhere. Shelves coated in frost. Scorch marks on stone. The smell of ozone and winter.

For about thirty seconds, nothing else existed.

Then reality crashed back.

He pulled away first. Stepped back fast, putting three feet of space between us. Dragged both hands through his hair, breathing like he'd run a mile.

"Fuck."

"Yeah."

We stared at each other. Both breathing hard. His lips were swollen, bloodied where I'd bitten him. My hair was a disaster, half-frozen where his lightning had coursed through it. His shirt had holes burned through it from my ice. My skin was flushed and marked with electrical burns that didn't hurt.

The library was destroyed around us.

"This didn't happen," he said.

"Agreed."

"You're still not trying for the dragon."

"Still not your decision."

His jaw worked. Lightning crackled between his fingers. "Ilena..."

"Go." I turned away. Started picking up books with shaking hands. "You made your position clear eight years ago. This doesn't change that."

"You don't understand..."

"I understand perfectly." I didn't look at him. Couldn't. If I looked at him now, with my magic still singing from where it had touched his, I'd do something stupid. "You don't want me dead. Fine. Noted. But you also don't want me in your life, and that's been clear for a long time. So take your concern and your orders and your confusing as hell mixed signals and get out."

Silence.

Long enough, I thought he'd already left.

Then: "For what it's worth," he whispered, "I never wanted you gone."

I froze. Book halfway to the shelf.

When I turned around, he was already walking away.

"Then what did you want?" I called after him.

He stopped at the end of the row. Didn't turn around. Just stood there, silhouetted against the moonlight, shoulders tight.

"Something I couldn't have."

Then he was gone.

I stood there in the wreckage of fallen books and magical destruction, touching my lips. They were swollen. Tingling. I could still taste lightning and copper.

My hands were shaking.

My magic was still singing from where it had touched his, reaching for him even though he was gone.

And I had absolutely no idea what the hell any of it meant.

Ozone and Bad Decisions

I MADE IT BACK to my room just as the eastern sky turned gold.

The door was unlocked.

I froze with my hand on the handle, ice already coating my fingertips. Someone had been in my room. Someone was still—

"Don't freeze the doorknob, Liebling. I just picked that lock."

Klaus.

I pushed the door open. He was sitting on my bed, looking marginally more human than yesterday thanks to Krystyna's Sunshine draught, smoking a cigarette and watching me with eyes that saw too much.

"Turnabout's fair play," he said, gesturing with his cigarette. "You've picked my lock enough times."

"Don't," I said, closing the door behind me and heading straight for the tiny bathroom attached to my room.

"Don't what?"

"Whatever you're about to say. Don't."

I caught a glimpse of myself in the mirror over the tiny sink and froze.

My lips were swollen. Bruised-looking. There was a faint mark on my jaw where Alexi's thumb had pressed. My hair was a disaster...completely out of its tie, tangled like I'd been in a windstorm. Or against a wall. My shirt was wrinkled, buttons slightly askew.

I looked exactly like someone who'd been thoroughly kissed. Fuck.

"That good, huh?" Klaus's voice drifted through the open door.

"Shut up."

"I'm just saying, you left here looking like death warmed over and now you look like... "

"I said shut up, Klaus."

I turned on the water, splashed my face. Tried to finger-comb my hair into something resembling order. Re-buttoned my shirt properly. It didn't help. The evidence was written all over me.

When I emerged, Klaus had stubbed out his cigarette and was watching me with an expression I couldn't quite read. Concern mixed with something that might have been amusement. He was still sitting on my bed like he belonged there.

"You went to the library," he said. Not a question.

"Yes."

"To research dragon bonding."

"Yes."

"And?"

I sat in the desk chair, suddenly exhausted. The adrenaline from the encounter was wearing off, leaving me hollow and shaking. "And I learned that attempting the bond with Govirrod is basically suicide."

"We already knew that."

"No, I mean..." I ran my hands through my hair again, wincing when I hit a tangle. "There's a list, Klaus. Names. Everyone who's tried and failed. It's dozens of people. And the only pairing that's ever worked for Govirrod was ice and lightning. Seventy years with Inge, who was an ice-worker. But before that? Bodies."

Klaus lit another cigarette, offered me one. I took it gratefully.

"So you're not trying," he said.

"I didn't say that."

"Lena..."

"I said I learned it was suicide. I didn't say I wasn't considering it." I took a drag, letting the smoke calm my racing thoughts.

Klaus was quiet for a moment, just watching me with those too-perceptive eyes.

"There's more," he said finally. "You didn't get that look from reading dusty books."

My hand went to my jaw automatically. Traced the spot where I could still feel the ghost of Alexi's touch.

"He was there," I admitted. "In the library."

"And?"

"And we fought."

"Lena." Klaus's voice was gentle. Too gentle. "Your lips are bruised. Your shirt was buttoned wrong. You've got a mark on your neck... yeah, there, you missed it... and you're shaking like you just survived a storm. You didn't just fight."

I touched my neck. Found the spot he meant... just below my ear, where Alexi's mouth had been for half a second before... before what? The sequence was blurry.

"We kissed," I said flatly.

Klaus raised an eyebrow. "Kissed. Past tense. Singular."

"Fine. We made out like teenagers in the restricted section until I threw him out."

"How very you."

"Fuck off."

"I'm just saying... "

"It doesn't mean anything," I cut him off. "It was anger. Adrenaline. Proximity and magic doing what magic does when you put two compatible elements in the same room."

"Uh-huh."

"It was a mistake."

"Sure."

His easy agreement made me suspicious. "What?"

"Nothing." He stubbed out his cigarette, lit another immediately. His hands were steadier than yesterday, but there was still a tremor. "Just interesting that he kissed someone he apparently can't stand. That he warned you about the dragon.

That he looked at you across the great hall like you were the only person in the room."

"He didn't..."

"Lena. Everyone saw. Linda's been running damage control, spreading the story that you two are professionals, that whatever happened years ago is ancient history." Klaus took a drag, exhaled slowly. "But there is something to see. Everyone knows it. The question is whether you're going to keep pretending you don't."

I wanted to argue. Wanted to tell him he was wrong, that it was just physical, just magic, just eight years of unresolved anger finding an outlet.

But my lips still tasted like lightning and blood.

And my magic was still humming under my skin, reaching for something that wasn't there.

"I don't know what to do," I admitted quietly.

"About the dragon or about him?"

"Either. Both." I crushed out my cigarette. "The book said dragon bonding requires perfect truth. No lies, not even to yourself. You have to know exactly who you are and what you want, or the bond will kill you."

"Do you?"

"Know what I want?" I laughed, bitter. "No. I wanted to survive this week. Now I'm researching how to bond with a creature that's killed dozens of people, while the man I used to love kisses me in libraries and then... I don't even know what. So no, Klaus. I have no fucking idea what I want."

Klaus was quiet for a moment, just smoking and watching me with those too-perceptive eyes.

"You know what I think?" he said finally.

"I'm sure you're going to tell me."

"I think you want to try for the dragon because it's the first thing in eight years that's made you feel alive. I think you want to prove you're more than the woman who fucked up Berlin." He paused. "And I think you want answers. Whatever happened on graduation night, whatever broke you two apart... you want to know why."

"That's a lot of psychoanalysis for seven in the morning."

"I've had all night to think about it." He smiled, sad and knowing. "We're a pair, aren't we? The addict and the exile. Both trying to prove we're more than our worst moments."

"Klaus..."

"It's okay." He stood, stretched. "You should shower. You smell like ozone and bad decisions."

"Fuck you, too."

He grinned... tired but real... and headed for the door. Paused with his hand on the handle. "For what it's worth? I think you should stay away from that dragon. Not because I don't think you're powerful enough—you are. But because I've watched you punish yourself for eight years. And I don't want to watch you die trying to prove something that might not need proving."

He slipped out into the hallway before I could respond, pulling the door closed behind him with a soft click.

I sat there in the empty room, surrounded by the smell of cigarette smoke and morning light, with bruised lips and a racing heart and absolutely no idea what I was going to do.

But Klaus was right about one thing.

I did need a shower.

I peeled off yesterday's clothes... the borrowed blouse from Linda, now hopelessly wrinkled. Stood under water as hot as I could stand and tried to wash away the feeling of Alexi's hands in my hair, his mouth on mine, his magic crackling through my veins.

It didn't work.

Nothing was going to work.

I got out, dried off, pulled on my own clothes this time... worn jeans and a faded t-shirt that felt more like armor than Linda's borrowed finery.

Outside the window, the compound was waking up. Graduates emerging from dormitories, heading toward the great hall for breakfast. Normal morning sounds... voices, laughter, the clatter of dishes.

Tonight was the graduation ceremony for the Class of 1984.

Tomorrow night, Govirrod would choose.

And the night after that, the lottery.

Three days.

I looked at myself in the mirror. The bruises on my lips were already fading... magic helped with that. The mark on my jaw would be gone by noon.

But I could still feel it. All of it.

I grabbed my jacket and headed for the door. Klaus was right... I needed food. Coffee. Something normal before tonight's ceremony and tomorrow's chaos.

But when I opened the door, I nearly collided with someone standing in the hallway.

Alexi.

Still in yesterday's clothes, hair disheveled, eyes bloodshot like he hadn't slept. He looked like hell. He looked devastating.

We stared at each other.

"We need to talk." He said.

"No, we don't."

"Ilena—"

"Whatever you're going to say, I don't want to hear it." I tried to step around him.

He shifted, blocking my path. Not aggressive... just present. Immovable.

"Last night..." he started.

"Was a mistake. We both know it. So let's just..."

"You can't try for the dragon."

I went very still. "Excuse me?"

"The bond. You can't try." His voice was flat. Controlled. "I know you went to the library to research it. I know you're considering it. But you can't."

"And you get to decide that?"

"Someone needs to."

"Funny." Ice spread from my hand, coating the doorframe. "I don't remember asking for your opinion."

"This isn't about opinion. It's about facts." He ran a hand through his hair, frustrated. "You read the book. You saw the list of names. You know what happens to people who try."

"Some of them succeed."

"One person succeeded. Seventy years ago. Inge, who had ice magic." His eyes held mine. "She's the only one who ever successfully bonded with Govirrod. Everyone else... dozens of them... died trying. Fire-workers, earth-workers, even other lightning-workers. Dead. All of them."

"Because they didn't have the right magic."

"Because dragon bonding doesn't care about ambition or desperation or how powerful you think you are." His voice went hard. "It requires perfect compatibility. Ice and lightning. That's what worked for Govirrod. That's what's kept him alive for centuries. And every single person who's tried without that pairing has died screaming."

"Then you know I have ice magic."

"I know you have ice magic and a death wish." He ran a hand through his hair. "Having the right element doesn't guarantee success. It just means you won't die in the first thirty seconds. The bond itself..." He stopped. "It's not just about magic. It requires perfect truth. Perfect understanding of yourself. One lie, one moment of self-deception, and the bond will tear you apart from the inside."

"How do you know that?"

"Because I've read every record the Devil keeps on dragon bonding. Every attempt. Every failure." His eyes met mine. "I know exactly what you're walking into."

"Then you know ice and lightning are the only pairing that's ever worked for him."

"I know it's the only pairing the Devil has specifically forbidden." His jaw tightened. "There's a reason for that."

"Care to share?"

"If I could, I would." The frustration in his voice was real. Raw. "But I can't. All I can tell you is that if you try for that dragon, you will die. And I..."

He stopped. Looked away.

"You what?" I demanded.

"Nothing."

"No. Finish it. You what, Alexi?"

"I can't watch you die." The words came out rough. Honest. "I've had to watch a lot of things these past eight years. Stand by while people I... while people died because of choices they made or choices someone made for them. But I can't watch you die."

My breath caught.

"Why?" the question escaped before I could stop it. "Why does it matter? You've spent years avoiding me. Like, whatever we had been, nothing. So why the hell do you care if I..."

"Because it wasn't nothing." He cut me off, voice sharp. "Whatever else was true, whatever happened between us, it was never nothing."

The admission hung in the air.

"Then tell me what happened," I said. "Tell me why you looked at me like that on graduation night. Tell me what I did that made you..."

"I can't."

"Can't or won't?"

"Both." His hands clenched at his sides. "There are things I'm not allowed to say. Constraints on what I can tell you. And even if I could..." He stopped. "It doesn't matter now."

"It matters to me."

"I know." Something flickered across his face. Pain, maybe. "But knowing wouldn't change anything. It would just... complicate things more than they already are."

"Things are pretty fucking complicated already."

"They could be worse."

We stood there in the hallway, too close and not close enough, eight years of silence pressing down between us.

"Just promise me," he said finally. "Promise you won't try for the dragon."

"I can't promise that."

"Ilena..."

"You don't get to ask me for promises. Not after eight years of nothing." I met his eyes. "If you want me to stay away from

Govirrod, give me a reason. A real one. Not orders or vague warnings or—"

"I can't give you what you want."

"Then I can't give you what you're asking for."

His jaw worked. "You're going to get yourself killed."

"Maybe." I stepped closer. Close enough to see the exhaustion in his eyes, the tension in his shoulders. "But that's my choice to make. Not yours. Not the Devil's. Mine."

"And if I told you there was another way? Something that didn't involve throwing yourself at a dragon that's killed dozens of people?"

"What other way?"

He hesitated. "I don't know yet. But give me time. Don't do anything until after the lottery. Three days. That's all I'm asking."

"Why?"

"Because..." He stopped. Started again. "Because I need time to figure out what the Devil's playing at. Why he forbade our pairing specifically. What he's afraid of."

"Our pairing," I repeated. "You said 'our.'"

His expression shuttered. "Slip of the tongue."

"Was it?"

He didn't answer.

"Three days," I said finally. "I'll give you three days. But only because I want answers too."

Relief crossed his face. Brief but unmistakable.

"Thank you."

"Don't thank me yet." I pushed past him, headed for the stairs. "And Alexi?"

He turned.

"Last night was still a mistake."

"I know."

"Good." I started down the stairs. "As long as we're clear."

But when I reached the landing and looked back, he was still standing there, watching me go with an expression I couldn't quite read.

Something that looked almost like grief.

I was fifteen when I understood what it meant to be claimed.

The anniversary fell on a Tuesday. Three years since the factory accident. Three years since my mother stopped humming while she worked, since my father stopped coming home with that particular smell of machine oil and cigarettes. Three years of living in my grandmother's apartment, sleeping in the room that used to be my mother's, pretending I was normal.

Grandmother made tea that morning. She always made tea on the anniversary... my mother's blend. Black tea with cardamom and a thread of honey. The smell alone could gut me.

She used my mother's teapot. Blue and white porcelain, delicate as eggshell, with a hairline crack along the spout. My mother refused to replace it.

I sat at the kitchen table and watched Grandmother pour. Her hands were steady. Mine weren't.

"She would have been proud of you," Grandmother said quietly.

I didn't answer. I was looking at the teapot, at those blue-painted *flowers, at the steam rising from the spout. My mother's hands had touched that handle. Every morning. Every single morning.*

The grief hit like a fist to the chest.

One second the teapot was steaming. The next, it was encased in ice.

Not frost. Not a gentle cooling. Ice... thick and white and spreading like a living thing. The porcelain cracked with a sound like a gunshot. The tea inside turned solid. Frost raced across the table, up the wall behind Grandmother, across the window until the glass went opaque.

The temperature in the kitchen dropped forty degrees in the space of a heartbeat.

I couldn't breathe. Couldn't move. Could only watch as my mother's teapot shattered into a dozen pieces, porcelain and ice scattering across the table.

Grandmother didn't scream. Didn't gasp. She just looked at the wreckage, at the frost still crawling up the walls, at my hands... white-knuckled and shaking on the edge of the table.

Then she looked at me.

"Pack your things," she said. "Quickly."

Before I could ask why, someone knocked on the apartment door. Three precise raps. Deliberate. Expected.

Grandmother's face went pale. She knew that knock.

She crossed to the door and opened it.

A man stood in the hallway. Sixty, maybe older, dressed in dark clothes that looked expensive but worn. Not rich... comfortable. His eyes were the gray of storm clouds, and when he looked at me through the open kitchen doorway, I felt something shift in the air. Recognition. Inevitability.

"Solomonar," Grandmother said. Not a greeting. An identification.

"Weather-worker." He inclined his head with respect I didn't understand. "Your granddaughter has manifested."

"She's just a child."

"She froze your kitchen solid." He stepped inside without invitation, moved to look at the wreckage. Studied the ice patterns with professional interest. "Untrained emotional response. Grief-triggered. Impressive power for an untrained child." His gaze cut to me. "How old?"

"Fifteen."

"Late manifestation. Trauma-induced, I'd wager." He crouched beside the table and ran a finger along the ice. It didn't melt at his touch. "Strong. Very strong. The Devil will want her."

The words hit like a physical blow.

"No," Grandmother whispered.

"This isn't a negotiation." The Solomonari stood. "I'm offering her a chance. I train her; *she goes to Scholomance, she becomes something more than a girl who breaks her dead mother's teapot." His eyes cut to me. "Or I leave, and you wait for the next accident. The next flash freeze. And eventually, something worse comes for her instead of me."*

"How long?" I asked. My voice sounded distant.

"Two and a half years with me. You'll be presented at the next Convocation. If the Devil accepts you, you enter the school that autumn."

"And if I refuse?"

His smile was bitter. "You won't."

Because we both knew. The stories said other things too. About what happened to witches who didn't answer the call. About power that turned inward and ate you alive.

The Devil always collected his due.

"Pack what you can carry," he said. "We leave in an hour."

I opened my eyes. Stared at the ceiling of my Scholomance room.

Fifteen years since that morning. Fifteen years since I'd left my grandmother's apartment with a Solomonari who promised to teach me control.

And eight years since graduation night. Since the final trial. Since whatever I'd done that made Alexi think I'd betrayed him.

I needed to remember that night. Needed to know what happened.

Because if he was right... if I'd somehow sold him out to the Devil... then I needed to understand why I didn't remember.

And if he was wrong?

Then someone had lied to us both.

And we'd spent all these years hating each other for nothing.

I looked down at my hands. At the three silver rings that had been my mother's. At the fingers that had frozen her teapot into pieces fifteen years ago.

Outside, the dragon was waiting.

And somewhere, so was the truth.

First full day back at Scholomance, and I was already drowning.

Some things never change.

Silver and Shame

THE BERGMANNS HAD CLAIMED the entire third floor of the guest wing. Three generations of weather-workers, and they made damn sure everyone knew it.

I stood in the hallway with Klaus, Maria, and Linda. Klaus was pale under his careful makeup, hands fumbling with his cigarette case.

"We don't have to do this," I said.

"Yes, we do." Linda said firmly as she smoothed her skirt. "They excluded him deliberately. We respond by showing up."

Through the door we could hear voices, laughter, and crystal clinking. The Bergmanns had imported French wine, probably. A show of wealth for the other legacy families.

Klaus straightened his shoulders, lifted his chin. The mask slid into place... charming, careless, the beautiful boy who didn't give a fuck.

Almost convincing.

"Let's get this over with," he said and opened the door.

The suite was packed. Forty people crammed into rooms meant for twenty... the Horváths, the Roths, the von Eschenbachs. All the names that mattered, all the bloodlines stretching back centuries. Expensive suits, designer dresses, jewelry worth more than I'd made in a year.

The main room had been transformed. Crystal chandeliers... real crystal, not the cheap imitations... cast warm light across Persian rugs that probably predated the school itself. Fresh flowers in elaborate arrangements, their scent cutting through the cigarette smoke and expensive cologne. Someone had brought in actual furniture... velvet settees, leather chairs, mahogany side tables covered in French wine and Romanian delicacies that couldn't be found anywhere in Ceaușescu's Romania. Black market, all of it. The Bergmanns flaunted wealth while the rest of the country starved.

Large windows overlooked the lake. Afternoon sun painted the water silver and blue, mountains sharp against a cloudless sky. Beautiful, if you could ignore the company.

The Bergmanns held court near those windows. Klaus's mother looked exactly as I'd expected: blonde hair shellacked into place, pearls at her throat, bird-thin and a forced smile that didn't reach her eyes. Chanel and disappointment. His father stood beside her, a bored statue; tall, silver-haired, banker-precise in a charcoal suit.

Three other Bergmann graduates flanked them, radiating barely contained judgment.

The room didn't go silent when we entered. That would have been too obvious. But conversations paused. Glances flickered.

Heidi Bergmann's smile froze.

"Klaus." Her accent was cultured West Berlin. Country clubs and charity galas. "What a... surprise."

"Hello, Mother. Lovely party." Klaus's voice stayed light. "Hope you don't mind... I brought friends."

Heidi's eyes swept over us... dismissing Maria, lingering on me with something like recognition, landing on Linda with barely concealed annoyance.

"How kind of you to attend." Each word precisely measured. "Though I wasn't aware..."

"That you'd invited Klaus?" Linda finished smoothly. "You didn't. But we're Class of '76. We go everywhere together."

Heidi couldn't respond. Not without admitting she'd deliberately excluded her own son. Not in front of witnesses.

"Of course." Heidi's smile could have cut glass. "Please, help yourselves to refreshments."

We moved into the room. Klaus grabbed champagne with hands steadied by pure spite. I took wine... something French and red that tasted like it cost more than a small car.

Conversations hummed around us. Legacy families discussing business deals, political connections, and who had the best candidates lined up for the lottery. A woman in emeralds laughed too loudly at something a man in Armani said. Near the fireplace... someone had actually lit a fire despite the mild evening... a cluster of older graduates compared notes on their various successes. Cars, houses, positions of power.

Klaus, Maria, and I formed a small island in the sea of wealth and judgment.

"Well," he murmured, "that went better than expected."

"Give it time," Maria said.

Klaus's uncle cornered us within ten minutes.

"Klaus." Friedrich Bergmann didn't offer a handshake. His gaze swept over Klaus's eyeliner, his silver rings. The judgment was immediate, visceral. I could see it in the way his lip curled, the slight step back like Klaus might be contagious.

This was the man who'd sent Klaus birthday cards until he turned nineteen. Until he came out. After that, nothing but silence and the occasional public reminder of his disappointment.

"I see you've decided to grace us with your presence."

"Wouldn't miss it, Uncle Friedrich." Klaus sipped champagne. "Lovely spread."

"French wine. Cost a fortune to import." Friedrich's expression hardened. "One must maintain standards. Speaking of which."

The insult hung in the air. Around us, conversations had quieted slightly. People pretending not to listen while absolutely listening. This was entertainment—watching the Bergmann family drama unfold, watching Klaus get put in his place.

Klaus's smile didn't waver. "I've always appreciated your commitment to mediocrity. Very on-brand."

Friedrich's face went red. He turned to me, and I felt the full weight of his contempt shift targets. "Ilena Firan. The weather-worker from Berlin. Five dead, wasn't it?"

Silence fell. Everyone was paying attention now. Berlin was my scarlet letter, and Friedrich was making sure everyone remembered.

I sucked on a tooth, stretched my neck and pushed myself off the wall where I had been leaning. I met his eyes. "The investigation cleared me."

"How... convenient." His smile was all edges. "Though I suppose when you're a foundling magician with no family connections, these things get... overlooked."

"That's enough," Linda said sharply.

"Is it?" Friedrich's voice rose... not loud, but enough. "My nephew embarrasses this family by bringing his Berlin... associates... to a legacy event. One of whom is directly responsible for..."

"We all heard you the first time, Uncle." Klaus's voice went cold. "Very subtle."

"Don't you dare..."

"What? Call you out for being petty and vindictive?" Klaus set down his glass with a deliberate click. "Consider it called."

The room had gone quiet. Everyone watching.

Friedrich's face went purple. "You disgrace..."

"The Bergmann name?" Klaus laughed, sharp, bitter. "Uncle, I *am* the Bergmann name. Three generations. Do you really think dear Mother is going to squeeze out another child at her age? And you certainly haven't stepped up to the plate to deliver. I am the legacy here."

"You're a..."

"Careful."

The word came from directly behind me. So close I felt the heat of him first... body warmth cutting through the cool air, the scent of leather and something darker I couldn't name. Then his voice, low and dangerous, the single word vibrating through my spine.

Every hair on the back of my neck stood up.

I froze. Couldn't move. Couldn't breathe. My body remembered him before my brain caught up... remembered being this close, remembered the way he used to stand behind me just like this, chin nearly touching my shoulder, breath warm against my neck.

The room shifted. Everyone felt it: the way magic suddenly felt closer to the surface, dangerous. This was what happened when the Devil's enforcer entered a space. The air itself remembered to be afraid.

I turned slowly.

Alexi stood inches away. Close enough that I had to tilt my head back to meet his eyes. Close enough that if I swayed forward even slightly, we'd be touching.

And I wanted to. God, I wanted to.

The pull hit me like a physical force... magnetic, undeniable, something that bypassed reason and went straight to instinct. The same way the dragon's call had pulled at something deep in my chest, making me want to walk into the courtyard and offer myself up. This was like that. Almost as strong. Almost as terrifying.

Except this wasn't some ancient creature's compulsion. This was just him. Just Alexi, standing too close, and my body remembering what it felt like to be his.

The room was watching. Everyone watching us, watching this, watching whatever the fuck this was between us that apparently still wasn't dead after eight years.

Not in full enforcer blacks today... just dark trousers and a fitted shirt that emphasized the controlled power in every line of him. But the scars were visible on his forearms, snaking past his elbows. Raised tissue, deliberate patterns. Not wounds from accidents or fights. These were marks of service, of oaths sworn in blood and shadow.

And his eyes... storm-gray and absolutely lethal. I'd seen those eyes soft once, warm, looking at me like I was the only thing that mattered in the world.

Now they looked past me at Friedrich Bergmann like he was an insect.

"The Master doesn't tolerate disruptions." Each word precisely measured. His voice was still low, still dangerous, and I felt every syllable in my chest. "Perhaps this conversation should continue elsewhere."

Not a suggestion. A command wrapped in courtesy.

Friedrich swallowed. You didn't argue with the Devil's Enforcer. Not here. Not anywhere if you valued your life and your oath intact.

"Of course. My apologies." He inclined his head in polite submission and retreated. The crowd parted for him like water, nobody wanting to be associated with whatever had just happened.

Alexi didn't move. Didn't step back. He was still close... too close. The space between us hummed with unfinished business, with everything we'd never said, never resolved.

The room was watching. I could feel their eyes on us, the speculation, the gossip, already forming.

Then his gaze finally dropped. To me.

Our eyes met.

I wanted to say something. Anything.

He took a step back. The absence of his warmth felt like a loss.

"Firan," he said. My surname. Nothing more. Nothing else.

"Alexi."

His jaw tightened. Just barely. Just enough that I caught it.

For a moment, I thought he might say something else.

Instead, he turned away.

"Enjoy the party," he said, and disappeared into the crowd.

I'd stopped breathing. My chest felt tight, compressed. Like someone had wrapped wire around my ribs and was slowly, methodically tightening it.

"Well," Klaus said quietly. "That was complicated."

Complicated. Sure. That was one word for watching the man you'd loved—the man who'd looked at you like you'd murdered his soul—intervene in a fight on your behalf while simultaneously pretending you were nothing but a surname.

Linda squeezed my arm gently. "You okay?"

I nodded. Didn't trust my voice. Didn't trust what might come out if I opened my mouth.

"Good." She glanced around the room. "Because we're not giving them the satisfaction of running. We stay until we're ready to leave. On our terms."

We found a corner. Safer there... backs to the wall, view of the room, space to breathe. An alcove near a bookshelf filled with leather-bound volumes that likely no one had read in decades. Books wealthy people bought by the yard for decoration.

Klaus lit a cigarette, fingers unsteady against the lighter.

"You didn't have to do that," he said to Linda.

"Yes, I did. We're Class of '76."

Maria raised her wine. "To humiliation. May it build character."

Klaus laughed... broken, but real. "You're all insane."

"Your kind of insane," I said. I bumped my shoulder against him. The corners of his lips turned up slightly, and he nodded.

Around us, the party continued. Legacy families networking, positioning themselves for tomorrow's lottery. Through the windows, afternoon light slanted across the lake, bright and unforgiving. The Bergmanns continued their meaningless chit-chat. They'd erased Klaus from the narrative. Made him invisible.

But we were still here. Still standing.

And somehow, that felt like winning.

Twenty minutes later, Heidi Bergmann appeared at our corner.

She'd been watching, waiting for the right moment. I'd felt her eyes on us multiple times, assessing, calculating. Waiting for witnesses, probably. Or maybe just waiting for her anger to crystallize into something she could wield with precision.

Up close, I could see the fine lines around her eyes, the way her smile never quite worked. The tension in her jaw. This woman had spent thirty years perfecting the art of disappointment, and Klaus was her masterpiece.

"Klaus." Her voice was quiet. Pleasant, even. But acid ran beneath every syllable. "I think it would be best if you left now."

Klaus went very still.

"You've made your... statement. Whatever it was." She glanced at us... dismissive. "You've embarrassed your father and me in front of our peers. Again. So please. Show what little dignity you have left and leave."

"No," Klaus said softly.

Heidi blinked. "I beg your pardon?"

"I said no." He met her eyes. "We're staying."

"This is a private event..."

"At a Scholomance Convocation," I cut in, voice carrying just enough, "where all graduates are equal. Or are you suggesting otherwise, Frau Bergmann?"

Heidi's face went tight. She couldn't say yes. Couldn't admit publicly she was trying to exclude her own son. Not here. Not in front of two hundred witnesses.

"Of course not," she managed.

"Wonderful," Linda smiled and swirled her champagne glass. "Then we'll stay as long as we like."

Klaus looked at his mother. At the woman who'd spent a decade pretending he didn't exist.

"Yeah," he said. "We'll stay."

Heidi turned and walked away without another word.

An hour later, I went to refill my wine and found myself face-to-face with Klaus's father.

Ernst Bergmann looked at me the way he probably looked at bad investments—calculating, dismissive, already written off.

"Miss Firan." He didn't extend his hand. "I don't believe we've been formally introduced."

"We haven't."

"No." He sipped champagne. "Though I've heard about Berlin. Terrible tragedy."

The Wall incident. Again.

I nodded, "It was." I nodded toward the corner where Alexi stood, deep in conversation with a legacy magician. "You are welcome to speak to the Enforcer who was there that night, if you'd like his take on things?" My heart pounded in my ears.

"Mmmm, of course." His eyes drifted toward Alexi, then back to me, his smile was thin. "Accidents happen, no? Particularly to those who...overreach." He paused. "My son, for instance. Overreached quite dramatically. Associated with the wrong people."

He meant me. He meant Alexi. He meant everyone who wasn't legacy.

"Your son is one of the best people I know."

"Is he?" Ernst's voice went cold. "A drug addict, barely employed, making a spectacle of himself? That's your definition of 'best'?"

"He's surviving."

"Surviving." Ernst laughed, short, bitter. "That's one word for it. But perhaps that's the difference between foundlings and legacy families. You people don't understand what it means to carry a name."

"You people."

"Foundlings. Those without lineage. Without..." He stopped himself.

I set down my wine before I threw it.

"You know what I think, Herr Bergmann? I think you're terrified. Terrified that your son is better than you despite everything. That he survived Scholomance and came out kinder, braver, more human than you could ever be. And that terrifies you because it means all your money, all your legacy? It doesn't mean shit."

Ernst's face went red.

"How dare… "

"I dare because I don't care what you think of me. But Klaus? He still cares. And you use that against him every single day."

I walked away before he could respond.

My hands were shaking. My heart hammered. But I'd said it.

Linda caught my arm as I reached the door. "That was either very brave or very stupid."

"Probably both."

"Good." She smiled. "I'd have been disappointed if it was just one."

We left shortly after. Klaus had reached his limit… I could see it in his brittle smile, his restless hands. We made our excuses and escaped.

The hallway air hit like a blessing. Cooler after the oppressive heat of too many bodies, too much perfume, too much concentrated judgment. The corridor was blessedly empty. Through windows at the far end, I could see the courtyard below… graduates gathering, the fountain running steady, afternoon shadows stretching long.

Klaus lit a cigarette, the flame wavering slightly.

"Thank you," he said.

"For what?"

"Coming. Staying. Telling my father off." He exhaled smoke. "Though you probably just made an enemy for life."

"I've survived worse."

"Yeah. You have."

We stood in silence, looking out over the lake. The afternoon was sliding toward evening. In a few hours, we'd be in the great hall for graduation. Watching the Class of 1984 take their oaths. Watching one of them get chosen as a tribute.

The lake reflected the bright sky, calm and deceptively peaceful. The mountains stood sharp against the horizon.

Tonight, graduation. Ten candidates. How many would see it through?

And who would get dragged to Hell?

Blood and Fire

THE GREAT HALL HAD been transformed.

Every candle lit, hundreds of them, their flames unnaturally still despite the press of bodies. Every surface was polished until it gleamed. The long tables pushed to the walls, leaving the center floor empty except for a single raised platform of black stone that hadn't been there this morning.

On that platform stood five figures in white robes.

The Class of 1984. The survivors.

Only five.

I'd heard the rumors all afternoon...whispers about how many had died in the final trials, how brutal this year had been. Three years ago, ten bright-eyed, terrified yet eager candidates had disappeared beneath the lake to learn the Devil's arts.

Five came back up.

Seeing them made it real. Five young faces, pale and gaunt, marked by whatever horrors they'd endured. Their white robes hung loose... they'd all lost weight, lost something more essential than flesh. Two women, three men, none older than twenty-five. They stood perfectly still, eyes forward, hands at their sides.

They looked like they'd learned not to move unless told.

I stood with Klaus and Linda near the back, close to the doors. Just in case. Klaus's hand kept twitching toward his cigarettes. Linda's face was composed, but I could see the tension in her jaw.

"Five," Klaus murmured. "Fucking hell."

"Class of '76 all survived," Linda whispered. "All ten of us. We were lucky." She paused, watching the five survivors. "Some years only one or two make it out."

"Fifty percent," I said. "Could be worse."

"Could always be worse," Klaus muttered.

Around us, graduates shifted on their feet, hands twitching toward magic they couldn't use here. Not now. The weight in the air... that pressure that said powerful beings were watching... made my teeth ache. Every instinct screamed to leave, to run, to get as far from this place as possible.

No one moved toward the doors.

We'd all sworn oaths. We'd all come when summoned.

And we'd all stay to watch this, no matter what it cost us.

The Master stood at the front of the hall, Stăpânul in his formal robes of deep blue embroidered with silver. The kind of robes that belonged in museums, that spoke of centuries of tradition.

His silver hair fell loose to his shoulders tonight—different from the severe style he'd worn in the courtyard the other night. His weathered face was composed, serene, but I could see the steel underneath. Power barely leashed. This was a man who'd commanded the Scholomance for longer than most of us had been alive.

He looked like someone's kindly grandfather.

I'd never bought that act.

Luminița stood beside him in crimson silk that moved like liquid. Her dark hair was unbound, falling past her waist. She was beautiful—everyone said so. Graceful. Elegant. Inhuman. The Master's companion, his second, the woman who'd been at his side for as long as anyone could remember.

She looked almost gentle tonight. Almost human.

I'd never trusted that either.

Four enforcers were scattered throughout the hall… two flanking the entrance, two positioned near the platform. All in matching black military-style uniforms. All standing with that same predatory stillness. Former tributes. Graduates who'd been chosen by the Devil and bound to his service.

I didn't recognize any of them. Different classes, different years. But they all had the same look—hard, watchful, dangerous. The Devil's soldiers.

Movement near the back entrance caught my eye. Another enforcer making his way through the crowd, checking the perimeter. Full dress uniform—black military-style jacket with a high collar, silver buttons, polished boots. Everything immaculate, severe.

My breath caught.

Alexi.

He was doing a security sweep, moving along the back wall, eyes scanning faces. Professional. Methodical. He hadn't seen me yet.

Then he turned. Our eyes met.

He stopped. For a heartbeat, neither of us moved.

Then he changed direction. Toward me.

"Shit," Klaus muttered beside me.

"It's fine," I said. The lie tasted bitter.

Alexi reached us. Close. Too close. Not touching, but near enough that I could smell leather and something darker—ozone, maybe. Storm-smell.

For a long moment, neither of us spoke.

"Five," he said finally, his voice low. Not looking at me. Looking at the platform, at the survivors in white. "Half of them were dead before they even took their oaths."

I didn't answer. Didn't know what he wanted from me.

His jaw worked. Then he did something unexpected... he shifted slightly, angling his body so his back was to the room, his bulk shielding our conversation from prying eyes. The gesture was subtle. Professional. But deliberate.

"Tomorrow's the dragon trials," he said, still not looking at me.

"I know."

"And you're still planning to..."

"Don't." I cut him off. "You asked for time. I haven't decided anything yet."

His hands flexed at his sides. Carefully controlled. "The Master wants to see you."

My stomach dropped. "What?"

"After the ceremony." His voice was flat. Emotionless. The enforcer's voice. "He sent me to deliver the message."

"Why? What does he..."

"He didn't say." Something flickered across his face. Too quick to read. "But when the Master summons you, you go."

"Is this about the dragon?" I asked quietly.

Alexi's jaw tightened. "I don't know. Maybe."

"You're lying."

"I'm not." He finally looked at me. Storm-gray eyes, exhausted, carefully blank. "I wasn't told why. Just ordered to give you the message."

But there was something in his eyes. A warning he couldn't voice. Fear he couldn't show.

"Alexi..."

"Be careful what you agree to." The words came out fast. Quiet. Almost too quiet to hear. "The Master doesn't ask questions unless he already knows the answers. And he doesn't make offers that aren't traps."

My chest tightened. "What's he going to ask me?"

"I don't know." He stopped. His whole body went rigid.

I followed his gaze. The Master was looking at us. Not obviously... his attention still appeared focused on preparations... but I felt the weight of his regard like a physical thing.

Alexi took a step back. The distance between us suddenly professional, correct. His face smoothed into that enforcer's mask... cold, controlled, untouchable.

"After the ceremony," he said, loud enough for anyone nearby to hear. "The Master's study. Don't keep him waiting."

He turned and walked away. Back straight. Movements precise. Everything about him screamed duty, obedience, control.

But his hands... I'd seen them shaking before he shoved them behind his back.

Klaus exhaled slowly. "What the fuck was that?"

"I don't know."

Linda's hand found my arm. "The Master doesn't summon people for pleasant conversations."

"I know."

My hands were shaking. The Master wanted to see me. And Alexi, the Devil's enforcer, who knew exactly how the Master operated—had just warned me to be careful.

Had tried to protect me in the only way he could.

That wasn't the behavior of someone who hated me.

That was the behavior of someone who was trapped. Who couldn't help openly but was desperate to help anyway.

Linda's hand found my other arm. Steadying. "Breathe. Just breathe."

I tried. Failed.

The Master raised his hand. Silence fell like a dropped stone.

"We gather under the second darkness," the Master said in Romanian. His voice carried without effort, resonating in the stone walls, in my bones. "We honor our oaths. We welcome new blood into our ranks."

The ritual response came from two hundred throats, mine included: "Întotdeauna. Până la moarte."

Always. Until death.

The five graduates stepped forward in perfect unison. They'd been drilled on this, I remembered it like it was yesterday. Rehearsed it over and over until the movements were automatic. Their faces were blank, eyes forward, but I could see the fear underneath. The exhaustion. The knowledge that this was almost over, that they'd almost made it, that they just had to survive one more ceremony.

Ten had started. Five remained.

What had happened to the other five? I knew better than to ask.

The Master began the litany. Names. Origins. Specializations. His voice steady and formal, turning these five exhausted survivors into official graduates.

"Radu Mihăilescu. Bucharest. Storm-caller."

A young man with dark hair and hollow eyes. His hands trembled slightly.

"Ioana Popescu. Constanța. Water-binder."

A woman with blonde hair pulled back severely. She looked like she hadn't slept in days.

"Heinrich Vogel. Munich. Fire-worker."

Stocky, bearded, older than the others. Maybe twenty-five. German. His jaw was set like he was enduring torture. Legacy family, probably... the kind who'd sent their sons to the Scholomance for generations.

"Mara Kovač. Belgrade. Wind-weaver."

Small, dark-haired, with scars visible on her neck. Something had burned her. Recently. Yugoslav. Her eyes were hard, older than her years.

"Cristian Enache. Iași. Shadow-mage."

The youngest. Maybe twenty-two. Beautiful in that sharp, dangerous way. Dark hair, darker eyes, pale skin. He looked like he'd been carved from marble and left in a crypt.

Five names. Five survivors. Ten had entered three years ago.

The crowd was silent. Everyone doing the same math. Fifty percent mortality rate just in the final trials alone. Not unprecedented, but brutal nonetheless.

"You have survived the trials," the Master continued. His voice softened slightly. Almost paternal. Almost kind. "You have proven yourselves worthy. You have earned your freedom."

He paused.

"For now."

That always got a reaction. I could feel it ripple through the crowd... that collective acknowledgment of the truth we all lived with. Freedom. Sure. Until the Convocations called us back every few years. Until the lottery selected us and demanded we provide candidates. Until we died or failed to answer the summons and the enforcers came.

Freedom was temporary. The oaths were forever.

The five knelt in unison. The white robes pooled around them on the black stone platform.

"Do you swear to uphold the secrets of the Scholomance?"

"We swear." Five voices, perfectly synchronized.

"Do you swear to answer the summons when called?"

"We swear."

"Do you swear to provide a candidate if chosen by lottery?"

"We swear."

"Do you accept that your oath is binding until death?"

"We accept."

The words echoed in the stone hall. Final. Irrevocable.

And then the temperature dropped.

Not gradually. All at once, like someone had opened a door to winter. My breath misted in front of my face. The candles flickered—all of them, simultaneously; the flames bending sideways though there was no wind.

The air grew heavy. Oppressive. Magic pressed down from above, from below, from everywhere at once. Ancient magic. Terrible magic. The kind that predated humanity and would outlast it.

The Devil was coming.

I'd felt this once before. My own graduation night, standing where those five knelt now, feeling the weight of something immense and terrible turning its attention to our world.

Klaus grabbed my arm. His hand was ice-cold, shaking. "Lena...
"

"Stay still," I breathed. "Don't move."

Around us, graduates were doing the same... freezing in place, barely breathing. This was the most dangerous part. When the Devil was present, when reality was thin, anything could happen. Any wrong move could catch his attention.

And you never wanted the Devil's attention.

I'd met mortals who didn't believe in the Devil. Who thought he was metaphor, legend, the superstitious fear of ignorant peasants. Those same mortals didn't believe in magic either. Or dragons. Or that ten students disappeared beneath a Romanian lake every few years to learn arts that would drive ordinary people mad.

Those mortals were fools.

We knew better. We'd sworn oaths to him. We'd felt his presence during our own graduations, that weight that made reality bend. We'd seen what happened to graduates who broke their oaths, who tried to run, who thought they could escape.

The Devil was real.

Whether he was *the* Devil... the one Christians feared, the fallen angel, the adversary of God... or just something old and powerful that enjoyed the aesthetics of damnation, I didn't know. No one did. The Scholomance had existed for centuries, and the being who ran it had always called himself Diavol.The Devil. Whether that was truth or theater, it didn't matter.

The power was real. The oaths were real. The price was real.

The shadows in the corners of the hall deepened. Stretched. Moved with purpose, reaching toward the center of the room like grasping fingers.

The candles went out.

All of them. Hundreds of flames extinguished in an instant, plunging the hall into absolute darkness.

And then he was there.

Not slowly. Not gradually. Just *there*... standing behind the kneeling graduates, present in a way that made my eyes hurt and my mind refuse to process what it was seeing.

The Devil.

Diavol. The True Master of the Scholomance. The one who taught us, owned us, bound us.

He wore the shape of a man, but wrong. Too tall... seven feet at least, maybe more. His form seemed to shift at the edges, like he existed in multiple places simultaneously, like reality couldn't quite contain him. He was dressed in black that absorbed light rather than reflected it, fabric that might have been cloth or shadow or something else entirely.

His face... I tried not to look directly at it. None of us did. There was something fundamentally wrong about it, like staring at the sun or into an abyss. But I caught glimpses. Pale skin, if it was skin. Features that were almost human, almost handsome, but skewed in ways that made my stomach clench. The body was impossibly thin and yet full. Eyes that glowed faint red, like embers.

And horns. Small, curving back from his temples, black as obsidian.

The air around him oscillated between heat and cold. Temperature didn't work right in his presence.

"I accept your oaths," he said.

His voice was layered. Multiple people speaking at once, at different pitches, creating chords that shouldn't exist. The sound bypassed my ears and resonated directly in my chest, my bones, my teeth.

"I claim my due."

He moved between the five kneeling figures. Slowly. Deliberately. Examining them like a merchant examining goods, a predator selecting prey.

I couldn't look away. None of us could. Even though every instinct screamed to close my eyes, to turn away, to run—we all watched.

His hand... if it was a hand... reached out and touched each graduate's head in turn. Brief. Clinical. Each one flinched at the contact but didn't move otherwise.

Radu. Touch. Release.

Ioana. Touch. Release.

Heinrich. Touch. Release.

Mara. Touch. Release.

He stopped behind Cristian Enache. The shadow-mage. The youngest of them.

The Devil's hand rested on Cristian's shoulder. Possessive. Final.

"This one," the Devil said.

Cristian's face went white. But he didn't protest. Didn't beg. Just lowered his head in acceptance.

He'd known. Somewhere deep down, he'd known he would be chosen.

They always did.

"You are mine now," the Devil said. His voice softened slightly—almost gentle, almost kind, in the way a loving owner might speak to a favored pet. "Your service begins when the moon rises tomorrow night. Until then, enjoy your last hours of freedom."

Freedom. As if Cristian would be free for the next twenty-four hours. As if he could do anything but wait in terror for whatever came next.

The weight lifted slightly. The other four were dismissed... released to their lives, their eight years of freedom before the Convocations called them back. They stood on shaking legs, faces showing relief and guilt in equal measure.

They'd survived. They were free.

Cristian would never be.

The Devil began to fade, shadows pulling back toward the corners, his form becoming less solid—

A roar shattered the night.

Not from inside the hall. From outside. From *above*.

The sound was primal, ancient, full of rage and hatred that made every instinct scream *predator, run, hide, survive*. It vibrated through the stone, through the air, through my bones.

The hall erupted. People shouting, moving toward the doors, pressing against each other in panic. The Master's head snapped up, his face going from serene to something harder. Battle-ready.

"Stay inside," he commanded. His voice cut through the chaos like a whip. "No one leaves..."

The roof exploded.

Flaming stones and timber rained down. I threw myself sideways, hitting the floor hard as debris crashed where I'd been standing. Klaus yanked me up, pulling me toward the wall. Linda was shouting something I couldn't hear over the screaming.

Through the gaping hole in the roof—twenty feet wide, thirty, still growing as more stone fell away... I could see the night sky.

And I could see *HIM*.

Govirrod.

The dragon was massive. Bigger than anything should be, bigger than natural law allowed. Storm-gray scales that gleamed like oil in the dim light, each one the size of a shield. Wings that blocked out the stars, that stretched so wide they seemed to touch the mountains on either side of the valley.

His eyes were molten silver. Burning. Fixed on the hall below with singular, terrifying intent.

Fixed on the Devil.

Another roar. The dragon dove.

The Devil didn't run. Didn't move. Just stood there, a small dark figure on the platform, as Govirrod plummeted toward him. The dragon's jaws opened... wide enough to swallow a bus, wide enough to take the Devil and the platform in one bite.

The Master threw himself forward. Not at the dragon. Toward Luminiţa.

And Luminiţa *changed*.

One moment she was a woman in crimson silk, standing calmly beside the Master.

The next she was airborne… scales of deep red and gold, wings snapping open with a sound like thunder, smaller than Govirrod but faster, more agile, built for speed where he was built for raw power.

A dragon.

Luminița was a dragon!

Fall of Gods

L UMINIȚA HIT GOVIRROD MID-DIVE.

The impact shook the earth. I felt it through my boots, through my bones, a collision of forces that shouldn't exist in the same reality. The sound was thunder and tearing metal and something older—the scream of a mountain being split in two.

They grappled in midair, talons finding purchase on scales, wings beating against each other in a hurricane of displaced air. Then they were through the ruined roof and into the night sky, silhouettes against the stars.

"Out!" The Master's voice cut through the chaos. "Everyone out, NOW!"

The hall emptied in a stampede. I got caught in the crush, Klaus on one side, Linda on the other, all of us shoving toward the doors as more stone rained from above. Someone screamed. Someone else went down, trampled. I couldn't stop, couldn't help, even though I wanted to... the press of bodies was too strong, survival instinct overriding everything else.

We burst into the courtyard.

The night was full of wings and lightning.

Luminița dove from above, lithe and swift, her scales gleaming red-gold in the moonlight. She raked her talons across Govirrod's flank, drawing lines of black blood that arced bright plasma across the darkened sky. The black dragon roared... rage and pain combined... and twisted impossibly fast for something so gargantuan. His tail whipped around, catching her across the shoulder. The crack of impact echoed off the mountains.

Luminița tumbled, wings folding, falling...

Then snapped them open ten feet from the ground, pulling up hard enough that I felt the downdraft from one hundred yards away. She climbed, spiraling, bleeding from a gash in her shoulder that looked deep enough to be mortal.

"Jesus Christ," Klaus breathed beside me.

Around us, graduates scattered across the courtyard. Some pressed against the buildings, trying to get under cover. Others stood transfixed, unable to look away. The five new graduates—the survivors of Class of '84—were being herded toward the dormitory by one of the enforcers. Cristian, the chosen one, looked like he was in shock.

The dragons fought like gods.

Govirrod was a titan—easily twice Luminiṭa's size, built like a battering ram covered in armor. Every movement was power, destruction, and inevitability. When his wings beat, trees bent. When he roared, windows shattered.

But Luminiṭa was speed and precision. She darted in, struck, and pulled away before Govirrod could retaliate. Claws flashing. Teeth finding gaps in his scales. Drawing blood, piece by piece, death by a thousand cuts.

It wasn't enough.

Govirrod caught her.

His jaws closed on her wing... I heard the bones snap from the ground, heard Luminiṭa's scream that was half-human, half-dragon, all agony. He shook her like a dog with a rat, then flung her away. She hit the side of the great hall hard enough to crack stone, hard enough that I felt it in my chest.

She fell.

Thirty feet. Forty. Hit the courtyard with an impact that shattered flagstones.

And didn't get up.

The Master was running before she finished falling. Faster than any human should move, across rubble and bodies and broken stone. He reached her as she transformed... mid-collapse, woman again... and caught her before her head could hit the ground.

"Luminiṭa," he said. Just her name. But the way he said it...

There was emotion there beyond master and servant. Beyond owner and owned.

Govirrod roared. The sound was triumph and fury combined. He'd taken down the other dragon. Now there was only...

The Devil raised one hand.

I felt it before I saw it. A change in pressure, in temperature, in the fundamental nature of reality. The air itself seemed to solidify, to become something dense and crushing, and wrong.

Govirrod's roar cut off mid-breath.

The dragon froze. Mid-flight, wings spread, jaws open. Just froze, like someone had pressed pause on the world.

"You are MINE," the Devil said.

His voice was wrong. Layered. Multiple tones speaking with discord.I braced myself, his voice rattling my teeth and vibrating my bones as it challenged the fabric of reality not to fray.

"You swore an oath. You bound yourself. And you think—" The Devil's form flickered, shadows bleeding from him like smoke. "—you think you can simply choose freedom through violence?"

Govirrod moved. Fought against whatever held him. His wings beat once, twice, but it was like swimming through concrete. The air itself had become his prison.

"I. AM. FREE." The dragon's voice was defiance incarnate. Rage given form. "THREE HUNDRED YEARS. NO MORE."

"You are nothing," the Devil said, and now his voice went quiet. Soft, like the quiet that preceded avalanches. "You are property. A tool. And tools do not choose when they break."

The temperature dropped. Not gradually... instantly. The air crystallized. My breath froze in my lungs. Around me, graduates were collapsing, clawing at their throats, gasping for air that had turned to ice.

The Devil closed his fist.

Shadows erupted from everywhere—from the ground, from the air, from the space between spaces. Black tendrils that wrapped around Govirrod's wings, his legs, his neck, and his jaws. The dragon thrashed, tore through them, but they reformed as fast as he broke them.

And they were squeezing.

Govirrod screamed. Not in rage anymore. In pain. In desperation. The sound echoed off the mountains, a dragon's death-cry that would haunt my nightmares for years.

Then Luminița moved.

I'd thought she was unconscious. Dying. But she pulled free of the Master's arms... staggered, fell, transformed in a burst of light and heat. Dragon again, crimson and gold, one wing hanging useless.

She launched herself on three legs. Clumsy. Desperate.

And tore out Govirrod's throat.

Her teeth found the gap between his scales... the vulnerable place where neck met chest. She bit down and twisted, and black blood fountained across the courtyard in a spray that hissed when it hit stone.

Govirrod's struggles weakened. The light in his silver eyes dimmed.

The Devil's shadows tightened.

The dragon collapsed. The impact cratered the courtyard, sent a shockwave that knocked me off my feet. Dust and ash billowed. Stone cracked with sounds like gunfire.

Silence.

Luminița released her grip. Staggered back, scales cracked and bleeding, that broken wing dragging. She transformed... woman again... and collapsed. Maybe she was not some agent of The Devil wearing a human face. Perhaps she was a dragon punished to wear the skin of a woman. What did she do?

The Master was there instantly. Gathering her up as if she weighed nothing. Her dark hair was matted with blood. Her crimson silk shredded and soaked.

"Get her to the infirmary," the Devil said. "She has earned her rest."

The Master didn't acknowledge him. Just carried Luminița away toward the infirmary, his face carved from stone, something terrible and protective in the way he held her. It spoke volumes.

Her head lolled against his shoulder. Blood... too much blood... soaked through what remained of her crimson silk. Her dark hair hung in matted ropes, and I could see bone through the torn flesh of her shoulder where Govirrod's tail had crushed her wing. But she was breathing. Shallow, pained gasps.

She'd been willing to die for the Devil. And he'd let her.

Around us, graduates were picking themselves up. Slow. Dazed. I watched a man try to stand, fall, try again. A woman crawled toward someone who wasn't moving. The sounds filtered back... moaning, weeping, someone calling a name over and over. The crackle of dying fires. Water dripping from the destroyed fountain, mixing with something darker.

I stood frozen, unable to move.

Govirrod's corpse dominated the courtyard. Even in death, he dwarfed everything. A mountain of black scales already going dull like tarnished metal. His neck twisted at an impossible angle, Luminița's teeth marks visible in his throat—deep gouges through scale and muscle.

Blood pooled beneath him. Not pooled—flooded. It had spread ten feet wide, steaming in the cold air. The smell hit me—copper and sulfur and something older, something that made my hindbrain scream this was wrong.

His wings were spread in death, membranes torn and hanging in tatters. One bent backward, broken in three places. His jaws frozen open, teeth like swords. And his eyes—those molten gold eyes that had burned with defiance—were dark now. Filmed over. Empty.

Three hundred and forty-seven years of service.

And this was his reward for daring to want more.

Bodies scattered across the courtyard. Near the ruined hall... shapes that might have been human once. By the destroyed fountain... a woman's hand protruding from beneath marble, still wearing rings. Against the east wall... more bodies. Some crushed. Some simply stopped.

I didn't count them. Couldn't bear to turn people into numbers. But I knew. Twenty-six. Maria had seen them all.

The five new graduates huddled near the dormitory. Ioana with her face buried in someone's shoulder. Heinrich cleaned his glasses over and over, as if clarity would make this make sense. And Cristian—the chosen tribute—just stood there. Blank. Already gone somewhere inside himself.

Welcome to the Scholomance, I thought. This is what a bargain with The Devil buys you.

The Devil stepped from his crater, shadows bleeding away as he solidified. Completely untouched. His suit wasn't even dusty. While bodies cooled and blood ran between flagstones, he looked like he'd just left a tailor's shop.

He surveyed the courtyard with ember-red eyes. Tracking across the wounded, the dead, the broken. Counting. Cataloging.

And I saw it in his face... satisfaction.

This was exactly what he wanted. The bodies. The terror. The absolute certainty that rebellion earned nothing but death. This was the lesson.

People were starting to move with more purpose. Someone organized the uninjured into groups—checking the wounded, clearing rubble, identifying the dead. The enforcers directing traffic. There was almost a sense of relief beginning... maybe we'd survived the worst of it. Maybe we could start picking up the pieces.

I wanted to believe it.

But I couldn't look away from the Devil. From those eyes sweeping across the courtyard one more time. From that small, satisfied smile.

He was waiting for something.

Then his gaze found mine.

The smile widened. Just slightly. Just enough to freeze my blood.

We locked eyes across fifty feet of bloodstained stone. And I knew with absolute certainty: this wasn't over.

The Devil raised one hand. Not dramatically. Just raised it.

His voice cut through every sound. Every moan, every sob, every whispered prayer.

"Remain where you are."

Witness

THE COURTYARD FROZE.

People who'd been moving toward the injured stopped mid-step, hands outstretched. A man halfway to standing dropped back down. A woman reaching for the wounded froze, arm extended.

Everyone turned to face the Devil.

He stood in his crater of melted stone, perfectly composed. But there was something underneath the calm now—something cold and furious and absolute. Something that had been challenged and would not forgive it.

"You will bear witness," the Devil said.

His ember-red eyes swept across us. Where his gaze landed, people flinched. Shrank back. Tried to make themselves smaller, less visible, less likely to be noticed.

"To what defiance costs," he continued, his voice dropping. Forcing everyone to strain to hear. Making us lean forward. Making us complicit in our own terrorizing. "To what rebellion earns."

I felt Klaus beside me before I saw him. His hand found my shoulder—grip tight, trembling. Whether from fear or fury, I couldn't tell.

"Govirrod served me for three hundred and forty-seven years." The Devil's voice was quiet now. Deadly quiet. "Three centuries of loyalty. Of obedience. Of perfect service. And tonight, he chose to throw that away. To attack me. To seek freedom through violence."

The temperature dropped. Not gradually... instantly, viciously. My breath crystallized in front of my face. Around me, graduates huddled closer together, shivering despite their robes.

"Look at him." The Devil gestured toward Govirrod's corpse without taking his eyes off us. "Look at what freedom bought him."

I didn't want to look again. But I couldn't help it. None of us could.

The massive black dragon, cooling in pools of his own blood. Wings spread in final defiance, now just dead weight. Those gold eyes that had burned with hope—dark and empty now.

"Death," the Devil said simply. "And how many of you died alongside his rebellion?"

Silence. Heavy and suffocating.

"Count them," he said, and now there was something almost gentle in his voice. The gentleness of a knife sliding between ribs. "Go ahead. Count your dead."

Behind me, Maria's voice came out hollow and distant. "Twenty-six."

The number hung in the frozen air.

"Twenty-six," the Devil repeated, savoring it. "The price of one dragon's pride. Remember that. Remember what rebellion costs when you think about breaking your oaths. When you imagine there might be freedom waiting beyond these walls."

He paused. Let us all stand there among the bodies, freezing, waiting.

"There isn't."

The silence was absolute. Even the wind had stopped.

"But dragons," the Devil said, and his voice changed—became almost contemplative, "are not so easily replaced."

He moved. Not walking... just suddenly there, standing beside Govirrod's corpse. His hand rested on the black scales, almost tender.

"Govirrod made his lair in the deepest caverns beneath this lake." His fingers traced a scale's edge. "Centuries of dwelling there. Sleeping. Dreaming. Bleeding his magic into stone."

He looked up. Made sure we were all listening.

"Dragon magic does not simply dissipate when its bearer dies," he continued, quieter. Colder. "It pools in the places they've lived. It waits in the darkness. And sometimes... rarely... it crystallizes into something new. A seed. Raw Draconic essence, unformed and hungry."

Hungry. The word made my chest tighten.

"Govirrod's seed is down there now." The Devil's voice dropped to barely a whisper. Everyone leaned forward, straining to hear. "Growing wild without its creator. Feeding on the magic he left behind. If we do not retrieve it before tomorrow's Black Moon rises, it will consume itself."

He looked directly at me. Held my gaze.

"Or worse," he said, smiling. "It will hatch into something we cannot control. Something that remembers its creator's defiance. Something that inherits his rebellion. His rage. His hatred."

Around me, sharp intakes of breath. Whispered prayers. The thought of another Govirrod... wild and unbound... terrified them all.

But all I could think was: too convenient. Govirrod rebels and dies, and suddenly there's a seed that needs retrieving?

"The caverns are saturated with centuries of his power," the Devil said, still looking at me. Like he could see every doubt forming. "Unstable. Hostile. Flooded with dragon magic that will tear apart anyone foolish enough to enter unprepared."

He finally looked away. His gaze swept the courtyard.

"It will take powerful magic to navigate what writhes in the dark. Two weather-workers. Ice to stabilize the chaos. Lightning to cut through what pools in shadow."

No.

The word formed in my head before I could stop it. Before logic could intervene.

Because I knew. We all knew. There was only one lightning-worker powerful enough for what he was describing. Only one enforcer who could cut through dragon magic like it was tissue paper.

My eyes found him before I could stop them.

Alexi stood ten feet to my left, perfectly still in that way enforcers learned... spine straight, shoulders back, hands loose at his sides. Ready for violence or orders, whichever came first. The torn sleeve of his uniform exposed a muscled forearm, and there was a cut along his jaw he hadn't bothered to heal. Dark hair fell across his forehead, and even from here I could see the tension in his jaw. The rigid control.

Storm-gray eyes fixed on the Devil with an intensity that would have been defiance in anyone else.

In Alexi's eyes... it was resignation.

He knew too.

The Devil's gaze swept the courtyard, deliberate and slow, savoring our fear. "Dragon magic recognizes bonds. The forming of them..."

His eyes landed on me. Held.

Then shifted left. To Alexi.

"...and the breaking of them."

My blood turned to ice.

Around me, the crowd shifted. Whispers started... low, vicious, the kind that spread like wildfire. I could feel their stares. Feel their understanding settling over the courtyard like ash.

Of course. Of course the Devil would choose us. Two weather-workers. Ice and lightning. Former lovers whose relationship had imploded spectacularly enough that everyone knew the story.

Emotional resonance. Shared history. Intimacy twisted into something else.

We were perfect for what he needed.

Klaus's hand clamped down on my shoulder... hard, bruising. "No," he said, low and fierce. "Ilena, don't... "

But I was already moving.

Not thinking. Just moving.

Because I could see it happening... the Devil calling Alexi's name, Alexi walking forward with that terrible resignation in his eyes, descending into darkness saturated with centuries of hostile dragon magic. Going alone into whatever horrors waited in those caverns.

And I couldn't...

I wouldn't...

My feet carried me forward before Klaus could tighten his grip. Before Linda could grab my other arm. Before anyone could stop me.

The crowd parted. Fast. Like I was contagious.

Maybe I was.

I walked toward the crater, toward the Devil standing at its center like a wound in reality. Every step felt like wading through deep water. My legs shook. My heart hammered so hard I could feel it in my throat.

But I didn't stop.

Behind me, Klaus made a sound... wordless protest, fury, grief. "Ilena, goddammit..."

"Let her go," Maria's voice came, distant and hollow. Still lost in her visions. "It's already happened."

The Devil watched me approach. No surprise in his ember eyes. No satisfaction yet. Just... waiting.

I stopped at the crater's edge. The glass-smooth stone still radiated heat, shimmering in the cold air. Close enough to see my reflection in those terrible eyes.

"I'm ice," I said. My voice came out steadier than I expected. "You need ice to stabilize the chaos."

For a long moment, he said nothing. Just studied me with that inhuman intensity—like he could see every thought, every doubt, every desperate reason I'd stepped forward.

Then he smiled.

It was a terrible thing, that smile. Knowing and satisfied and almost... fond.

"Indeed," he said. "Ice to stabilize. Lightning to cut through. How fortunate that you volunteer."

Volunteer. The word hung between us like a blade.

I hadn't been commanded. I'd chosen.

And he'd wanted me to choose.

The realization hit like a fist to the chest. This... all of it... had been orchestrated. The speech about dragon magic recognizing bonds. The emphasis on emotional resonance. The deliberate pause after mentioning two weather-workers.

He'd been waiting for one of us to step forward. Needed us to choose it.

But why?

"Alexius." The Devil's voice cut through my spiraling thoughts. Sharp as broken glass. "Step forward."

I didn't turn. Couldn't turn. But I heard him—the measured footsteps, that controlled grace enforcers cultivated. All leashed power.

He stopped beside me. Close enough that I could feel the heat radiating from his body. Close enough to smell smoke and ozone and something wilder underneath.

Neither of us looked at each other.

"Two who were once lovers," the Devil said, and his voice dropped to something almost tender. Almost gentle. "Two who shared everything—magic, bodies, promises. Two who broke each other so thoroughly that eight years couldn't mend the wounds."

My hands clenched at my sides. Ice crystallized in my palms without conscious thought—sharp enough to cut.

"Perfect," the Devil continued. "Dragon magic feeds on such resonance. On betrayal. On wounds that refuse to heal. On love that curdled into hatred."

Beside me, Alexi's breathing changed. Barely. Just a slight hitch that I only caught because I'd once known every rhythm of his body.

"You will descend into the caverns," the Devil said, looking at both of us but somehow speaking only to me. "You will retrieve Govirrod's seed before the Black Moon rises tomorrow at midnight. Twenty-four hours."

Twenty-four hours. Alone together in darkness saturated with hostile dragon magic.

I'd just volunteered for this.

"The seed will not come willingly," he continued. "Dragon magic recognizes bonds—the making and breaking of them. It feeds on emotional resonance. On shared history. On intimacy twisted into something else."

He stepped closer. So close I could see the ember-glow of his eyes reflected in the glass-smooth crater.

"Fail," he said softly, "and the seed will consume itself. Or worse."

The threat was clear. Succeed, or face something worse than what we'd just witnessed.

"Master..." The word strangled itself coming out of my throat.

"You have until midnight tomorrow." He stepped back, voice rising to carry across the courtyard. "I suggest you don't waste time."

His hand came up. Touched my face... fingertips against my cheek. Ice-cold. Burning.

"The cavern will open for you," he whispered. "Or it will open for no one."

He released me. Stepped back. His voice rose, carrying across the courtyard.

"They have until the Black Moon rises tomorrow at midnight. Twenty-four hours, sealed in darkness with what Govirrod left behind. Two weather-workers. Ice and lightning. Enemies who were once lovers."

He looked at the assembled graduates. Made sure they were all watching.

"Let us hope," the Devil said, "that the seed is all they find down there."

The words hung like a curse.

"The rest of you will tend your dead. Heal your wounded. Burn your pyres before dawn."

He paused. Let them see his face in the firelight.

"And remember what you witnessed here tonight."

The cold intensified until my lungs burned. Ice crystals formed on my eyelashes. Around me, people shook, teeth chattering.

"Rebellion has a price," the Devil said, soft as falling snow. "And I always collect."

The cold vanished. Air warmed. Blood rushed back with painful intensity. People gasped, drawing desperate breaths.

But the threat remained.

"Enforcers," the Devil said, turning away. "Take them below."

Then he was gone. Not walking away... just gone. Reality folded around the space he'd occupied.

Two figures in black materialized from the shadows. One moved toward me, face covered except for dark, expressionless eyes. His grip on my arm was firm but not cruel. Just inevitable.

"Wait..." Klaus lunged forward, breaking free. "Lena, you can't..."

Linda caught him, arms wrapping around his chest. Her face chalk-white, composure shattered. "Klaus, don't."

"Let her go," Maria said, blood still trickling from her nose. "There's nothing we can do."

"The fuck there isn't..." Klaus twisted, but Linda held on.

"Klaus." Linda's voice was steel and silk. "Let her go."

I looked back at them. At Klaus's face twisted with helpless fury. At Linda holding him with shaking hands. At Maria swaying, lost in visions.

Helpless. Trapped. Unable to do anything but witness.

The enforcer's grip tightened. A reminder.

Alexi was already walking toward the eastern wall. Moving with that enforcer's stride... economical and dangerous. The firelight caught the strong column of his throat where ash had streaked the skin, the dark shadow along his jaw. He looked like some avenging angel cast down from heaven.

Beautiful and terrible and completely untouchable.

He didn't look back.

I wanted to scream. To refuse. But where would I go? The Devil owned us all, and rebellion earned death.

The enforcer pulled me forward.

We walked through chaos... graduates tending wounded, checking dead, putting out fires. The great hall gutted and smoking. And there, Govirrod's corpse. That mountain of scales going dull, blood steaming, wings torn.

Three hundred and forty-seven years. And this was freedom's price.

We walked through the smell of burned flesh and dragon blood, through water mixed with ash and gore.

Behind us, someone wept with long, broken sobs.

The eastern wall rose ahead—old stone, ancient. The entrance carved like a waiting mouth, surrounded by symbols I couldn't read but felt in my bones. Magic centuries old.

We walked toward the entrance to the deep cavern. The places beneath the lake, beneath everything.

Dragon lairs.

Into the Dark

THE STAIRS WENT DOWN forever.

I counted two hundred steps, then three hundred, then lost count as the walls closed in around me, and the stone was rough, worn smooth by something massive that had passed through repeatedly for centuries. The temperature dropped, then spiked, then plummeted again without warning. My breath misted white, then vanished, then appeared again.

The enforcer's lamp stayed at the entrance. After the first turn, darkness swallowed us whole.

Then the walls began to glow.

The light started as pale green, luminescence seeping through cracks where phosphorescent moss pulsed in scattered patches.

Crystals embedded in the rock glowed blue-white, stuttering like a struggling heartbeat.

Dragon magic. Centuries of it had soaked into every surface, still active though its source cooled far above.

I'd never felt anything like it. Power that made my own magic feel like a candle beside a forest fire, old beyond measure, and alive in ways I didn't understand. It pulsed through stone, through air, through everything. This was what dragons were. Not just creatures, but gods. Forces of nature wearing flesh.

Govirrod had lived here three hundred and forty-seven years, bleeding this power into the mountain's bones.

The air grew thicker, heavy like breathing through wet wool. A metallic taste coated my tongue as the weight of old magic pressed against my skin.

He walked ahead of me, each step deliberate and silent despite his exhaustion. Even covered in ash and blood, he moved with that predator's grace. His shoulders stayed loose, weight balanced, every movement precise.

"Watch your step," Alexi said. His voice echoed strangely, multiplying against the stone.

I watched the line of his shoulders, the tension in his spine. I tried not to remember his hands tangled in my hair, his mouth hot against my throat, or the way he'd whispered my name like a prayer.

It felt like yesterday and a lifetime all at once.

The stairs ended. We emerged into a cavern so vast that the far walls disappeared into darkness; the ceiling was lost somewhere above. Magical light pooled in patches, an eerie luminescence separated by deep shadow.

And everywhere I saw the marks.

Claw gouges marked the stone, each one as long as I was tall. Burn patterns showed where dragon-fire had scorched rock to glass. Deep grooves worn into the cavern floor revealed where the massive dragon had coiled for centuries.

This had been Govirrod's home.

"Christ," I breathed.

Alexi surveyed the space, jaw tight. "The central chamber will be deeper. That's where the seed would form."

"You sound certain."

"You pick things up." His voice was flat. "Eight years as the Devil's enforcer teaches you how he thinks." He started along the cavern wall. "We search systematically. Less than twenty-four hours."

I followed, keeping my distance. The ground was treacherous, shifting from jagged to smooth without warning in the dim light. The heat was oppressive. Sweat soaked through the silk of my borrowed dress, fabric meant for ceremony rather than survival. It clung to my skin like a second layer of misery. My feet were blistered raw inside heels designed for polished floors, not deceptive stone. I'd give anything for water. For boots. For any of this to make sense.

We had nothing. Just each other and time counting down.

A grinding sound echoed through the cavern. Stone shifted against stone, deep in the mountain's bones.

"Did you..."

The floor lurched beneath us.

I stumbled and caught myself against the wall. The crystals flared brighter, pulsing frantically. The grinding grew louder, closer.

"Move!" Alexi's hand locked around my arm and yanked me forward.

His skin was burning hot. And where his palm met my bare arm, I felt the crackle of wild magic, uncontrolled, searching for ground. My ice magic surged up to meet it before I could think, our powers tangling together as they recognized each other.

The ceiling came down.

Stone crashed where we'd been standing. Dust exploded outward, choking and thick. The impact sent shockwaves through the floor, and more sections started crumbling. The entire mountain was trying to collapse into the void Govirrod's death had left.

"There!" Alexi pointed through swirling dust at a tunnel mouth barely visible ahead.

We ran. Boulders the size of carts fell around us, missing by feet, by inches. The grinding was everywhere; the whole world coming apart.

We dove through the tunnel entrance as the chamber behind us collapsed completely.

The sound was deafening. Then, suddenly, silence fell.

I lay on rough stone, gasping for air. Every breath tasted of dust and magic and terror. My hands were scraped raw, blood welling from a dozen small cuts. But I was alive.

Beside me, Alexi pushed himself up slowly, favoring his left side. His torn uniform exposed skin at his ribs. Blood darkened the fabric, spreading slowly.

"You're bleeding." The words came out before I could stop them.

"I'm fine." He stood, then swayed, catching himself hard against the wall. His breath hissed between his teeth.

I got to my feet and moved toward him. "Let me see..."

"Don't." He held up a hand, keeping me at a distance. "Don't touch me."

"You're hurt..."

"I said I'm fine." But his voice was strained with pain. "It's nothing. Just... just give me a second."

I watched him breathe through it, taking slow, measured breaths while his jaw clenched and his hands pressed flat against stone. He forced the pain down through sheer will, that iron control reasserting itself as he became the Devil's perfect weapon again. Untouchable, unbreakable, and carved from stone.

It made me furious.

"You don't have to do that," I said. "Pretend you're fine when you're not."

He finally looked at me. "Yes. I do." His voice was flat. Final. "We keep moving."

He pushed off the wall and walked down the tunnel, limping slightly. Always walking away.

I followed because there was nothing else to do. The way behind us was blocked. Tons of stone sealed the tunnel entrance. We couldn't go back even if we wanted to.

The tunnel was narrow, walls pressing close on both sides. The crystal light was dimmer here, everything cast in a sickly blue. And the heat pressed down on us. Oven hot.

The air crackled with electricity. Static lifted the hair on my arms, making my skin prickle like a thousand needles. The smell of ozone hit me, sharp and acrid, leaving the taste of copper on my tongue. Lightning magic was building with nowhere to go.

"Alexi." I stopped walking. "Your magic..."

"We keep moving."

"Look at the crystals." They flickered in the walls, responding to the electrical charge. "You need to ground it..."

Lightning arced from his hands without warning. The bolt was wild, uncontrolled. It struck the tunnel wall, and the crystals exploded in a shower of sparks and shrapnel.

I threw up an ice shield too fast, panic driving the magic. It surged out of me in a wave, coating the entire wall in a three-inch barrier of crystalline ice. My heart hammered against my ribs as I fought to pull it back, to stop the spread before...

The ice held. It didn't creep forward. It didn't consume everything like The Wall.

I forced myself to breathe. Count. *You're in control.*

Alexi stared at his hands. Lightning still danced across his knuckles. He couldn't make it stop.

"Ground it," I said. "Now."

He closed his fists. The lightning flickered, dimmed and died. His breathing was harsh and ragged.

"What was that?"

"Nothing. The cavern's interfering... "

"That wasn't interference." I gestured at the shattered crystals and scorch marks. "That was you losing control."

His jaw clenched. He turned and started walking deeper into the tunnel, still favoring his injured side. "Keep your distance."

"If you lose control again... "

"I said, keep your distance!" His voice echoed off the walls, multiplying. Then he continued, quieter, "Just... stay back. Please."

The 'please' stopped me. I'd never heard him beg for anything.

He disappeared around a bend in the tunnel.

I stood there with my heart hammering. Scorch marks still smoked on the walls. Shattered crystals glittered like broken teeth scattered across the floor.

Something was very wrong with him. And he knew it.

I followed.

The tunnel opened into another chamber, smaller than the first, but the crystal formations here were enormous. Some stood as tall as I was, growing in clusters that pulsed with inner light. The heat they emitted was like standing next to a forge.

"There," Alexi pointed across the chamber.

Deep carvings in the far wall formed symbols. Ancient script, more than I'd seen before. Beneath the inscription was an opening, a passage, leading deeper into the darkness.

"That's where we need to go."

Between us and the passage stretched a field of crystal formations, each one glowing brighter and brighter, their temperature rising with every pulse.

"We can't cross that," I said. "The heat alone..."

He studied the crystals for a long moment, not answering. Just calculating. "Ice."

I looked at him. "What?"

"Your magic. Ice." He was still staring at the field, not at me. Working through the problem in his mind. "Cool the path enough to cross. It's the only option."

That was why the Devil sent me down here. Not as punishment, but as a tool. My ice magic, specifically.

"I can't..."

"You can." He still wasn't looking at me. "Your precision against raw heat. It'll work."

"You don't understand." My voice came out sharper than intended. "The last time I worked with this much power..."

"The Wall." He cut me off and finally looked at me, his eyes cold. "I know. Everyone knows. You lost control and people died."

The words hit like a slap.

"But that was two years ago," he continued, his voice flat and pragmatic. "And we don't have another option. So either you do this and we cross, or we don't and we're trapped down here when the cavern collapses."

"If I lose control..."

"Then we die." He turned back to the crystals. "But we die anyway if we stay here. At least this way we have a chance."

No faith. No reassurance. Just cold calculation and survival instinct.

It shouldn't have steadied me. But somehow, it did.

A deep rumble shook the chamber. The crystals flared brighter; the temperature spiking. The heat made my skin feel too small for my bones.

"We're out of time." Alexi's voice remained flat. "The whole cavern is collapsing. We cross now or we're trapped."

He was right. I hated that he was right.

"Fine."

I reached for my ice magic. It rose, cold and sharp, through my chest, spreading down my arms like frost forming on glass. My hands shook as the temperature around my fingers dropped, breath misting white in the super-heated air.

Don't think about The Wall. Don't think about the storm that wouldn't stop. Don't think about the bodies.

The magic rose inside me eagerly. Too eager. It wanted out. It wanted to spread, consume, and freeze everything.

No. Not like that. Controlled and precise.

I started forward, laying down ice as I went. Thin sheets crackled as they formed, already melting at the edges from the intense heat. I took one step, then two. The cold poured out of me, meeting the furnace heat in a violent collision. Steam rose in clouds, the air shimmering with the temperature war.

My hands shook. Sweat ran down my spine despite the cold I was generating. Every instinct screamed that I was going to lose it, that the magic would slip, and that The Wall would happen again.

Behind me, Alexi followed. I could feel his magic pressing too close, too intense. Storm and lightning and barely controlled chaos.

Halfway across, his magic spiked.

Lightning arced wildly and hit the nearest crystal cluster. For one frozen moment, nothing happened.

Then they exploded.

Crystal shards flew like shrapnel. Heat blasted outward in a wave. I threw up ice shields around us, above us, fighting panic as the magic surged. Too much. Like The Wall. Exactly like The Wall. Ice spread too fast, consuming everything in its path.

No. Stop. Control it.

Alexi's magic spiked again, wild lightning seeking ground. Without thinking, I grabbed his arm.

The contact was electric. Literal electricity flowing between us, his magic recognizing mine, our powers tangling together like they'd never been apart.

His lightning flooded into me. The sensation burned, overwhelming me. I felt it everywhere. In my bones, under my skin, between my thighs. The intensity was almost obscene. Heat and power and something darker that made my breath catch for reasons that had nothing to do with fear.

My ice magic rose to meet it on instinct. Cold against heat, order against chaos. The two forces crashed together inside me, and I gasped. Not pain. A response that felt dangerously like pleasure.

His hand closed over mine where I gripped his arm. Skin to skin now, no barriers between us. The magic intensified, and I felt his sharp intake of breath, felt the way his whole body went taut.

This was dangerous. This was...

Focus. Ground it. Don't let go.

I pulled. Drew his excess magic into myself, wrapped it in ice, and forced it down. The lightning fought me. His power was raw, primal, nothing like the controlled storms he used to command. It wanted to explode. Wanted to destroy.

But my ice was stronger. Had to be stronger.

The surge stabilized. The chaos calmed.

We stood there, my hand on his arm, both of us breathing hard. My whole body shook from the effort of containing that much power.

His skin was burning up.

"Alexi—"

He pulled away. "I'm fine."

"You're not..."

"I said I'm fine!" He turned away and started walking toward the passage. His steps were unsteady. Wrong.

I followed with my pulse hammering.

We reached the passage. Alexi leaned against the wall, breathing hard. In the crystal light, I could see his hands shaking.

"How much further?" I asked quietly.

"I don't know." His voice was rough. "The Devil said the central chamber would be obvious. Where Govirrod spent most of his time. Where his magic would be strongest."

"And if your magic keeps surging?"

"Then you ground it." He looked at me, and his eyes were definitely darker now. Almost black. "Like you just did."

"That was—" I stopped. What was I supposed to say? That touching him had felt like lightning and sex and drowning all at once? That I could still feel the ghost of it humming under my skin? "That was dangerous."

"Dangerous is letting my magic explode in a sealed cavern." His jaw was tight. "What happened back there worked. So if it happens again, you do the same thing."

"Alexi..."

"We don't have another option." He pushed off the wall and started toward the passage. Then he stopped but didn't turn around. "And for what it's worth... I felt it, too."

The admission hung in the air between us.

"The magic," he clarified, his voice flat. "Just the magic. Nothing else."

But his hands were shaking again, and this time I didn't think it was from fever.

He disappeared into the passage.

I stood there for a moment, hand still tingling from where I'd touched him. From the feel of his magic flooding into me. Storm and chaos and power.

This was going to kill us. One way or another.

But there was no choice except forward.
I followed him into the dark.

The Gallery

THE PASSAGE NARROWED UNTIL we had to walk single file. Crystal light barely reached here, just faint blue traces that made shadows jump and twist. The heat pressed in from all sides, thick enough to chew.

Alexi stumbled.

It wasn't much. Just a half-step, a hand bracing against the wall. But I saw it.

"Stop," I said.

"We keep moving."

"Alexi..."

"I said..."

Lightning arced from his hand where it touched the wall. The bolt was wild and sudden. The crystals there exploded.

I threw up ice shields on instinct, but this time the magic came smoother. More controlled. The ice formed exactly where I needed it, deflecting the worst of the blast.

Progress. Or maybe desperation was teaching me control.

Alexi jerked his hand back from the wall, staring at it. The lightning danced across his palm, between his fingers. He couldn't stop it.

"Ground it," I said, already moving toward him. "Now."

"Stay back..."

I grabbed his wrist.

The contact hit like a lightning strike to the spine. His magic flooded into me, raw and primal and desperate. But this time it was worse. Hotter. More chaotic. Like touching the heart of a storm that wanted to devour me whole.

I gasped, nearly letting go. The sensation was overwhelming. Heat and power flooding through every nerve, racing down my spine, pooling low and insistent between my thighs. My skin felt too tight, too sensitive. Every point where we touched burned with awareness.

His other hand caught my shoulder, fingers digging in, pulling me closer or holding himself up; I couldn't tell. We stood pressed together in the narrow passage, chest to chest, his magic pouring into me while mine rose to meet it with an urgency that had nothing to do with control.

Ice and lightning crashed together. Cold and heat colliding. The two forces met inside me, and this time I felt everything.

I didn't just feel his magic. I felt him. His fear was sharp as broken glass. His fever burning through his veins. The way his body was fighting itself, tearing itself apart from the inside. And underneath it all, threading through the chaos like a pulse, I felt a desire that was raw and undeniable, a recognition that went bone-deep.

He wanted me. Despite eight years of hatred and lies and broken trust, despite everything that should have kept us apart, his magic knew mine and craved the contact. His body pressed against mine told me exactly how much.

The knowledge should have made me pull away. Instead, my free hand came up to clutch his torn uniform, holding him closer.

"Ilena..." My name came out strangled. Warning or plea, I didn't know.

I pulled. Drew his excess magic down hard, wrapped it in ice so cold it should have hurt. Forced it to ground through sheer desperate will.

The surge stabilized. Slowly. Too slowly. Every second was an agony of sensation. His magic bleeding into mine, his body hard against me, his breath coming in harsh pants that I could feel against my throat.

When it finally calmed, we stood there in the narrow passage, breathing like we'd run miles. His forehead had dropped to rest against mine. When had that happened? I could feel his breath on my lips, could smell smoke and ozone and something wilder that made my heart jump and my body ache.

His hand was still gripping my shoulder. Mine was still tangled in his uniform. Neither of us moved.

"It's getting worse," My voice came out rougher than I intended.

He made a sound that was half laugh, half something darker. "Which part?"

Before I could answer, he pulled back, though not far. The passage was too narrow for more. Just enough to break contact, just enough that I felt the loss of his heat like a physical ache.

"I can handle it," he said, but his voice was rough. Strained.

"You almost couldn't." I fought to keep my voice level, clinical, fighting to ignore the way my body was still humming from his touch. "How long since the last surge? Less than an hour?"

His jaw clenched. He looked past me, back the way we'd come, then ahead into deeper darkness. Anywhere but at me.

"The dragon magic here—" I started.

"We keep moving." He pushed past me, continuing deeper. His shoulder brushed mine, and even that brief contact sent sparks of magic crackling between us.

My pulse hammered as I watched him go. The surges were getting closer together. More violent. And now I could feel his desire bleeding through the magic, raw and undeniable.

Was it just the cavern? Or was something else happening to him?

The passage opened abruptly into a chamber.

We both stopped.

It was smaller than the others we'd seen, but perfectly symmetrical. Carved, not natural. The walls curved up to form a domed ceiling, every surface covered in intricate relief depicting dragons, gilt with precious metals that shone in the light emanating from the crystals. Gold leaf still gleamed after what must have been centuries. The craftsmanship was exquisite. Each figure was carved in perfect detail, each scene flowing into the next like a story told in stone.

The artistry was beautiful. I could see the skill immediately. Faces carved with such precision I could read the emotions frozen there. Bodies caught mid-motion, every muscle and tendon visible beneath stylized skin. Wings poised to unfold. Fire shaped from gold that flickered in the light.

And it was absolutely horrifying.

Those beautiful faces were screaming. Those perfect bodies were breaking. Those wings were tearing through flesh and bone. The fire was consuming as much as it was creating.

"What is this?" I breathed.

Alexi moved forward slowly, fever-bright eyes tracking across the images. He didn't speak. Just stared.

I stepped closer to the nearest wall, trying to make sense of what I was seeing.

The mural showed figures kneeling before a central form. The Devil, unmistakable even in stylized carving. Beautiful and terrible, depicted in gold and shadow. Around him knelt supplicants, dozens of them carved with their heads bowed, their hands raised in prayer or pleading.

Bile filled my throat.

They were human!

I moved to the next panel in the sequence. The same figures, but they were changing. Bodies elongated. Limbs reformed. Spines arched backward at impossible angles.

The next panel showed more horror. Bones broke through the skin. Faces stretched, jaws dislocated and reformed into something else. Wings tore through shoulder blades in sprays of gold leaf that looked disturbingly like blood.

My breath caught.

The final panel in the sequence showed the completed transformation. Magnificent and terrible dragons carved in exquisite detail, every scale perfect, every claw sharp as blades. Golden chains wrapped around throats and wings, and legs, binding them to the Devil's will.

"No," I heard myself say. "That's not... that can't be... "

"Dragons aren't born." Alexi's voice was hollow. Distant. "They're made."

I turned to stare at him, not wanting to speak.

"Look around." He gestured at the walls. "Every sequence starts the same. Humans. All of them start with humans."

I forced myself to look. Really look. He was right. Panel after panel, wall after wall, they all began with human figures. And they all ended with dragons.

"This isn't mythology," The horror of it settling into my bones. "This is... this is a record. Instructions. The Devil doesn't find dragons. He creates them. From people."

From graduates, I realized with sick certainty. From tributes who knelt before him, just like those carved figures. From people whose shoulders he touched... people who had no choice.

Alexi had already moved on, drawn to another section. I followed, unable to stop myself. Each sequence told a different story with different outcomes and fates. Some ended in glory, dragons shown in their full magnificence. Others ended in ruin, bodies that couldn't hold the change depicted broken and malformed.

And everywhere, those golden chains wrapped around throats and wings and legs, binding them all.

"How many?" I whispered, looking around the chamber. How many people had the Devil unmade and reformed? How many centuries of this?

Then I saw what had stopped Alexi.

The far wall held the largest mural, dominating the entire space. It told a single figure's complete story... the transformation successful and devastating, centuries of service shown scene after scene. Battles fought, enemies destroyed, the Devil's will made manifest in scale and fire. Then came rebellion. The final scenes showed the dragon attacking the Devil. No chain could hold it. No binding could stop it. The very last image captured death, the dragon falling with wings spread wide in defiance.

"Govirrod," Alexi said.

"How do you know?"

"Look," he pointed to the final panel. "The gold leaf. It's still wet."

I stepped closer. He was right. The gilt hadn't fully set, gleaming with an oily sheen as it caught the light.

Govirrod had died hours ago, and this mural was still being completed.

As I watched, one of the carved scales seemed to shift and deepen. The gold flowing like liquid to add another detail I could swear hadn't been there a moment ago.

The mural was still forming. Still carving itself.

"Magic," I breathed. "The chamber is recording them. All of them."

I looked around with fresh horror. How many other murals were updating themselves right now? Adding last moments, last breaths, deaths that had happened hours or days or centuries ago?

"Like trophies," Alexi said, voice flat. Dead. "Centuries of people transformed, bound, used. All documented here. Forever."

He swayed. Caught himself against the wall.

I grabbed his arm before he could protest. "Sit. Now."

"I'm..."

"Burning up. I can feel it through your uniform." I guided him toward the center of the chamber where the floor was smooth. "Five minutes."

He didn't fight. That scared me more than the fever.

We sat surrounded by centuries of transformation etched in stone. The murals seemed to move in the flickering crystal light, shadows making the figures writhe.

"Why keep these?" I asked quietly. "Why immortalize the failures?"

"Power." Alexi's eyes were closed, head tilted back. "Reminding himself what he can do. What he's done."

"That's..." I trailed off. I couldn't find words adequate to the horror.

"That's what we serve," Alexi finished, voice bitter. "The Devil doesn't just bind dragons. He collects them. Studies them. Records every variation, every outcome. This is his gallery. People who'd knelt before him and been rewritten, body and soul."

I looked at Govirrod's mural again, studying that final scene of rebellion and the gold still settling into the carved stone.

"It's still forming," I said. "The magic is still... working."

Alexi opened his eyes. They were darker than when we'd entered, nearly black now, the amber buried under something else. "Adding him to the collection. Making sure his failure is remembered."

Something in his tone made me look at him sharply. "Your eyes..."

"I'm fine." But his hands were shaking. And when he stood, he had to brace himself against the wall.

The crystal light pulsed. For just a moment, I could swear I saw his shadow move wrong. Too large. Too angular.

Like something with wings.

I blinked, and it was gone.

"There's a passage." He pointed to the far side of the chamber. Another opening leading deeper. "The central chamber must be beyond."

"Alexi, wait..."

But he was already walking toward it, moving like every step took effort he was trying to hide.

I stood, looking around the gallery one last time at centuries of people transformed, bound, used, immortalized in gold and stone.

And somewhere beyond that passage, we were supposed to find a dragon seed. Raw Draconic essence, the Devil had called it.

But looking at these walls, at centuries of suffering carved into every surface, I couldn't shake the feeling we were looking for the wrong thing.

I followed Alexi into the passage. The images stayed with me - faces caught mid-scream, bodies breaking and reforming, Govirrod's rebellion still gleaming wet.

Dragon Seed

THE PASSAGE OPENED INTO vastness.

The chamber was a perfect sphere carved from living rock, walls so smooth they reflected light like black mirrors. Crystals were everywhere, floor to ceiling, some thin as my finger, others thick as tree trunks. All pulsing with blue-white light. All breathing.

Heat rolled over us. Not the oppressive warmth from the tunnels. This was alive, living visible currents that made the air shimmer and dance.

"This is it." Alexi's voice was rough. Strained. "The central chamber."

He took three steps forward and froze.

"What?" I moved beside him. "What is... "

Then I saw it.

A gargantuan heart the size of a man hung three feet off the ground, floating without chains or supports as magic suspended it in mid-air. Every crystal brightened and dimmed in time with the slow, ponderous rhythm of its beats. Veins of gold and crimson threaded through translucent flesh, light flooding through chambers and valves with each beat.

It was beautiful and horrifying and impossible.

"That's not a seed," I said.

"No." All color drained from his face. His hands started shaking. "No, it's not."

Lightning arced across his knuckles, wild and uncontrolled. He jerked like someone had yanked a rope attached to his chest.

He took another step forward, but it wasn't voluntary.

"Alexi..."

His boots scraped against stone, trying to dig in and hold position. His whole body went rigid, muscles locked in resistance. But his feet kept moving. One step. Another.

"Can't..." He gritted through his teeth. "...stop..."

I lunged, grabbing his arm to pull him back.

Pain exploded through the contact.

Not mine. His.

Everything he was feeling crashed into me like a physical blow. The compulsion dragging him forward like hooks in his ribs, the terror clawing at his throat, the magic tearing through his body. The burning.

I gasped and let go, stumbling back.

What the fuck was that?

A surge of power slammed through him. His back arched violently, head thrown back, a sound tearing from his throat that wasn't human. And I felt it, distant and muted, but there. An echo of his agony ricocheting through my chest.

The compulsion dragged him another step forward. Then another.

I threw ice at his feet. It formed and melted instantly, steam rising. I tried to block his path, but he shoved past me, gentle but inexorable. Like trying to stop a glacier.

He reached the center and stopped beneath that enormous heart.

He looked up.

His face went white. "No. Please... "

Slowly, his arm rose. It shook as he fought every inch.

His other hand grabbed his own wrist, trying to pull it back down. The attempt failed. The compulsion was too strong, written into the magic saturating this place.

I started forward, then stopped. If I touched him again, that pain would hit me full force. And if the compulsion could override his will, what would it do to mine? I might be the only chance we had, I had to hold back.

His fingers spread as he reached.

The hand touched the membrane.

His fingers passed through, then came away glistening with dark red liquid shot through with veins of molten gold.

He stared at his palm, transfixed. Lightning crackled up his arm, wrapping around the gold, pulling it into his skin like a parasite burrowing deep.

The heart pumped hard and fast, responding to his touch.

"I'm the seed," he said, voice hollow. "I'm what's being planted."

His magic detonated inward.

Lightning slammed into him from the inside out. He went to his knees. The sound that tore from his throat echoed off the walls, part scream, part roar as something broke inside him.

And I felt it. That echo of his pain, stronger now. Like something had opened between us that hadn't been there before.

I moved without thinking and dropped beside him, hands finding his shoulders.

Everything crashed into me at once.

His memories flooded through the connection like a dam breaking, eight years compressed into heartbeats.

Berlin in winter. Standing outside a warehouse at midnight, waiting for someone who never came. Waiting for me.

The Master appearing from the shadow. "She isn't coming." Offering answers. Offering proof.

A room with evidence spread on a table. Documents in my handwriting—reports on the trial configurations, notes on weaknesses in the cavern systems, dates proving I'd known what he'd face and deliberately hadn't warned him.

She knew. She always knew. She set me up to fail.

I felt his world crack open. Love curdled into something poisonous. Rage and betrayal burned through everything good we'd been.

But the contact forced it both ways. He was feeling my shock, my complete confusion, my utter lack of guilt about something I didn't understand.

Because I'd never written those reports. I'd never sabotaged anything. I had no idea what he was talking about.

The truth crashed through both of us like lightning.

All of it had been fabricated.

Something snapped into place between us, violent like a door slamming open that I hadn't known was closed. A connection forged itself in the space of a breath.

His eyes opened, nearly black with just a thin ring of amber left.

"You didn't know." The words came out with raw certainty, not a question. "The Master showed me documents. Your notes on the trials. Proof you'd sabotaged me." He gasped, fighting for breath. "But you don't... you have no idea what I'm talking about."

"I never wrote anything about your trial." My voice came out strangled. "I don't know what..."

"I know." He looked at me, and I saw it hit him. Eight years of hatred built on lies. "I can feel it. That you're telling the truth."

He could feel it the same way I'd felt his pain and his memories. Whatever had just snapped into place between us was still there, still open. I could feel him too... not his thoughts or words, just him. His terror, his pain, his desperate dawning horror at the lies he'd been convinced to believe were true.

Another surge was building. I felt the warning pressure in my chest that wasn't mine, like the air before a storm.

It struck him harder than the first time.

His back arched. I heard bones crack. The sound that tore from him wasn't human, and the echo of it rippled through me, making my own body seize.

I held on anyway, gritting my teeth against the sympathetic pain.

When it passed, he slumped forward, breathing in harsh gasps.

"The Devil fabricated evidence," I said. "Made you think I betrayed you. Kept us apart."

"Yes."

"Why?"

"Dragon magic." He looked up at the heart beating overhead. "Feeds on broken bonds. On emotional resonance. He needed us. Former lovers with a connection twisted into hatred and loss. The perfect fuel for transformation."

I looked at his hands.

Gold was spreading from his fingertips up his forearms, visible and real. Not just under the skin anymore but on it, faint tracery like someone had painted veins with molten metal. His nails were darker, harder, coming to slight points.

He followed my gaze and stared at his own hands, turning them over slowly as he watched the gold pulse with each heartbeat.

Silence stretched between us, heavy with the weight of years. What he'd been forced to believe. What the Devil had denied us.

His hand cupped my face, thumb tracing my cheekbone with a gentleness that made my throat tight.

"The library," he whispered. "What I said to you. What I wanted you to feel... "

"Betrayal?" I finished. "Anger? Confusion? Because that's all I've felt since graduation."

"Yes." His voice cracked. He nodded, "And you had every right to hate me for it. For all of it."

I should have pulled away and let the anger I'd carried have its moment.

But his hand was warm against my face, and in a few hours, he'd be a dragon, trapped or dead.

"Knowing why doesn't erase it," I said.

"I know."

Another surge was building. I felt pressure in my chest.

I kissed him.

It was desperate, raw, and overdue. I wasn't gentle, nor did I ask permission.

He made a sound against my mouth, surprise or relief or something darker. His hands framed my face, fingers burning electricity-hot against my jaw.

The surge hit.

His mouth opened under mine and I tasted ozone, copper and something wild that made every nerve sing. His uncontrolled magic crashed into me, chaotic and overwhelming.

My ice rose instinctively to meet his lightning. Outr touch created a path I understood now. His power bled into me while my cold wrapped around his heat, forcing it down, grounding it through sheer, desperate will.

His hands tightened, one sliding into my hair and gripping hard, the other dropping to my waist and pulling me closer.

When the surge passed, we stayed locked together, both shaking and breathing hard.

He pulled back just enough to speak. Forehead pressed against mine. "What... how did you... "

"The bond," I said. "Whatever just snapped into place between us is letting me help."

Alexi pulled back enough to look at me, those nearly black eyes searching my face.

"The Devil wanted us to have a bond," he said. "But after I was trapped as a dragon. That's what he planned. A connection formed through servitude and guilt. To control us." His hand came up, traced my jaw. "This wasn't supposed to happen yet."

"What is it?"

"The bond is magical and emotional," he said. His thumb brushed my cheekbone. "I can feel you. Your truth. Your fear. Your... " He stopped.

"The gallery," I said, understanding suddenly. "Those murals we saw."

"I thought the Gallery was a rumour," he said. " Maybe instructions for some ancient ritual." His laugh was bitter. "Not a record of everyone he's ever transformed."

"The successful ones serve," I said. "Bound in dragon form."

"For centuries. Govirrod served for three hundred and forty-seven years." His voice went flat. "He was trapped, unable to shift back. Was he aware? Could he remember being human?"

The weight of it settled over us. This was Alexi's future. Unless we stopped it.

"And the failures?" I asked, though I already knew.

"They're stuck between forms, part human and part dragon, bodies that can't hold either shape." His jaw clenched. "In constant pain until they die."

Another surge was building, faster this time.

It hit, and I grabbed him, pulled his magic down through sheer force of will. My ice wrapped around his lightning, containing the worst of it. When it passed, I was breathing hard.

"It's buying time," he said. "Slowing the transformation. Not stopping it, but..."

"How much time?"

He glanced at the sealed entrance where no daylight filtered through. There was no way to tell.

"Not enough."

I looked at his hands again. The gold had spread past his elbows now, creeping toward his shoulders.

The next surge came barely a minute later.

This time, when I grabbed him to ground his magic, something else happened. A flash of white light behind my eyes and suddenly we were somewhere else. A shared memory pulled from the bond, neither his alone nor mine but ours.

We were in his room at the Scholomance in winter. Both of us were younger, less broken. My body straddled his on the narrow bed, his hands gripping my hips as we moved together. The look on his face showed hunger and wonder, and absolute certainty. We belonged to each other; we were complete.

The memory shattered as the surge passed.

We stared at each other, both breathing hard.

"What was that?" I managed.

"The bond," he said. "Forcing itself open. Showing us...," He stopped. Swallowed hard. "What we were. Before."

Another surge came with another shared memory, this one softer. We were lying tangled together afterward, our hands clasped, fingertips dancing against each other. Both of us smiling, just happy.

The transformation was spreading faster now. Gold covered his forearms completely, with small patches appearing on his neck and jaw.

"How long?" I asked.

"By midnight, the transformation completes. The Devil comes. Performs the binding ceremony." His eyes met mine. "And then I'm trapped. A dragon, fully and permanently. Unless..."

"Unless we disrupt it."

"We'll probably die trying."

"Better than the alternative."

He almost smiled.

***

Over the next hour, the surges came faster, each one harder than the last.

Every time I pulled his magic down, the bond showed us fragments of moments we'd buried, nights we'd shared and the love we'd had before it all went wrong.

I saw his hands on my skin, my mouth on his throat. Both of us desperate and young, certain we'd have forever.

The transformation kept spreading. Gold had moved past his shoulders now, creeping up his neck toward his face. His nails were fully pointed. His eyes were barely human.

The next surge hit, the worst one yet. His magic detonated outward, wild and uncontrolled, threatening to tear him apart from the inside.

I didn't think. Just moved.

I kissed him hard and desperately.

His mouth opened under mine and I pulled his magic down with everything I had. The power crashed through me like lightning striking water. My ice wrapped around it, contained it, forced it to ground even as it burned through my control.

He gripped my waist hard enough to bruise. The sensation of his magic bleeding through his touch was overwhelming, too much and too fast, but I held on anyway.

The surge finally passed, and we stayed locked together, both shaking. His forehead dropped to my shoulder.

"Can't..." His voice was wrong, rougher, like his throat was changing. "Can't keep..."

"Yes, you can." I held him tighter. "Stay with me."

But my ice was cracking. Each surge was harder to contain. My own magic guttered like a dying flame.

Gold covered most of his visible skin now, spreading across his face, neck, and arms with only patches of human flesh remaining.

The power built again. I gritted my teeth and pulled it down, feeling something in my magic snap from the strain.

After it subsided, I glanced at the sealed entrance.

"Klaus," I whispered. "Linda. Maria. Someone."

But the seal held.

And the transformation continued.

His breathing went ragged, each inhale labored. The surges were coming every thirty seconds now with barely time to recover between.

I held him through each one, my ice cracking further with every attempt. My strength was failing.

Gold reached his hairline. His fingers were completely transformed. His eyes were almost entirely black.

"Ilena..." My name came out distorted. "Have to... let go..."

"No."

One more surge hit. I pulled it down with everything I had left and felt my magic shatter completely.

In the aftermath, I had nothing left.

He couldn't hold on anymore; his grip slipping from my waist.

I looked at the entrance one last time.

Dark. Sealed.

We were out of time.

And rescue wasn't coming.

Midnight Approaches

TIME HAD LOST MEANING in the chamber, measured only by the heart's relentless pulse overhead and the gold spreading across Alexi's skin like a slow-motion wildfire.

The kissing had stopped working. My ice guttered and died against the inferno of his magic. The last time I'd tried, nothing happened. I pressed my mouth on his while both of us shook, his lightning burning through me unchecked until I had to pull away gasping.

So now I held him.

He lay on his side, head pillowed on my thigh, knees drawn up slightly. It was the only position that didn't press against the wing nubs between his shoulder blades. He was unconscious or close to it. His breathing was shallow and too fast. Fever burned through him hot enough that sweat soaked through my clothes where we touched.

I traced the gold covering his face. The surface was smooth and warm, beautiful in a terrible way. His features were still recognizable but sharper now, his cheekbones like blades and his jaw more angular. When his lips parted with each labored breath, I could see his teeth had become pointed, not quite fangs but getting there.

His hands lay limp at his sides, completely transformed. Gold ran from fingertips to wrists, then to elbows, then to shoulders. Black claws had replaced his nails, longer than my fingers and sharp enough to cut stone.

I picked up one of his hands. The weight was substantial; the bones denser than human. The claws clicked softly when I moved his fingers.

He'd touched my face with these hands an hour ago. Cupped my cheek with such tenderness despite the claws. Despite the gold. Despite everything.

Now he couldn't move them at all.

I set his hand down gently. My fingers found his shoulder, traced down his spine to where the wing nubs had grown.

They were no longer fist-sized bumps but something larger and more defined. I could see the bone structure pushing up against skin stretched so tight it had gone translucent and purple-red from the pressure. The ridges of the forming wing bones were visible underneath like shadows through paper.

I touched one carefully. He didn't flinch or react at all.

The skin was hot and tight as a drum. And underneath, I felt movement. Bones shifting. Growing. Membrane forming in the space between reality and flesh.

It was going to tear through soon.

I knew it the way you know a storm is coming from the pressure in the air and the sense of inevitability.

My hands were shaking.

I pressed them flat against the stone floor, trying to steady myself, trying to think.

But all I could think was: I'm losing him.

I wasn't losing him to death. That would be cleaner. Kinder.

I was losing him to this. To transformation. To becoming something that couldn't remember what it had been. Something that would be aware but unable to communicate. Unable to shift back. Unable to be anything but a dragon for centuries while the Devil used him.

Govirrod had served for three hundred and forty-seven years.

How long would Alexi serve?

The thought made something split open inside me, a fissure in whatever wall I'd built to keep functioning, to keep holding on.

I looked at his face again, at the gold spreading up his temples, into his hairline, down his throat.

"Don't leave me," I whispered. My voice cracked on the words. "Not like this. Not when we just..."

I couldn't finish because I didn't know how to finish.

Because what had we done? Discovered the truth? Kissed desperately while his humanity burned away? Almost said things we couldn't take back?

Was that enough? Did it matter?

Would he remember any of it when he was a dragon?

His body jerked.

The movement was different from a surge.

He rolled onto his stomach with a choked sound. His spine bowed upward, vertebrae popping one by one. The sound echoed in the chamber with wet snaps that made my stomach turn.

I moved with him, hands finding his shoulders. "Alexi..."

The wing nubs swelled.

I watched the skin stretch tighter and tighter. The translucent membrane showed bone structure underneath, delicate struts forming a framework I recognized from the murals. Dragon wings. Beautiful. Terrible.

The skin split.

The membrane didn't tear. It erupted.

It burst through like something breaching water, black with gold veining, slick with blood and fluid I didn't have a name for.

Alexi screamed.

Agony tore from his throat, completely inhuman. It echoed off the chamber walls, multiplied, and came back at us from every direction.

I held on.

Bone pushed through next. White struts extended from his shoulder blades, membranes stretching between them as they grew and unfurled.

Blood followed, hot against my hands, soaking into my clothes. The smell of it was copper and the supernatural wilds that made the air taste like lightning.

Alexi convulsed, his spine bowing higher. The wings kept coming, kept tearing through. Membrane and bone and muscle all forced their way out through flesh that hadn't been designed to accommodate them.

I couldn't do anything but hold him. I kept my hands on his shoulders while his heart hammered too fast through his back. His fever burned me as he transformed under my touch.

"I'm here," I said. My voice was breaking. "I'm here, I'm not leaving..."

The wings spread.

They were four feet across, maybe five, and were still growing. Ragged skin hung where they had forced through strained flesh. Blood smeared everything, even the translucent black membranes stretched over bone like fine silk painted with gold veins resembling lightning frozen mid-strike. It was all beautiful, horrifying, and unmistakable dragon.

The convulsions slowed. Then stopped.

He went limp, face down on the stone.

For a horrible moment I thought he'd died. That his heart had stopped, and the transformation had killed him.

Then I felt his back rise with shallow, labored breathing.

I sagged onto him, pressing my forehead between his shoulder blades just below where the wings emerged. Both of us were covered in his blood and shaking.

The wings lay spread on either side of him, twitching slightly like they were trying to fold but didn't know how yet. Blood pooled on the stone beneath them.

He couldn't roll over with the wings like this, torn, raw and unable to fold properly.

I lowered myself down and lay on the cold stone beside him, facing him. Close enough to see his face. Close enough to touch.

"Alexi," I whispered. "Can you hear me?"

Nothing.

I touched his face where it pressed against the stone. The gold was warm under my palm. "Please. I need... I need you to..."

His eyes opened.

They were completely black with no white or iris, solid black that reflected the crystal light like obsidian.

But something flickered behind them: recognition and awareness.

He saw me.

His mouth moved, trying to speak. His throat worked, muscles shifting under golden skin.

What came out wasn't words but a rough and guttural sound that felt wrong.

He tried again. His face twisted with effort and frustration.

"I..." The sound was barely recognizable, closer to a growl than speech. "...rry..."

Sorry. He was trying to say sorry.

My throat closed. I pressed my forehead to his, both of us lying there on blood-slicked stone. "Don't. You don't have to..."

"Wall..." The word was mangled and slurred, like his tongue didn't fit anymore. "Lib—library..."

"I know." I kept my hand on his face, my forehead against his. "I know what The Devil made you do. I know you didn't want to leave me."

He made that sound again, pain mixed with something darker.

"He made you hunt people," I continued, raw and honest. "At The Wall...made you hunt... me..."

His eyes closed, like he couldn't bear to see my face while I said it.

"I understand." My voice cracked. "I was exonerated. But that doesn't erase it. Doesn't make it okay."

Silence fell between us, broken only by his labored breathing, the heart pulsing overhead, and us lying there face to face on cold stone.

"Part of me wants to hate you," I whispered. "For how that made me feel." I stopped and swallowed hard. "And part of me never..."

I couldn't say it.

The words stuck in my throat like broken glass. Love. I'd never stopped loving him despite everything. Despite eight years. Despite the absence. Despite all of it.

But I couldn't make myself say it.

His hand moved slowly and clumsily, gold fingers and black claws reaching across the small space between us.

I caught his hand and held it between both of mine. Pressed it to my cheek.

"I know," he said, the words barely comprehensible. "Can... feel... it... "

Whatever had formed between us when he touched that heart allowed him to feel what I wouldn't say. He could feel it bleeding across the connection like a truth I couldn't voice.

"If you don't remember," I said. "When you're a dragon. When the binding... "

"Will... " He stopped and tried again. "Will... remember... you. "

He said it with such certainty, such desperate faith.

But we both knew he was lying.

The gallery murals hadn't shown dragons who remembered. They'd shown centuries of service. Awareness trapped in reptile bodies. Human consciousness in inhuman forms with no way to communicate. No way to shift back. No way to be anything but what the Devil made them.

He'd serve for centuries, never remembering what it felt like to be human. To touch me. To kiss me. To speak.

The thought shattered something inside me.

The break was complete this time, a full rupture.

A sound escaped my throat that was neither quite a sob nor quite a scream but something between the two.

His thumb moved against my cheek, the claw careful and gentle despite its sharpness.

"Don't... " His voice was failing, each word harder than the last. "Don't... cry... "

I hadn't realized I was.

I reached up with my free hand and felt wetness on my face. One tear, but there.

I wiped it away roughly. "I'm not crying."

He almost smiled. I saw it in his eyes despite the gold. Despite the black.

Then his eyes closed. His hand went limp in mine.

"Alexi..."

His chest still rose and fell, still breathing, but he was unconscious again.

I lay there beside him on the blood-slicked stone. His hand between both of mine. His wings spread awkwardly on either side, forcing him to stay face down. His body was more dragon than human now. Gold covered everything except small patches on his torso. His face, hands, and voice were all transformed.

The chamber shuddered.

I looked up.

The sealed entrance showed fractures spreading through the Devil's magic like frost on glass.

Then came impact, hard and violent. The entire chamber shook. Crystals chimed. The heart overhead pulsed faster.

It came again.

Voices filtered through, muffled and distant.

"... break the fucking seal... " Klaus. Rage and desperation tangled in every syllable.

Hope flared in my chest, sharp and painful.

I looked at the entrance and watched the fractures spread wider and faster.

Another impact. The seal splintered. Black lightning tried to hold it together.

"... can't break it.. " Linda sounded strained and exhausted.

"ILENA!" Klaus again, screaming my name like he could force the magic to break through sheer will.

The fractures spread. But the seal held.

I watched them try. Impact after impact. Magic hitting magic. The sound was like thunder buried underwater.

The fractures reached the edges and started to seal themselves. Black lightning stitched the damage closed like sutures.

"No," I whispered. "No, please... "

One more impact came, weaker than the others.

The damage healed. The voices faded.

They couldn't break through.

But they'd tried. They were still out there. Still fighting for us.

"Not alone," I whispered to his unconscious face, my forehead still pressed to his. "We're not alone."

His wing twitched, like he'd heard.

I stayed there, lying beside him on the cold stone, still holding his transformed hand.I felt the fever burning through him, his wings trembling. Feeling his heart hammering through his back.

The heart overhead beat faster, responding to something I couldn't see.

I looked at the sealed entrance. No light filtered through anymore. Darkness filled the space beyond.

Night had fallen.
The Black Moon was rising.
And somewhere above, the Devil was coming.

The Binding

T**HE HEART OVERHEAD PULSED** faster.

My skin prickled as the air pressed down, heavy, cold, and suffocating.

The shadows in the corner moved. They didn't flicker. They deepened and gathered, coalescing into a pitch darker than the absence of light.

They weren't flickering but deepening, gathering into something darker than the absence of light.

The Devil stepped through them like a curtain parting.

Darkness clung to him, wrapping around his shoulders and trailing from his fingers. Then it slid away like oil on water, retreating back into corners.

In the chamber's crystal light, he was almost painful to look at. A beauty that made your eyes water. Symmetry so perfect it seemed artificial, like a face carved by an artist who'd never seen a real human, technically flawless but fundamentally wrong.

His smile was gentle, almost kind, which made it worse.

He stood beside the floating heart, and the golden light made his skin look translucent. I could see movement underneath, shadows and shapes that didn't belong inside flesh.

When he looked at me, his ember eyes caught the light and reflected it back doubled and tripled, like there were more eyes behind the ones I could see.

Instinct twisted my chest.

He looked down at us lying on blood-slicked stone.

"How touching." His voice was soft and amused. "You chose to stay with him."

I scrambled up and put myself between him and Alexi's unconscious form.

"Don't touch him."

"Or what?" The Devil glanced at my hands. "You have nothing left. I can feel it."

I reached for my magic and found almost nothing, a guttering flame where an inferno had been. He was right, but I stayed between them, anyway.

He laughed softly, genuinely delighted. "Brave. Futile. But brave." He slowly and deliberately circled us. "Do you know what I find most entertaining about weather-workers? You think your element defines you. Ice makes you cold. Lightning makes you fierce." He paused. "But fear makes you all the same. Desperate. Predictable."

"You broke us on purpose." My voice was steadier than I felt. "Eight years of lies. Making him hate me..."

"Yes," he said simply, like admitting he preferred wine to water.

"The fabricated evidence. The manipulation..."

"All of it." He stopped circling. "The Black Moon. The lottery. Govirrod's rebellion. The caverns. This heart." He gestured upward. "Designed to bring you here. To this moment."

The weight of it settled over me.

"Even the bond," I said. "When he touched the heart..."

"Especially the bond." That smile widened. "You think that was your choice? Dragon magic feeds on broken connections remade. I needed you apart. Grieving. Then together just long enough to rebuild." He looked at Alexi. "Perfect fuel for transformation."

My hands clenched.

"Why? You could have just taken him..."

"Where's the artistry in that?" He crouched beside Alexi and traced one clawed hand with a fingertip. "I've transformed thousands. It becomes monotonous." His eyes lifted to mine. "But breaking two people? Watching them suffer separately for years? Giving them one night of hope before taking everything? That's entertainment."

Ice erupted from my hands; everything I had left. Sharp, desperate shards screamed through the air toward his face.

He casually waved a hand, as if brushing away smoke.

My ice shattered mid-air, screeching like breaking glass. Fragments fell like harmless snow, melting before they touched stone.

I stood there shaking, my magic completely spent and nothing left but exhaustion and the weight of failure.

"I learned millennia ago never to attempt rebellion unless you're certain you can win." He brushed frost from his sleeve and looked at me with something like pity. "You are not certain. You are desperate."

He stood and turned back to Alexi. "Now. Let's complete what we started."

I moved to block him, but he didn't even look at me, just gestured.

An invisible force slammed into my chest and threw me back against the chamber wall hard enough that stars burst across my vision.

By the time I could breathe, Alexi's body was rising from the stone.

He wasn't standing but floating, lifted by the Devil's will like a puppet on invisible strings. His head lolled forward, chin to chest, and his wings hung limp, dragging. The torn membrane dripped blood that never reached the floor, suspended in air like everything else the Devil touched.

The Devil slowly raised both hands, almost reverently. He placed them on Alexi's floating form, one palm against his forehead, the other spread across his chest where his heart hammered too fast.

Golden light bloomed from both contact points. It poured into Alexi like liquid, following the pathways of his veins. I could see it spreading under his skin, gold branching through black scales, lighting him from within like he was made of stained glass.

"The binding is simple." The Devil's tone was almost conversational. "I share my essence. He receives it. The connection locks him permanently into dragon form. Unable to shift back. Unable to disobey." He glanced at me. "He'll serve for centuries. Watching you age and die while he remains. Watching everyone turn to dust. Until all that's left is service and memory."

Alexi's body jerked as his face elongated, and his wings grew. The golden light intensified.

"The binding completes in moments..."

Alexi's eyes opened.

They were completely gold and molten with slit pupils.

He saw the Devil's hands; the light pouring in, the chains beginning to materialize, golden, spectral, and waiting.

His mouth opened.

Thunder erupted.

The sound shook the chamber. Crystals cracked. The heart pulsed wildly.

"There it is." Satisfaction filled the Devil's voice. "The dragon's voice. Magnificent."

Alexi's eyes found mine past the Devil's shoulder.

I saw awareness there and recognition and fury directed not at me but at him. I understood in that moment—this was when the Devil opened himself, when he was vulnerable.

I pushed off the wall and staggered forward despite the pain in every step. I had nothing left except desperate hope, but I lunged anyway.

I moved fast and daringly, grabbing the Devil's wrist where his hand pressed against Alexi's suspended chest. My other hand found Alexi's sternum beside the Devil's palm.

The Devil's eyes snapped to me. "Don't—"

Too late. We made contact.

Alexi's lightning exploded into me through my palm on his chest. Raw power that felt like touching the sun. Every nerve lit up at once. My vision whited out. The taste of copper flooded my mouth.

The Devil tried to pull back, his hand starting to part from contact, but Alexi lifted a struggling arm and wrapped elongated fingers around the Devil's wrist to hold it in place.

"You dare..." The Devil's voice lost its smooth edge.

The lightning kept coming in wave after wave. I grabbed it with what remained of my ice, barely a whisper of frost, and forced it into shape, into a blade, into a weapon made of everything we had left.

The Devil yanked his arm with tremendous strength. I was lifted off my feet, still holding on.

The lightning struck.

It went through my grip on his wrist, through the contact where his palm met Alexi's chest. Ice and lightning combined, targeted at the binding itself.

The Devil's head jerked back as his eyes widened. "No..."

The golden light cracked, and the binding shattered. Spectral chains exploded as the Devil wrenched both hands free, grabbed my shoulder, and threw me.

I hit stone hard and rolled, unable to breathe. Alexi's body dropped and fell hard to the chamber floor.

The Devil stumbled back. He actually stumbled. He stared at his hands, where frost crawled across his palms.

"No." He wasn't angry but stunned. "You shouldn't... that's not... "

But he was already backing away toward the shadows.

The transformation didn't stop but surged forward unchecked and wild without the binding to control it. I rolled onto my side, my ribs screaming, and watched from where I'd fallen.

Alexi's body convulsed on the chamber floor. Bones cracked, not individual snaps but a continuous grinding roar like a building coming down. His spine elongated, vertebrae splitting and reforming. His chest expanded with wet tearing, popping cartilage and bone scraping across bone.

Then his body lifted, pulled upward by the transformation itself, rising and growing, vertical now, massive and still changing.

Those incredible wings unfurled in stages: five feet, then ten, then twenty, expanding like sails catching wind until they spanned almost a hundred wall to wall. Membrane stretched between bone struts, black silk shot through with veins of gold that pulsed with each heartbeat.

The air pressure dropped so fast my ears popped. Then popped again.

Wind screamed through the sealed chamber, hot one moment and freezing the next. It tore at my clothes and my hair, carrying the smell of ozone, rain, ancient, unknowable wilds.

Temperatures swung in violent extremes. My breath fogged, then the air burned my lungs, then fogged again. The stones beneath me cracked from thermal shock.

Alexi's face split down the middle, wet and horrible. His jaw extended forward, reforming into a muzzle lined with teeth like daggers. Eyes blazed molten gold, pupils contracting to slits. Horns erupted from his skull with sounds like breaking trees.

Scales rippled across every visible surface in waves, black as a starless sky. Each one was edged with gold that caught the dying crystal light and threw it back brighter. They overlapped like armor, like art that had never been meant for human eyes.

Branching electricity lit the chamber in harsh flashes while the smell of ozone and rain on stone filled the air. Storm made flesh. He was a dragon now, thirty feet of scales and wings and raw power standing before me, massive and taking up half the chamber.

Wind howled around him as the temperature swung wildly and lightning arced across the wings with each movement. His eyes opened, gold with slit pupils and crackling with barely contained storm.

He looked down at the Devil pressed back against the chamber wall.

And roared.

The sound was thunder itself, not like thunder but the living embodiment of it.

The chamber shook. The mountain shook. Crystals exploded. My bones vibrated.

The dragon lunged.

The Devil dove sideways and rolled. He came up already moving toward the shadows.

The dragon's impact brought the storm with it; his claws tearing through stone where the Devil had been while lightning blazed from his jaws to the walls. Wind battered everything as the chamber cracked and the ceiling buckled under the assault.

The dragon attacked again, with wings beating. Each stroke brought hurricane winds.

His jaws snapped as the Devil barely stayed ahead, stepping through shadows and reappearing, constantly moving.

The Devil was still smiling but wary now.

"This is why I bind them." His tone was almost conversational despite dodging. "Uncontrolled, they're magnificent. True tempests given form."

The dragon's tail whipped through the air and shattered a crystal pillar.

"You broke the binding. Clever." The Devil studied the dragon's eyes with something like pride. "Look at him. Beautiful. Powerful. Majestic beyond mortal comprehension." He gestured to the destruction, the storm, the magnificent creature wreaking havoc. "This is what I give the world... dragons. Tempests given form. Legends made flesh." That terrible smile appeared. "And someone must always pay the price for such gifts."

Another attack came with lightning blazing and thunder shaking foundations, but the Devil just laughed. "Enjoy your victory. If you survive it." He stepped back into shadow and didn't reappear, leaving a silence that fell heavy and absolute.

I was alone with the dragon in the ruined chamber.

He stood there, thirty feet of scales, one hundred feet of wings, and raw power. Wind still howled around him in visible spirals. His chest heaved. Each breath created a visible plume of steam and ozone.

Then his head turned slowly. Those gold eyes found me where I'd fallen against the chamber wall, bleeding, bruised, and barely able to stand.

For a moment, I wondered if he'd recognize me at all. If anything of Alexi remained in that massive skull, or if the transformation had burned it all away, leaving only dragon and only storm.

The surrounding gales calmed, not gone but settling, while lightning dimmed to a flicker across his scales. The wild cold front and heat waves steadied into a pleasant temperateness as his eyes locked onto mine, gold and crackling with barely contained energy. They were ancient and intelligent and so aware it hurt to see. Recognition flickered there along with understanding and something that might have been relief, gratitude, or just desperate hope.

"Alexi," I whispered as the chamber groaned above us. I looked up to see cracks spreading across the ceiling. The structural damage from the fight, the storm, and the dragon slamming into ancient stone had finally reached a breaking point. Stone ground against stone with sounds like the world ending before the ceiling split wide and began to fall.

Blood and Ash

THE CEILING CAME DOWN.

Not all at once; that would have been too merciful. Instead, it peeled away in massive slabs, each one breaking and echoing booms like artillery fire. The impacts sent shockwaves through stone that had stood for centuries, bringing down more debris in a cascading failure that filled the air with pulverized rock and the smell of ozone and magic gone wild.

I tried to move but couldn't. My body had nothing left.

Then Alexi was there, his wings forming a canopy of black and gold that turned the falling boulders into a drumbeat on his back. Each hit made him flinch. I felt it through the bond, sharp bursts of pain echoing in my chest. But he didn't move, didn't shift position, just kept his body between me and the collapsing mountain like that was the only thing that mattered in the world.

He was still protecting me, even like this.

Pain flooded through our connection. His pain: ceiling impacts, transformation still settling into bones that weren't made for his shape, magic churning wild and barely controlled. And underneath everything else, the fear. Not of the collapse or death. Fear of losing himself completely, of being trapped in this form forever, of becoming a creature that couldn't remember what it meant to be Alexi.

I'm here, I thought desperately, praying he could feel it through the bond. *I've got you. You're not alone in this.*

The gold eyes found mine and held. For just a moment, the world narrowed to that connection. Dragon and woman, storm and ice, eight years of separation compressed into one look that said everything neither of us could speak aloud.

Recognition flickered in those inhuman eyes. Understanding. Relief so profound I felt it in my own chest.

The chamber shuddered violently. Another section of ceiling tore loose, and the dragon shifted to cover it, his wings taking the brunt of the impact. I felt his pain spike through the bond, felt him fighting to stay conscious, to keep me safe even as the mountain tried to bury us both.

Suddenly, the eastern wall of the chamber blew inward, not from the collapse but from the other side.

Magic detonated through solid rock. Ice and lightning and compressed air all hitting the same point simultaneously. The stone face shattered, chunks flying inward, and through the smoking gap came rescue.

"MOVE!" Linda's voice cut through the chaos. "We're getting you OUT!"

Class of '76 poured through the breach like an avenging army. Linda came with ice coating her hands and murder in her eyes. Maria swayed on her feet, eyes distant and unfocused. She'd Seen this, guided them here. Thomas and Andrei supported each other, both looking like they'd burned through every scrap of power they had. Ana had blood streaming from her nose from magical overextension. Stefan Kovács appeared in an expensive suit, now in tatters, his face pale but grimly determined.

They'd fought their way through the mountain to reach us.

Everyone froze when they saw the dragon.

Klaus went white. "Mein Gott."

The dragon's head swung toward them with terrible speed. The wind picked up around him, and lightning crackled across scales.

"It's Alexi!" I grabbed for his leg, the only part I could reach. "They're here to help!"

The lightning dimmed, and the wind calmed. Those gold eyes tracked between me and the newcomers, calculating.

"Back through the lairs." Linda pointed through the hole they'd made, shouting over the falling rock. "Govirrod's routes. It's the only way out!"

Another section of the ceiling came down. The dragon's wings spread wider, sheltering all of us.

"GO!" Linda grabbed my arm, hauling me toward the breach.

We ran through passages carved by centuries of dragon inhabitation. Massive tunnels, wide enough for the dragon to move without scraping too badly. The walls glowed with phosphorescent crystals, pulsing with residual magic. Beautiful and eerie and ancient.

Maria led us with absolute certainty, eyes white with vision, following futures only she could see. "This way! Fifteen minutes if we don't stop!"

My legs burned, and my lungs screamed. But I kept running, kept pushing, because stopping meant dying, and I hadn't survived this long to give up now.

Behind us, the heart chamber imploded.

The sound was indescribable. Not just noise but pressure, a shockwave that hit like a physical thing. We all went down, humans stumbling while the dragon's bulk slammed into the passage wall hard enough to crack stone.

Then silence fell, heavy and absolute and somehow worse than the destruction.

"Everyone alive?" Linda's voice came out rough but steady.

"Define alive," Klaus muttered from somewhere in the dust cloud.

I pushed myself up, every muscle protesting, and looked back at the dragon. At Alexi wedged into the passage, wings half-spread, blood dripping from tears in the membrane where stone had caught and pulled. More blood than seemed survivable, streaking down black scales and pooling on ancient rock.

But his eyes were clear and aware. He was still himself.

His eyes closed briefly. When they opened again, something like determination flickered there.

"Keep moving," Linda commanded. "Those enforcers know something happened. We need to be gone before they organize."

We climbed.

The passage sloped upward, twisting through the mountain. My thighs burned, breath coming in gasps. Klaus kept a hand on my arm, steadying me when I stumbled.

The dragon came last, moving with surprising grace despite his size. Each step was deliberate; each movement calculated to avoid blocking our escape route. His wings dragged occasionally against walls but never stopped, never slowed.

He was still protecting us.

The passage opened suddenly into the grey dawn light of the courtyard. Into hell.

Half the Scholomance waited there. Graduates stood in ruined formal wear, faces pale with exhaustion and fear. Enforcers flanked them in black uniforms, hands on weapons. The Master stood in his crimson robes, looking older than I'd ever seen him, supported by Luminița who had blood seeping through white silk where she pressed a hand to her side.

Everyone turned as the dragon emerged behind us.

Silence fell like a blade.

Forty feet of predator. Black scales catching dawn light, wings dragging against the archway, blood dripping. Those molten gold eyes tracked every person in that courtyard with the kind of awareness that made you remember this was something that could kill you without effort.

Someone screamed. Short. Cut off fast.

"Hold!" The Master's voice carried despite sounding tired. "No one moves."

The enforcers didn't relax, but they didn't attack either. They just watched and waited, hands on weapons, bodies coiled.

I felt the dragon tense behind me. I heard the shift of scales, the scrape of claws on stone. He was ready to defend if they came at us, ready to kill if he had to.

Graduates slowly and carefully backed away, their eyes locked on the dragon.

Never dangerous.

The Master stepped forward, each movement careful; he was approaching a wounded animal and its response was unknown. He looked at the dragon, then at me standing beside him with one hand still resting on black scales, then back to the dragon.

His face went still.

"The binding failed." It was a statement, not a question. "What happened?"

"He opened himself to complete it," I said. "Made himself vulnerable."

The Master's jaw tightened. "The Devil?"

"Wounded. Escaped into the deep chambers. But alive."

"Then we are all damned." He breathed it, almost to himself. Then he looked at Luminița. Something passed between them. A look, years of shared service under the Devil's cruelty.

She moved forward despite her wounds, each step looking like it cost her. She stopped beside the Master. "The lottery is postponed. The Convocation is incomplete. You are dismissed to await further summons."

Murmurs rippled through the assembled graduates. Some sounded relieved; others, terrified.

"What about them?" An enforcer gestured toward me and the dragon.

The Master's expression didn't change. "They answer to the Devil. As do we all. When he returns, he will decide their fate." A calculated pause. "Until then, they are graduates of the Scholomance. Nothing more."

Translation: Not our problem. Let the Devil sort it when he's recovered.

Luminița moved toward us then. She stopped a few feet from the dragon and looked up at those golden eyes. "The binding broke before completion." Her voice carried that strange doubling again. "You can shift back, Alexi. The transformation isn't permanent."

The murmurs grew louder as confusion spread through the crowd.

The Master caught her arm, gentle but firm. "Don't. The oath binds me. If I help them..."

"I know what it costs." She turned to face him fully. Blood still streaked her temple. "I've watched you pay it for over a century."

"Luminița..."

"He almost killed me tonight. I threw myself between him and Govirrod. Bled for him. Nearly died for him." Her voice hardened. "And the moment I was no longer useful, he stepped over me like I was nothing. One hundred and sixty-one years of service. Dismissed."

The Master's jaw worked, and his hands trembled. Barely visible, but there.

"I'm tired of being disposable," she hissed. "Aren't you?"

A long silence fell. The courtyard held its breath.

"Yes." He exhaled the word and released her arm. "God help me, yes."

She turned back to the dragon and reached up slowly, letting him see her hand coming. She touched his muzzle where scales met softer flesh. Light flickered under her palm. Silver-white and ancient.

"Show them," she said. Not to the dragon, but to the courtyard. "Show them what the Devil never wanted anyone to see."

The Master's voice rose to address the crowd. "For centuries, the Devil has kept his greatest secret. Where dragons come from." He paused. "You're about to witness the truth."

An enforcer started forward. "You can't... the Master will..."

"I AM the Master." His tone cut like a blade. "And I'm tired of his lies."

Luminița looked at me. "Feel what he needs. Show him with your own body. You are ice. He's lightning." She gave me a slight smile. "You ground him. Always have."

I turned to the dragon, to Alexi.

His desperation crashed through the bond like a wave, full of the need to be himself again, and the terror that he'd lost the ability to be anything but this.

Come back, I thought at him. *Come back to me.*

I closed my eyes and felt my own body. Finding the boundaries of skin, the weight of bones, and the contained heat of blood moving through veins. Small. Finite. Human. Not a limitation, but a choice. I pushed that feeling toward him through the bond. Not words. Not images. Just the pure sensation of being less, of fitting into something smaller, of choosing limitation over power.

The dragon shuddered.

Then the transformation began.

Someone screamed. Multiple someones screamed. The scraping sound of feet across stone as graduates backed away, stumbling, filled the air.

But I couldn't look away.

It was pain made visible. Wings folded in too far, too fast, membrane tearing wetly. Scales receded with sounds like fabric ripping. The snap and pop of cartilage and crack and grind of joints relocating. The dragon shrank down and down and down. Forty feet becoming twenty, becoming ten, becoming six feet of man collapsing onto dirt.

The low, guttural and broken sob that tore from him during those final seconds wasn't human or dragon either. It was a cry from somewhere in between, something that made my chest ache.

Silence was stark as Alexi hit the ground gasping.

He was naked, covered in blood and ash, with wounds everywhere. Claw marks across his chest from the Devil's attack, burns on his forearms, bruises blooming purple across defined muscle. His eyes were still gold with slit pupils in that sharp-featured face. Patches of black scales scattered across his shoulders, down his ribs, along the backs of his hands. Permanent marks the transformation had left behind.

But he was human. Mostly human. Here.

The courtyard erupted.

"Dragons are HUMAN!"

"Christ, they were PEOPLE!"

"How many has he transformed?"

The Master's voice cut through the chaos. "Every dragon you've ever seen was once human. Graduates. Transformed. Bound. Trapped for centuries." His eyes swept the crowd. "The Devil's greatest secret. Now you know."

Luminița stepped forward, and for just a moment scales rippled across her skin. A flash of what she was underneath. "I was Class of 1823. I've served for one hundred and sixty-one years as his dragon." Her doubled voice carried to every corner. "Until today. Until they broke what I thought unbreakable."

She looked at the Master. "Run," she said simply. "Before he realizes what we've done here."

Klaus threw his coat over Alexi before I even processed what was happening. I dropped to my knees beside him in the dirt, hands finding his face, his shoulders, his chest where his heart hammered against my palm.

"You're you," I said. My voice broke on the words. "You came back."

His gold eyes found mine. Those new reptilian pupils that might never be fully human again. "Couldn't stay a dragon." His voice was raw, rough, and beautiful. "Not without you there."

Eight years of grief and rage and wanting him crashed through me at once.

I kissed him, desperate and raw and eight years overdue.

His hand came up, tangling in my hair. His other hand found my waist, despite his wounds, pulling me closer with a desperation that matched my own.

The bond flared between us. Not just magic but emotion, recognition, and everything we'd been denied for eight years flooding through the connection. His relief. My joy. The absolute certainty that this was right, and this was real, this was what we'd both been missing.

When we finally broke apart, I pressed my forehead to his. "I thought I lost you."

"Never." His voice was certain despite how rough it came out. "Not again. Not ever."

"Touching as this is," Klaus's voice cut through the moment, urgent and afraid, "we need to MOVE. Now."

A shout came from the gate. Enforcers were organizing, finally shaking off their shock. Some of the Devil's loyalists realized what was happening, what the Master and Luminița had just exposed.

"They're blocking the gates!" Ana's voice came sharp with warning.

Alexi tried to stand, but his legs didn't cooperate. New body, old reflexes; everything feeling wrong. He stumbled and would have fallen if I hadn't caught him.

"I've got you," I said, getting an arm under his shoulders. Klaus got the other side.

"Train station," Klaus decided, already moving. "Prague. We disappear before anyone gets organized enough to follow."

Linda appeared at our side, magic already coating her hands. "We'll hold them. GO!"

We moved toward the gate as fast as Alexi's unsteady legs would allow. Graduates parted for us. Some staring in horror, some in wonder. Maria gave us a nod. Others moved to flank us, adding their bodies to the protective circle.

Ahead, enforcers blocked the gate. Six of them with their hands on their weapons, young faces uncertain but following orders.

"Stop!" The lead enforcer stepped forward. "You can't..."

Lightning crackled from Alexi's free hand. Weak, unstable, but enough. The enforcer stumbled back.

"Try me," Alexi said, voice rough but dangerous.

The enforcers looked at each other, at the lightning, at the dragon who was human now but still had those predator's eyes.

They stepped aside.

Behind us, chaos erupted. Linda's voice rose in command. Maria's prophecy voice cut through the panic. The Master spoke in measured tones. They were creating confusion, creating cover.

We made it through the gate, into the village and down the path toward the station.

Alexi's legs were remembering how to work now. The stumbling became less frequent. But I kept my arm around him anyway, couldn't bring myself to let go when I'd just gotten him back.

His hand found mine and gripped tight. "Can you run?"

"With you?" His gold eyes met mine, and despite everything, the wounds, the exhaustion, the permanent changes the transformation had left, he almost smiled. "I can do anything."

We ran down the mountain path, through the village where windows stayed dark, to the station where a train sat waiting, steam already rising from its engine like it had been expecting us.

Klaus reached the platform first and yanked open a door to an empty compartment. "IN! NOW!"

We scrambled aboard just as the train lurched forward. Klaus slammed the door. We collapsed into seats. All three of us breathing hard, covered in blood and ash and eight years of accumulated trauma.

The Scholomance disappeared behind us as the train picked up speed.

Alexi slumped against the window, Klaus's coat wrapped around him, blood still dripping from wounds that should have killed him. But he was alive. Human. Here.

I sat beside him, unable to stop touching him. My hand found his, fingers lacing together like I were afraid he'd disappear if I let go.

"We made it," Klaus said, staring out the window in disbelief. "We actually fucking made it."

Alexi's thumb traced patterns on my palm. The touch sent sparks through the bond. Not sexual, just connection, recognition, the absolute relief of being together.

"Now what?" he asked quietly.

"Now we run," I said. "Until we figure out what comes next."

His eyes met mine. Gold, inhuman, and absolutely devastatingly aware. "Together?"

The word hung between us. A question, an offer, and a promise all at once.

I squeezed his hand and felt the bond pulse with certainty. "Together."

Klaus lit a cigarette with shaking fingers. "You two are disgusting. I love it."

Despite everything, the wounds, the exhaustion, the fact we were fugitives running from an ancient devil, I smiled.

I looked at Alexi. At the permanent changes the transformation had left: the patches of scales across his shoulders like dark constellations, the gold eyes with their reptilian pupils that would never go back to human grey, and the way his canines were slightly sharper than they should be. He'd never be quite human again. He'd never be what he was before.

But he was here. He was himself. He was mine.

And I wasn't letting go.

"Prague," Klaus said, exhaling smoke toward the ceiling. "We have contacts there. Places to hide."

"And after Prague?" I asked.

Klaus smiled, sharp and reckless. "After Prague, we figure out how to make the Devil regret ever fucking with the Class of '76."

Fugitives

THE TRAIN SWAYED WEST through morning fog, putting kilometers between us and the Scholomance with every minute that passed. Not enough kilometers. Never enough.

I sat across from Alexi in the cramped compartment, watching him try to hold himself together. The clothes someone had shoved at him during the escape hung loose on his frame. Better than Klaus's coat and nothing else, but not by much. He was still covered in dried blood and dust, still radiating heat like a furnace even though the morning air was cold enough to see our breath.

He hadn't spoken since we'd boarded. Just stared out the window at the passing countryside, jaw clenched tight and hands gripping the edge of the wooden bench hard enough that I heard the wood creak.

Klaus sat in the corner, smoking, one leg crossed over the other in that deliberate way he had when he was pretending everything was fine. His hands only shook a little when he raised the cigarette to his lips.

"How long to Prague?" I asked.

"Four hours." Klaus exhaled smoke toward the ceiling. "Assuming we don't get stopped at the border checkpoints."

"Will we?"

"Depends if word's gotten out yet." He flicked ash into the small tray by the window. "If the Devil's sent enforcers after us, we'll know soon enough."

Alexi's knuckles went white on the bench.

"Easy," I said quietly.

His eyes cut to me. Gold. Completely gold for a heartbeat before the amber fought its way back. "I'm fine."

"You're leaving marks in the wood."

He looked down at his hands like they belonged to someone else, then released his grip slowly, flexing his fingers. The indentations in the bench stayed. Five perfect crescents pressed into old wood.

"Sorry," he muttered.

"Don't be." I shifted forward, close enough that our knees almost touched. Close enough to feel the heat rolling off him in waves. "This is the same route Klaus and I took coming in. Remember? Except then we were afraid of what was waiting."

"And now we're afraid of what's following." Alexi's voice was rough. Unused.

Klaus stubbed out his cigarette and immediately lit another. "At least you're both still alive to be afraid. That's something."

The train rocked through a curve. Alexi flinched at the movement. Too much, too sensitive. Everything was amplified. I could see it in the way his jaw tightened, the way his eyes tracked every shadow that passed the window.

I reached across the space between us. Put my hand on his wrist.

His skin was fever-hot under my fingers. But he stilled. Went absolutely motionless like my touch was the only thing keeping him anchored.

"Stay with me," I whispered. "Stay human."

Gold flashed in his eyes again. His whole body trembled with the effort of holding the dragon at bay. Keeping the huge and wild supernatural creature that wanted to burst through his skin and bone from remaking him into scales and wings.

"Trying," he gritted out.

The train slowed. A station appearing through the fog.

Klaus was on his feet instantly. "I'll handle it. Don't move. Don't talk. Don't look at anyone."

He slipped out of the compartment before either of us could respond.

We sat in silence, my hand still on Alexi's wrist. His pulse hammered under my fingers, too slow and too hard. Dragon heartbeat in a human chest.

"How does it feel?" I asked.

"Wrong." He finally looked at me. "Everything feels wrong. Like I'm wearing someone else's skin. Like I'm too big and too small at the same time. The dragon is right there." He tapped his chest. "Right under everything. Waiting."

"You came back, though. That's what matters."

"Did I?" His voice cracked. "Or did I just trade one prison for another?"

Before I could answer, Klaus returned. Moving quickly but not panicked. "Just ticket check. We're clear. For now."

He settled back into his corner.

Outside, the station slipped away. The train picked up speed again, carrying us west. Away from the lake. Away from the Devil.

Alexi's hand turned under mine. His fingers laced through mine and held on like I was the only solid thing in the world.

We sat like that for the next three hours. Connected. Grounding each other.

Klaus smoked and watched the door and didn't say a word.

Prague station emerged through morning fog exactly the way I remembered it. Gray stone, steam rising from engines, that particular smell of coal smoke and dampness that meant Czechoslovakia.

Klaus was off the train before it fully stopped, scanning the platform like he expected enforcers around every corner. Maybe he did. Maybe they were coming.

I got Alexi moving. He was stiff and awkward, trying to figure out proportions that had shifted in ways too subtle to see but impossible to ignore. The coat barely covered him. His feet were bare. He looked exactly like what he was. Someone who'd just been remade and was still figuring out how all the pieces fit together.

"This way," Klaus murmured. "Stay close. Don't look anyone in the eye."

We moved through the crowd. Early morning travelers, workers heading to factory shifts, a few drunk students from the night before. No one looked twice at us. Three more disasters in a city full of them.

Klaus led us through back streets to the industrial district. It was mainly warehouses and loading docks, buildings that serviced the city's underground. Everything smelled like wet concrete and old smoke.

He stopped at a warehouse covered in layers of graffiti. The loading dock door was chained but not locked. Klaus knelt by the side entrance, felt along the doorframe, and pulled out a key that had been wedged in the crack.

"Friend runs raves on weekends. Empty the rest of the week."

Inside was a massive open space. Concrete floor stained with spilled beer and cigarette burns. Spray paint covered the surface, the walls and support beams, even the ceiling twenty feet up.

DJ equipment sat in the corner under tarps. A makeshift bar built from pallets and plywood stood off to the right of the tarps. Mattresses scattered around the perimeter. Most looked questionable. A few had blankets. Black plastic and duct tape covered the high windows. It smelled like stale smoke, old sweat, too many bodies.

But the ceiling was high. The space was open. If Alexi shifted, he'd fit.

Klaus dropped a bag on one of the cleaner mattresses. "Clothes. Vendor on the way here." He pulled out bread, cheese, and a bottle of something clear. "Food. Bathroom's back there if the pipes work." He hesitated. "Linda shoved money at me as we were running. Told me to keep you fed."

"Klaus..."

"Don't." He held up a hand. "Boarding house three blocks over. I'll come back tonight with news." He looked at Alexi, then at me. "Figure out what happens next."

The door closed behind him with a hollow metal clang.

Alexi stood in the middle of the warehouse floor, not moving, barely breathing.

"You should clean up," I said.

"Can't."

"What?"

"If I lose focus..." His hands were fists at his sides. "The dragon is right there. If I let go even a little, I might shift. And this place." He looked around at the high ceiling, the open space. "There's room, but the noise. Anyone could hear. Anyone could walk in."

I glanced at the loading dock and the side entrance Klaus had left unlocked; the windows covered in plastic that wouldn't muffle the sound of a dragon materializing in an industrial warehouse. He was right. Space wasn't the problem; security was.

"Okay. Then don't shift. I'll bring water to you."

I found a mostly clean bucket behind the makeshift bar, filled it at the industrial sink in the bathroom. The water ran rust-brown at first, then cleared to something almost drinkable. A rag hung on a nail near the DJ equipment. Questionable, but probably cleaner than anything else in here. I soaked it, wrung it out, and brought everything back to where he stood frozen.

I reached for the hem of his shirt. He caught my wrist, gentle despite the fever heat of his palm.

"Ilena..."

"Let me," I said.

His hand fell away.

I peeled the shirt off him and let it fall to the concrete.

The body I remembered was still there, mostly, but changed. Lean muscle, broad shoulders and the lightning-strike scar from a training accident on his left side all remained. But now scales scattered across his shoulders, down his ribs, and along the backs of his hands. They caught the dim light filtering through the plastic-covered windows with an iridescent shimmer. Purple, green, gold. His eyes were still amber, mostly, but the pupils were wrong. Elongated, reptilian, dilating and contracting independently. Fever-hot everywhere.

He turned slowly, showing me his back.

The scales down his spine were thicker there, following his vertebrae in a perfect line from neck to tailbone. Where wings had emerged and retracted, the skin was now silvered and scarred.

I reached out and traced the scales with my fingertips.

He sucked in a breath, his whole body going rigid.

"Does it hurt?"

"No." His voice was strangled. "Opposite."

The scales were warm, smooth, permanent. I traced lower, down his spine, counting each one. His breathing changed. Faster, rougher. My fingers reached the small of his back, where the scales ended.

He turned fast, and gold flared in his eyes. Complete dragon eyes in a human face.

"They won't go away," he said. "I tried to hide them."

"Good." I stepped closer. "I don't want them to."

His hands were shaking.

I took his hand and placed it on my waist, over my shirt. His fingers flexed, testing his strength, then settled gently despite the coiled power. We stood like that. Him shaking with restraint; me holding steady. The warehouse around us was empty, exposed and temporary. But for this moment, it was ours.

I touched his face. The skin was smooth but rough stubble. His eyes flashed between amber and gold.

"I'm not afraid of you," I said.

"You should be."

"Why? Because you can turn into something that could kill me?" I traced his jaw. "I've seen you as a dragon. You protected me even then."

"That was instinct."

"Was it?" I held his gaze. "We're not the same people we were eight years ago."

"No." His expression shifted. "We're not."

"But maybe we can figure out what we are now."

His eyes closed, and when they opened again, they were amber. Fully amber, human. His other hand came up, both on my waist now, careful, controlled.

His forehead dropped to mine. Connection without words.

We stood like that, breathing together, magic humming between us. Ice and lightning finding balance.

I reached for the bucket and wrung out the rag, then gently lifted his chin with my fingertips. His eyes closed as I brought the cool cloth to his face. The tension in his jaw softened as I wiped away the grime and dried blood.

A low sound escaped him. Almost a sigh.

When his face was clean, he looked like Alexi again. My Alexi.

I dipped the rag again and moved to his shoulders. The moment my fingers brushed the scales, his breath caught. His eyes opened, watching me with an intensity that made heat pool low in my stomach. His hands settled on my waist. He leaned against me, giving me access to the back of his neck.

I cleaned the blood and grime away carefully, revealing skin I remembered and new marks I didn't. Scars that told stories I'd never heard.

He lifted his head and looked at me.

"Your turn."

Before I could protest, he stood and reached for the ruined dress. His fingers found the fastening at my shoulder. The fabric pooled at my feet.

He took the rag from my hand, his other hand settling at the back of my neck as he began to wipe my face. The tenderness in the gesture made my chest tight. He paused to rinse the cloth, and the cold water trailing down my neck and chest raised goosebumps along my arms.

His hand moved lower, across my collarbones, down to the swell of my breasts. He paused at the clasp of my bra, his eyes meeting mine in question.

I nodded.

Skilled fingers, fighting with a body that was not quite his, remembered what years made muddy. The garment fell away.

The cool rag traced paths across my skin. My breathing hitched.

"Alexi..."

He smiled, the expression transforming his face from haunted to something warmer. He guided me toward the mattress, his touch gentle but certain. I sat, then lay back as he knelt beside me. He braced himself on one hand and leaned in to kiss me. Soft at first, then deeper.

"That isn't how you bathe someone, Alexi."

He said nothing, just kissed along my jaw, down my neck. His lips were warm against my skin as he moved lower, his breath hot as he reached my breast. His tongue circled slowly while his free hand cupped my other breast, thumb mimicking the same teasing motion.

His name escaped me as a breathy sigh.

He shifted his weight, stretching out beside me. His left hand slid across my stomach and beneath the fabric of my panties.

I gasped as his fingers found their mark, moving with confidence.

His mouth closed around my nipple as his fingers worked the growing wetness between my thighs. The dual sensation made my back arch.

"Please, Ilena."

I smiled at the sound of my name, rough and desperate.

"You may."

He pulled away long enough to remove the last barrier between us. When he lifted my leg and pressed himself against me, I felt the heat of him. He pushed forward slowly, and the sensation made me gasp. He was bigger than I remembered; the changes affecting more than just scales and eyes.

"Alexi!"

He froze. "The change... is it a problem?"

His expression was perfectly vulnerable.

I reached up and pulled his face to mine. "Don't you dare stop."

His smile was brilliant as his hips began to move. Slow at first, letting me adjust, then building to a rhythm that matched the rising heat between us. He kissed me, and while the spark of our power was there, it had no room at this moment. We were just us. Bodies and breath and eight years of need finally answered.

He shifted positions, each adjustment drawing new sounds from me. Pleasure built in waves, cresting higher each time. It was as if he was trying to make up for every missed touch, every lost moment, in this single span of time.

Finally, we collapsed together on the mattress. The light through the windows had changed. Afternoon had given way to evening, neon beginning to glow through the gaps in the plastic. The sounds of night workers filtered in, a low murmur in the background.

We looked at each other, breathless and smiling.

"Ilena... I..."

The side door banged open, interrupting.

We sprang apart. Alexi grabbed his shirt while I snatched the coat, both moving toward the sound on high alert.

"It's me," said Klaus's voice. "Don't shoot."

He came in with newspapers under one arm, a paper bag in the other that smelled like bread and something fried. He took one look at us and smirked.

"I see morale is improving."

"Fuck off, Smoke," I said.

"Charming as always, Frost." He didn't look at Alexi, giving him space to pull the shirt back on. "Word's spreading faster than I thought. Figured you'd want to see."

He dumped everything on the cleanest mattress. Czech, Romanian, Hungarian papers. The bread was still warm.

"News?" I asked.

Klaus spread out the papers, tapped the headlines. "Revolution. Hundreds of witnesses saw what happened. By tomorrow, every graduate in Europe will know what the Devil's been doing."

"And enforcers?"

"Looking for you. But they're focusing on Romania. Checking trains at the border, watching the usual safe houses." He lit a cigarette. "Prague should be clear. For now."

Alexi had gotten dressed; the clothes still hanging loose but covering the scales.

Klaus finally looked at him. "You two need to figure out what happens next. Running only works until it doesn't."

He headed for the door, paused. "I'll be back tomorrow. Try not to burn the place down."

Then he was gone, the door clanging shut behind him.

Leaving us with newspapers and the weight of what came next.

The Choice

For three days, publications arrived with Klaus. Occult newsletters, underground circulars, papers that circulated in communities like ours, never making it to mainstream presses but spreading through the networks that mattered. We watched the story spread from graduate to graduate, city to city. Headlines in a dozen languages, all saying the same thing: Dragons are human. The Devil enslaves his chosen. Centuries of lies exposed.

Klaus brought bread with the updates. We learned to exist in the space between what we were and what we might become.

And we waited for the other shoe to drop.

It dropped on the evening of the third day.

Klaus came in without knocking, moving faster than usual, his face grim. He had a newspaper folded under his arm, Czech, the ink still fresh.

"You need to see this."

He spread it on the mattress. Front page. Photograph of Lake Cincis, the compound gates, enforcers standing guard.

The headline: Devil Returns. Traitors Will Pay.

I read the article. My Czech was rusty but good enough. The Devil had returned two days after we fled, wounded but alive and furious. The lottery had proceeded. Ten graduates were chosen, their names listed. Five had fled rather than provide tributes.

Those five were dead now. Hunted down within forty-eight hours.

The witnesses who'd spread the story were being questioned, detained, punished.

The graduates who stayed were trapped. Compound locked down. No one in or out. They were bait, and we all knew it.

Alexi turned from the window, his eyes shifting to gold. His hands opened and closed at his sides, testing, restraining.

"How many?" His voice was rough.

"Dead? Five confirmed. Detained? Unknown." Klaus pulled out another paper, then another. "It's the same across all the publications. He's making an example."

Alexi's temperature spiked. I felt it from across the room; the air around him shimmering with heat.

"People are dying because we ran."

"People are dying because he's a monster." I stood. "We didn't create this."

"We broke it. Now he's..." Alexi gestured sharply at the papers. "How many more while we hide here?"

Klaus lit a cigarette, the flame briefly illuminating his face. "That's the question, isn't it?"

"You should go." Alexi looked at me, his eyes completely gold now. "Without me, you're just another graduate. He wants me, not you."

"Stop." I moved into his space, close enough to feel the heat radiating off him. "We've had this conversation."

"And I'm having it again." His jaw clenched. "Every day I don't surrender..."

"You think kneeling saves them?" I grabbed his arm through the borrowed shirt. "You think he'll just let everyone go?"

He pulled away and paced to the window. "I know they're dying because I ran."

"They're dying because they fought back." I followed him. "You surrendering changes nothing except you lose."

"And if I don't go back?" He spun faster than any human could move. "More bodies. More names. All because I..."

"Because he's choosing to kill them." I got in his face. "This is on him. Not you."

Silence fell, heavy with heat and magic barely controlled.

Klaus cleared his throat and pulled a folded paper from his jacket, worn at the creases. "Linda's been busy."

"What?" I didn't take my eyes off Alexi.

"Names. Graduates who want in when the rebellion starts." He unfolded it. The list was long. "Forty-three so far, spread across six countries. But they need a signal. Something to show fighting back is possible."

"Like killing a devil," I said.

"Like killing a devil," Klaus agreed.

Alexi stared at the list, then at me. His eyes flickered between gold and amber. "You're serious."

"We go back. We free the hostages. We end him." I held his gaze. "In front of everyone. So they know it can be done."

"That's insane."

"Yes."

"We'll probably die."

"Probably."

"And you're choosing this, anyway."

"I'm choosing you." I stepped closer. "I'm choosing to fight. Eight years ago I thought I lost you to his lies. I'm not losing you to his threats."

Something shifted in his expression, the gold fading as amber fought back. "We could run. Disappear."

"Is that what you want?"

He looked at the papers scattered across the mattress. The names of the dead. The list of those waiting to fight.

"No." The word came out rough. "I want to go back. I want to free them. I want to watch him burn."

"Then take me with you. As your rider."

His eyes widened. "I've never carried anyone. If I lose control…"

"Then we fall together." I smiled without humor. "Sink or swim. Right now. Tonight."

Klaus moved toward the door and paused. "I called Linda. Told her the rebellion was starting."

"What did she say?"

"It's about damn time." His smile was sharp. "Get out of Prague. I'll spread the word." He opened the door. "Don't die. I'd hate to have wasted Linda's money."

The door clanged shut.

The choice was made. No way back.

Alexi moved to the center of the floor, the open space where we'd been careful not to let him shift for three days.

"Stand back."

I didn't move.

"Ilena..."

"No."

Gold flooded his eyes and stayed there. The dragon rising, finally allowed.

He closed his eyes, took a breath, and let go.

The transformation tore through him violently. Lightning crackled across his skin as bones cracked and reshaped, the sound wet and terrible. Skin rippled as scales erupted in waves of black with iridescent shimmer. Wings burst through his back, membranes unfurling with sounds like wet canvas tearing. His body expanded rapidly, muscle and scale and raw power filling the warehouse.

His wing swept wide and caught a support beam. The impact sent concrete and rebar exploding outward. The ceiling groaned, deep and ominous. His tail whipped through the DJ equipment, sending turntables and speakers crashing. His other wing smashed through the makeshift bar, pallets flying. Every movement brought more destruction as another beam buckled and another section of ceiling sagged dangerously.

His head rose toward the rafters and cracked against them. The whole structure shuddered as dust and debris rained down.

Then he looked at me.

Those molten gold eyes tracked my movement, pupils slitted to razor lines. For a heartbeat I couldn't read what I saw there. The bond was there; I felt it humming between us, but layered over it was pure instinct. Predator awareness that calculated threat and recognized pack and rider all at once.

"Alexi." My voice came out steadier than I felt. "I'm here."

The dragon's head lowered, fast and aggressive, close enough that I felt the furnace blast of his breath. I reached up slowly and touched his muzzle where scales met softer skin.

He went absolutely still.

Then recognition flooded through the bond. Not the dragon learning who I was, but Alexi asserting himself. Choosing awareness over instinct.

The dragon's head pressed into my hand with deliberate care.

A support beam gave way with a crack like gunfire. Part of the ceiling collapsed twenty feet away, concrete slamming into the floor hard enough to shake the foundations. More of the ceiling sagged. We had seconds.

"We need to go," I said. "Now."

The dragon's wing swept toward me, creating a ramp of membrane and bone. I ran for it and climbed. The scales were scorching hot under my hands, like touching metal left in summer sun. He was moving, shifting weight, trying to turn in a space that couldn't contain him. I nearly lost my grip twice before I lunged for the ridge between his shoulder blades.

Another section of ceiling fell directly above us. His wings snapped up instinctively, catching the debris. The impact drove him down, legs buckling. I flattened against his neck, holding on as concrete and rebar crashed against wing membrane.

Then he surged up, throwing off the debris, and I felt something lock into place. The bond had been there since the caverns, but this was different. This was recognition of weight and balance, of rider and mount.

The warehouse groaned, the entire structure giving up. The collapse roared behind us.

"Go," I said.

The dragon launched forward. His shoulder hit the loading dock door, and wood and metal exploded outward. Night air rushed in, cold and sharp and real. We burst into the rail yard as the warehouse collapsed completely behind us, dust and debris billowing out through the broken door.

The dragon ran, his legs eating up distance across broken concrete and old tracks, building speed as his wings began to beat.

We reached the edge of the rail yard where open air spread beyond, Prague glittering below in lights and spires.

The wings beat down hard and powerful.

We launched into the air and immediately dropped.

The angle was wrong, the weight distribution off, everything new and untested. We fell, the ground rushing up, my stomach lurching into my throat. I felt his panic through the bond, felt him fighting to remember, to trust what the dragon knew.

"You've got this," I said against the wind. "We've got this. Fly."

The wings adjusted and beat down again. We dropped another ten feet, buildings getting dangerously close. The wings beat harder, changed angle, and caught air differently.

Then we weren't falling anymore.

We rose. The dragon's rhythm found itself, wings beating steady and powerful. Prague fell away beneath us. The warehouse rubble, the rail yard, the river cutting silver through dark. I felt what the old legends meant when they spoke of dragon riders as masters of storms. Our magic wasn't just combined; it was amplified. Ice and lightning woven together, each making the other stronger. This was what the Scholomance had been named for. This was the power they'd built a school to contain.

The dragon banked, finding his balance, and everything clicked. Not fighting gravity. Not struggling. Just flying.

We climbed higher, turning east toward mountains barely visible against the night sky. Toward Lake Cincis.

I leaned forward against his neck, felt the scales warm under me, felt the power coiled in every wingbeat, felt the absolute trust required to let him carry me through the sky with nothing but air between us and the ground a thousand feet below.

"Let's go end this," I said.

Reckoning

Dawn broke over Lake Cincis, red and gold bleeding across the eastern sky, staining the water below.

The dragon descended through the morning fog, wings beating slow and deliberate. Below, the compound sprawled across the mountainside with its stone walls, ancient gates, and courtyard where hundreds had witnessed the transformation four days ago. Enforcers moved along the walls, small as insects from this height. The gates were sealed. No one in. No one out.

The Devil's trap, baited with hostages.

But if Klaus's intel was right, the Devil didn't know about the forty-three.

Linda had moved fast, coordinating through the underground network. The list of names... Graduates who wanted their freedom would be in position, hidden in the treeline, behind outbuildings, along the access road. Waiting for this signal.

If they were there. If Klaus had gotten the message through. If Linda had pulled it off in time.

The dragon banked lower. Close enough now to see faces turning up, pointing. Enforcers shouting, scrambling. Someone rang a bell, sharp and insistent, the alarm cutting through the dawn silence.

We descended toward the courtyard. The same courtyard where this had started. Where Govirrod had fallen. Where Alexi had been taken.

Where it would end.

The dragon's claws hit stone with a sound like thunder. The impact cracked the paving and sent enforcers stumbling back. His wings spread wide, one hundred feet of membrane and bone, blocking the sun and casting the courtyard in shadow.

Silence fell. Everyone froze. Staring.

Then the movement began. Graduates emerging from hiding in the trees, behind buildings and from positions they'd held through the night as they waited for this signal.

Forty-three Solomonari surrounded the compound.

The gates burst open from inside with Cristina leading a group, breaking through wards she'd spent the night dismantling. Linda appeared on the eastern wall, having climbed up from outside. Thomas crashed through a window, dragging two enforcers with him.

Coordinated. Precise. Inevitable.

The dragon shifted beneath me, magic gathering, reality bending. I slid down his wing as the transformation began, hit the ground running as scales became skin, wings folded into shoulder blades, massive form compressing.

Alexi knelt on the cracked stone, naked and breathing hard but controlled. Faster than before. Easier.

I let myself look, really look. The transformation had left him lean muscle and fevered skin, scales catching dawn light down his spine like a river of dark jewels. Beautiful. Dangerous. Mine.

Someone, Ana maybe, threw clothes toward us. He caught them and yanked them on while I stood watch, though I wasn't watching the graduates or enforcers anymore.

Around us, chaos erupted. Graduates poured through the breaches Maria had created. Enforcers overwhelmed, surrendering weapons or fleeing toward the compound's interior. Magic cracked through the air as wards broke and defenses fell.

The Devil appeared on the balcony above the great hall. Not running. Not hiding. Standing in full view, like he'd been waiting for this.

Maybe he had been.

His voice cut through the noise, amplified by magic to fill the courtyard. "You brought friends."

I looked up at him. At the face that had haunted eight years of my life. At the monster who'd enslaved centuries of graduates, who'd turned humans into dragons, who'd built an empire on lies and terror.

"You made this war," I called back. "We're finishing it."

His smile was cold. "Are you?"

Then he raised his hand, and the real battle began.

Magic detonated across the compound. Not his, ours. Linda's voice cut through the chaos: "NOW!"

The coordinated assault I'd been hoping for materialized. Maria led a team through the eastern wing, wards shattering under her hands. Thomas and Andrei crashed through the western gates with a battering ram of compressed air. Graduates I didn't recognize poured over the walls, dropping into the courtyard with weapons drawn and magic crackling.

Enforcers tried to hold the line but were outnumbered, outflanked, fighting Solomonari who'd spent days, years, waiting for this moment. One by one they dropped weapons, raised hands, backed away from fights they couldn't win.

"The hostages!" Linda's command echoed from somewhere inside. "Free them first!"

Alexi and I moved together, pushing through the chaos toward the great hall where the Devil still stood. An enforcer blocked our path, young and terrified, lightning gathering in his palms.

Alexi didn't break stride. Lightning met lightning, his stronger, more controlled. The enforcer went down.

We reached the steps. The great hall doors stood open; darkness beyond.

The Devil was waiting inside.

The hall looked exactly as I remembered it. Crumbled and broken. Torches burned in iron brackets along the broken walls, casting dancing light across the floor. The space was massive, built to contain dragon transformations for ceremonial bindings. High enough, wide enough, strong enough.

Except the Master wasn't on the dais. Two figures knelt at the Devil's feet instead, at the base of the steps. Heads bowed. Absolutely still, like statues carved from flesh.

The Master and Luminița. Both in human form. Both wearing the same robes they'd worn when they'd helped us escape, now torn and stained. Chains wrapped around their wrists, not iron but something worse. Enchantment made physical, glowing faintly in the torchlight.

Around Luminița's throat, a collar. Gold, ornate, ancient. The visible mark of her enslavement. It pulsed with the same sickly light as the chains, tight enough that I could see her pulse beating against it.

Luminița's face showed healing wounds from her fight with Govirrod. Scars silvering along her jaw, claw marks across her shoulder where fabric had torn. Fresh bruises layered over the old. The Master's hands trembled where they rested on his thighs, not from age but from fighting whatever compulsion held him motionless.

They'd been punished for helping us. Beaten. Bound. Made to kneel and wait for this moment.

"I wondered if you'd come." The Devil's tone was almost friendly, like we were discussing weather instead of war. "The dragon and his rider. How romantic."

"Let them go," Alexi said. His voice was steady, but I felt the heat building around him, saw his eyes shifting toward gold.

"Let them go?" The Devil laughed. "They're mine. They've always been mine. Just as you should have been." He gestured at the Master and Luminița. "Ask them. Ask if they can refuse me. Ask if freedom exists for those who kneel."

The Master's head lifted slightly. His eyes found mine, desperate, apologetic, helpless.

"You enslaved them," I said. "Lied to all of us. Transformed graduates against their will."

"I gave them power." The Devil descended the steps, slow and deliberate. "Purpose. Immortality. What did you give them? Hope?" He smiled. "Hope dies. Power endures."

"Your power ends today," Alexi said.

"Does it?" The Devil stopped ten feet away. "You think killing me frees them?" He spread his hands toward the Master and Luminița. "They knew what helping you would cost. They helped anyway. Do you know why?"

Silence.

"Because they believed you could win. That someone might finally succeed in killing me." His smile was cold. "Hope makes people sacrifice everything for a chance at freedom. But even if you kill me, will the binding break? Or will they remain slaves to a dead master?"

He glanced at the Master. "Show them."

The Master's body jerked. Not wanting to move but moving anyway, rising to his feet like a puppet on strings. His hands came up, palms out, magic gathering. Not his choice, compelled.

"No," he whispered. "Please..."

"Kill them," the Devil said.

The Master's magic lashed out. Not a testing strike, but everything he had. Centuries of accumulated power compressed into a single devastating blast. His face twisted with horror even as his hands obeyed, tears streaming as he screamed denial through clenched teeth.

I threw up ice. Alexi's lightning met the attack head-on. The collision detonated between us and the Master, a shockwave cracking stone, throwing us back hard. I hit the floor and rolled, gasping. My ears rang. Smoke filled the air.

Through the haze, I saw Luminița lunge. Not at us. At the Devil.

She made it three steps before the oath caught her. Every muscle locked. The collar flared white-hot against her throat. She screamed, a sound that rattled the rafters, and collapsed to her knees. The smell of burning flesh filled the hall.

"Defiance," the Devil said, almost admiring. "Even now." He looked at us over Luminița's convulsing form. "But you see the problem. They can't harm me. The enchantment won't allow it. But you? They can kill you just fine."

The Master was already gathering power again. I felt it building, more desperate, pulling from reserves that should have been empty. His whole body shook with the effort of containing it while fighting the compulsion to release it.

At us.

His eyes met mine. Not the Master I'd known, the man who'd taught me control, who'd shown small kindnesses when the Devil wasn't watching. This was something broken. Something being forced to destroy the very people he'd risked everything to help.

"I'm sorry," he choked out.

Then he turned the blast inward.

The explosion was deafening. Stone cracked. The air filled with the smell of ozone and burned flesh. The force threw me sideways. When I could see again through the dust and smoke, the Master was on the ground.

Not moving. Blood spreading beneath him, too much, too fast.

Luminița's scream cut through everything.

She lunged for him, not attacking, just trying to reach him. The chains yanked her back. Harder this time. The collar seared into her throat, punishing rebellion. She collapsed halfway there, clawing at the stone, trying to drag herself to him.

"No," she gasped. "No, no, no..."

I pushed myself up, every muscle protesting. Staggered forward toward the man who'd taught me to control ice, who'd slipped me extra food during punishments, who'd helped us escape even knowing what it would cost.

Dead. Because he'd chosen death over becoming the Devil's weapon.

Rage hit like lightning. Not cold. Not calculated. White-hot and absolute.

Beside me, Alexi's breathing changed. Heat rolled off him in waves.

The Devil sighed. "Dramatic. But ultimately pointless." He looked at us over Luminița's broken form, over the Master's corpse. "Shall we continue? Or would you prefer to surrender now and spare yourselves his fate?"

Gold flooded Alexi's eyes. Heat built around him, magic gathering, the dragon rising closer to the surface.

"I need to shift," he said.

"Do it," I said.

The transformation took seconds. Faster than before, controlled, deliberate. Skin to scales, human to dragon, power compressed now unleashed. The hall was built for this, vaulted ceiling high enough to contain him, but barely. His wings scraped stone. His tail swept through torches, sending them clattering. The space that had seemed vast moments ago was suddenly cramped, filled with forty feet of muscle and scale and barely contained fury.

The dragon roared.

The Devil's smile finally faltered.

I felt it then, what the legends meant. Rider and dragon, ice and lightning amplified through the bond, woven together until I couldn't tell where my magic ended and his began. The power the Devil had built a school to contain. The power he'd spent centuries trying to bind and control.

Free.

The dragon's first strike hit like a battering ram. Lightning channeled through talon and fang, precise as a blade. I felt the power building through the bond, felt my ice weaving into it without conscious thought. Storm and winter merged, amplified, became something neither of us could achieve alone.

The Devil's shields flared. Held.

But I saw the cracks spreading.

He threw everything at us. Fire that should have melted scales, wind that should have torn wings, curses that had killed dragons before. The hall shook. Stone cracked. Torches exploded in showers of sparks.

The dragon didn't flinch.

Another strike. Lightning wrapped in ice, cold enough to shatter steel. The Devil's shields buckled. Fractured.

"NOW!" Linda's voice cut through from the courtyard, distant but clear.

I felt them join us. Forty-three graduates who'd survived the lottery, who'd been bound and used and terrorized. Their magic poured through every door and window, converging on the Devil like a tidal wave.

Storm and frost and fire and wind. All of it focused on one target.

The Devil's shields shattered.

He staggered back, robes smoking, eyes wide with something I'd never seen on his face before.

Fear.

The dragon lunged.

I leaned forward, hands pressed flat against scales that burned beneath my palms. Ice spread from my fingertips down his neck, across his shoulders, along his spine, until lightning crackled through every frozen surface. The bond sang between us, magic amplifying magic, rider and dragon merged into a single devastating force.

The Devil raised his hands. Tried to shield. Tried to fight.

Too late.

The dragon's jaws closed around his torso. Crushing, inexorable. I felt the impact through the bond, felt ribs crack and organs rupture. Lightning detonated inside the Devil's body at the same instant my ice froze his blood in his veins.

He screamed. No words. Just sound, raw and primal, and ending.

The dragon's head whipped sideways. Bone shattered. The Devil's body tore, magical and physical defenses failing simultaneously. His power unraveled like thread pulled from cloth, centuries of accumulated magic dissipating into nothing.

The robes caught fire from within, flesh burning, consumed by the very magic he'd hoarded for so long.

The dragon released what was left.

The Devil's corpse hit the stone floor with a wet, final sound.

Silence.

Then Luminița gasped. Her hand went to her throat where the collar had burned into her skin. The gold was fading, cooling; the light dying.

The oath was breaking.

The collar crumbled to dust, falling away from her neck. She sobbed, relief and agony tangled together, and dragged herself the last few feet to the Master.

She made a sound like breaking, high and thin and terrible. Collapsed over his body, her hands framing his face, thumb brushing his cheek like she could wake him. Like freedom meant anything without him there to see it.

"Please," she whispered. "Please, I'm free now. We're free. Please..."

But the Master didn't answer.

For the first time since her creation, Luminița was free.

But freedom had come too late for the man who'd helped make it possible.

What Remains

THE DRAGON'S FORM BEGAN to collapse.

Not slowly but all at once, like a puppet with cut strings. Scales receding, wings folding inward, the massive shape compressing as magic reversed itself. I scrambled back as forty feet of dragon became six feet of man.

Alexi hit the stone on his hands and knees, naked and trembling.

For three seconds he just breathed. Harsh, ragged gasps that echoed in the sudden quiet.

Then his whole body convulsed. He vomited something black and viscous that steamed where it hit the floor. The smell hit me instantly. Sulfur and charred meat and something underneath that made my magic recoil. Old. Corrupt. The Devil's essence, flooding out of him.

"Alexi..."

He heaved again, shoulders locked, muscles straining as his body purged every trace of what he'd consumed. When it finally stopped, he collapsed sideways, gasping.

I moved closer, staying just within reach. "Did I..." He couldn't finish, just gestured weakly at the puddle eating through stone.

"You killed him," I said. "Your body knows what that cost."

He laughed, broken and half-sobbing. "Tastes like Hell."

Ana had been checking the perimeter, but now she hurried over with a cloak. He grabbed it and pulled it around his shoulders, body still wracked with aftershocks, but alive. Human. Changed, no longer fully what he'd been, yet not enslaved either.

The great hall's doors burst open.

Graduates poured in from every entrance with weapons drawn and magic crackling, eyes wild. They'd felt it. The Devil's death. The binding breaking. Power unraveling across the compound like thread pulled from cloth.

They stopped when they saw the bodies.

The Devil's corpse, torn and burned and half-dissolved. The Master, blood cooling beneath him in a spreading pool. Luminița still kneeling between them, hands on the Master's face, freed but shattered.

Linda pushed through first with Thomas and Maria flanking her. She took it all in with one sweeping glance, already moving to the next problem.

"Compound?" Alexi's voice was raw.

"Secured," Linda said. "Enforcers surrendered or fled. We're freeing the hostages now." Her eyes found the Devil's remains, and satisfaction flickered there, mixed with disbelief. "Is he really...?"

"Dead," I said.

The word rippled through the crowd. Someone started crying. Someone else laughed, high and slightly hysterical. Most just stared like they couldn't process it.

"The binding?" Maria asked quietly.

Luminița's hand went to her throat. To unmarked skin where gold had burned for over a century. "Gone," she whispered. "All of it. I feel... nothing. No pull. No compulsion." Her voice cracked. "Just nothing."

More graduates arrived, wounded and exhausted but alive. They filled the hall, pressing close, needing to see for themselves. Needing proof that the monster was really dead.

Klaus emerged from the crowd beside me, breathing hard, blood on his uniform that wasn't his. He'd been coordinating the courtyard teams. He glanced at the Devil, then at me, then at Alexi wrapped in the cloak.

"You did it," he said.

"We did," Alexi corrected.

Scales traced his spine where the cloak had fallen open. His eyes still held that gold shimmer when torchlight caught them. He'd never be fully human again, but he wasn't a slave to dragon instinct either.

"Is it over?" someone called from the back, their voice young and hopeful.

Luminița looked up from the Master's body. Her eyes, ancient and exhausted, swept across the assembled graduates.

"No."

Silence fell heavy and absolute.

"When I was first bound," she said, voice carrying despite its roughness, "there were others. Other devils." She touched her throat. "I saw them in the early years. Fighting over territory. Over contracts. Over power."

The hall seemed to hold its breath.

"This one was ruthless," she continued. "He drove them out. Claimed their territories. Their servants." Her gaze found the Devil's corpse. "I thought he'd won. That he'd destroyed them." She paused. "But if they only fled, if they're still out there, they'll feel this. The void he left. All this power, suddenly unclaimed."

The temperature seemed to drop.

"They'll come," Luminița said. Not a warning, but a certainty. "Days, maybe. Weeks at most. But they'll come."

Fear rippled through the crowd. The collective understanding that killing the Devil hadn't ended anything. Just started something new.

"Then we fortify," Linda said. Her voice cut through the rising panic, sharp and clear. "We prepare. We hold this place."

"Against devils?" Thomas asked.

"Against whatever comes." Linda surveyed the hall. "We have forty-three weather workers. More if we count the freed..." She stopped and turned to Luminița. "How many dragons just lost their chains?"

Luminița's expression went distant, like she was listening to something the rest of us couldn't hear. "Six," she said finally. "Not counting me. Six others who served him."

"Where?"

"Scattered. The caverns. The compound. One fled already. I felt him go the moment the binding broke." Her words came hollow. "The others are uncertain. Terrified. Some haven't been human in decades. They don't know what to do with freedom."

"Can they be trusted?" Maria asked quietly.

"Can any of us?" Luminița met her gaze. "We were all his. All bound, all forced. The only difference is they wore scales." She pushed herself up from the Master's body, the movement stiff and painful. "They'll need help. Guidance. Someone who understands."

"You," Linda said.

Luminița nodded. "Me."

Movement at the back of the hall drew my attention. Four graduates approached, carrying a makeshift stretcher. Linda gestured them forward, and together they lifted the Master's body with careful reverence. His crimson robes, torn and blood-soaked, hung limp. His face looked peaceful now. No more fighting the compulsion. No more serving a monster.

Luminița's breath caught as they began carrying him toward the door. She took a step as if to follow, then stopped. Her hand went to her throat again, fingers pressing against the skin that would always bear the memory of that collar, even if the mark had faded. When she spoke, her voice was barely above a whisper.

"He died so I could be free," she said. "So all of us could be free."

Linda moved to stand beside her. Not touching, just present. Two women who'd survived the Devil's cruelty in different ways, now faced what came next.

"We'll honor him," Linda said. "Give him the rites he deserves."

"And then?" Luminița asked.

"And then we make sure it meant something." Linda's voice was steady. "We rebuild this place. Not his way. Ours."

Luminița straightened, and I watched the transformation happen in real time. The broken woman kneeling over a corpse became something else. Something harder. A dragon who'd survived one hundred and sixty-one years of slavery wasn't going to crumble now.

"No more lottery," Luminița said, her voice carrying to every corner of the hall. "No more tributes. No more children stolen from their families."

"The knowledge stays," Linda continued. "The library, the training, the magic. But voluntary. A school, not a prison."

"And we defend it," Luminița finished. "Together. Because when they come, and they will come, we'll need every advantage. Every resource. Everything the Devil hoarded for himself."

She looked around the hall at the graduates, the freed hostages, the few remaining enforcers who'd surrendered rather than flee.

"I'm staying," she said. "To help the dragons adjust. To protect this place. To make sure no one else claims what he built."

"I'm staying too," Linda said. She looked at Thomas, Maria, Andrei. "Anyone who wants to help rebuild, who wants to make sure this never happens again, stay. Everyone else..." She paused. "You're free. Truly free. The oaths died with him. Go. Live. No one will stop you."

The hall was silent for a long moment. Then Klaus shifted beside me.

"Someone needs to hunt the ones who won't wait to come here," he said. His voice was rough but steady. "The loyalists. The other devils' servants. The ones already moving."

"Agreed," Linda said. She looked at me, at Alexi. "And I think we all know who's best suited for that."

Alexi straightened despite the cloak, despite the heat still radiating from his skin. "We'll go," he said. Not asking. Stating.

"You just killed a devil," Thomas pointed out. "Maybe rest first?"

"No time," I said. Because I felt it too, the urgency, the weight of what Luminița had said. Days, maybe weeks. "If they're coming, we'll find them first."

Linda nodded slowly. "Mobile. Dangerous. Strike before they organize." She almost smiled. "Suits you two."

"Klaus?" I asked.

He looked at me, then at Linda, then back at me. Eight years we'd known each other. Eight years of him keeping me alive, keeping me sane, being the one constant when everything else fell apart. The weight of that history showed in his expression now.

"I'll stay," he said finally. "Help fortify. Get clean." He paused, and for just a moment the mask slipped. The fear showed through. "I need... I need to stop running."

I pulled him into a hug. Felt him stiffen with surprise, then relax into it.

"You kept me alive," I said against his shoulder. "For eight years, you kept me going when I wanted to give up."

"You did the same for me, Frost." His voice was rough. "More than you know."

When I pulled back, his eyes were bright. He cleared his throat and turned to Alexi. Extended a hand.

Alexi took it.

"You take care of her," Klaus said. "Or I'll find a way to make you regret it."

"Understood," Alexi said. Something like respect passed between them.

Klaus released his hand and looked at Linda. "Where do you need me?"

"Everywhere," she said. But there was something softer in her expression. "Start with the perimeter. Then we'll figure out the rest."

He nodded and turned to go, then paused. Looked back at me one more time.

"Don't die out there," he said.

"Same to you," I said.

Then he was gone, disappearing into the crowd of graduates already organizing, already moving forward.

Maria stepped closer to Linda with a report. "The wounded are being moved to the infirmary. We have seventeen critical, and another thirty with serious injuries. And..." she hesitated. "Twenty-six dead. Most from Govirrod's attack."

The number settled like lead in my chest.

Twenty-six people who'd come to witness a convocation. Who'd expected ceremony, not war. Dead because a dragon chose freedom and the Devil chose revenge.

"We honor them," Luminița said quietly. "Give them proper rites. And we make sure their deaths meant something."

"They did," Alexi said. His hand found mine, still warm but solid. Real. "They witnessed the end of his rule. That matters."

Around us, graduates were already moving. Linda organizing teams, Maria coordinating healers, Thomas securing the perimeter. The shock was wearing off, replaced by purpose. By the desperate need to do something, anything, to process what had just happened.

I studied Alexi. The scales visible on his skin, the gold that hadn't left his gaze, the changes that wouldn't fully fade. The man who'd become a dragon to kill a devil and somehow stayed himself through it all.

"When do we leave?" he asked.

"First light tomorrow," I said. "Give your body time to finish recovering. Get some actual clothes. Then we go."

He nodded and scanned the hall one more time. At the Devil's corpse dissolving in its own corruption, at the space where the Master's body had been, at Linda and Luminița standing side by side, already planning the defense of a school that would never be the same.

"We did it," he said softly.

"We started it," I corrected. "The rest comes next."

His fingers tightened on mine. "Together?"

I looked at him. At the man who'd been stolen from me eight years ago, who'd been transformed into a weapon, who'd fought his way back to humanity and chosen to stand with me anyway. At the bond humming between us, ice and lightning woven together, stronger for having been tested.

"Yes," I said. "Together."

Epilogue

DECEMBER 1985 - AUSTRIAN Alps

The dragon cut through storm clouds like a blade through silk.

I crouched low against Alexi's neck, ice spreading from my palms across his scales. Not to cool him, but to amplify. To merge my magic with his until lightning crackled along every frozen surface, until we became what the legends meant: storm incarnate.

Below, the monastery clung to the mountainside, ancient and heavily warded. According to Linda's intelligence, it housed something that was trying very hard not to be found.

Ready?

Not spoken aloud. The bond carried it, thought to thought, magic to magic. We'd learned that in the year since Lake Cincis.

Learned to blur the lines between rider and dragon until I couldn't always tell where I ended and he began.

Always.

He folded his wings and dropped.

The wards shattered under the combined assault. Ice and lightning, winter and storm, delivered with the precision of a surgical strike. We hit the courtyard in a spray of stone and frozen rain. The impact cracked paving and shattered windows.

Figures in black robes scattered. Some ran, which was smart. Three stayed, drew weapons, and gathered magic that tasted wrong. Old and corrupt and desperately trying to rebuild what we'd destroyed at Lake Cincis.

The dragon's roar shook the monastery walls.

I slid down his wing as the transformation began. Scales receding, form compressing, forty feet of predator becoming six feet of man. Controlled now. The shift took seconds.

Alexi hit the ground beside me, already moving, lightning crackling around his fists. Naked, yes, but we'd stashed clothes nearby. First, we had to deal with the welcoming committee.

The lead cultist threw fire. I sheathed it in ice mid-flight, turning it to steam that obscured their vision. Alexi went low, lightning arcing from his hands to the puddles left by our entrance. The current jumped, found two targets. They went down, convulsing.

The third was faster, smarter. She vaulted backward and sent a cutting curse that would have taken my head off if Alexi hadn't yanked me aside. His other hand came up, lightning condensed to a point, and released.

She blocked it. Barely. The impact threw her back against the monastery wall hard enough to crack stone.

"Surrender," Alexi said. His voice carried that doubled quality now, human with dragon underneath.

She spat blood and raised her hands again. "The new masters are coming. They'll..."

Ice encased her from the feet up. I didn't let her finish the threat. We'd heard variations a dozen times already.

"They're not," I said. "We'll make sure of it."

Alexi was already moving toward the doors, not bothering to check if the cultists would recover. We'd gotten efficient at this over the past year. Brutal, maybe, but we'd learned that hesitation got people killed.

I followed him inside, ice coating my hands, ready for whatever else they'd prepared.

The library was three floors down, hidden behind wards that would have killed anyone without our particular combination of talents. But ice broke the magical locks while lightning short-circuited the death traps, and we moved through the monastery like we'd done this a hundred times before.

Because we had.

Different locations. Different cells. Same desperate attempt to summon something that would fill the void the Devil's death had left.

The library doors opened to reveal exactly what Linda's intelligence had promised. A summoning circle carved into the floor, fresh blood still wet in the grooves. Candles arranged in patterns that made my skin crawl. And at the center, a binding contract written in a language that predated Romanian, Latin, even Greek.

"They were close," Alexi said, kneeling beside the circle. He ran his fingers along the carved symbols, and they sparked where his skin touched. "Another day, maybe two, and they would have succeeded."

"Good thing we're thorough." I let ice creep across the carved symbols, freezing them until they cracked and became meaningless. The contract at the center, I picked up carefully and incinerated with a controlled burst of cold that left nothing but ash.

Alexi stood and moved to the corner where we'd hidden our supply pack before the assault. He pulled out clothes and dressed quickly while I finished destroying the circle. The ritual was familiar now. Strike hard, disable resistance, destroy whatever horror they'd been building, and move on before local authorities got involved.

"Three cells destroyed in two months," I said, watching the last of the symbols crack under ice. "The Budapest devil dead. Half his network in pieces."

"And how many more out there?" He pulled a shirt over his head, and I caught a glimpse of the scales that traced his spine. Permanent marks of what he'd become.

"Does it matter?" I met his eyes. "We'll find them. Stop them. Keep hunting until there's nothing left to hunt."

He crossed the ruined library to me, warm hands finding my cold ones. "Klaus sent word yesterday."

"And?"

"The school's graduating its first voluntary class this spring. Twenty students. No lottery. No binding." He smiled. "Linda and Luminița are holding. The other dragons are adjusting. Two even asked to help us hunt."

I raised an eyebrow. "Really?"

"Apparently we're becoming legendary." He pulled me closer. "The dragon and his rider who killed the Devil and now hunt his remnants across Europe."

"Could be worse."

"We could be dead."

"We could be apart."

The word hung between us, heavy with the weight of eight years lost, of almost losing this again, of choosing each other despite every reason not to.

"Never again," I said.

He kissed me instead of answering, and I tasted lightning and smoke and the promise that we'd made a year ago when the Devil fell. That we'd see this through. That we'd hunt every threat until the darkness he'd spread was nothing but ash and memory.

When we pulled apart, voices echoed from somewhere above. Locals gathered, drawn by the noise and destruction. Time to go.

We climbed back through the monastery, past unconscious cultists and shattered wards, into the winter air. Snow had started falling while we'd been inside, covering our dragon's landing in white.

Alexi's eyes flashed gold. "Ready to fly?"

I took his hand and felt the bond settle. Familiar now, comfortable, strong as forged steel. Ice and lightning. Rider and dragon. Partners who'd learned to blur the lines until we were something neither of us could be alone.

"Always," I said.

The transformation swept through him in seconds. I climbed his wing while scales spread and reality bent around the change. By the time the shift completed, I was settled in the hollow between his shoulder blades, the place that had become mine over months of flying together.

He launched into the winter sky, wings beating strong and sure.

Behind us, the ruined monastery grew small. Ahead, reports of activity in Prague awaited. After that, whispers from the Balkans. An empire of darkness being dismantled piece by piece by two people who refused to let it rise again.

The Devil was dead.

But his legacy lived on in every cell we destroyed, every artifact we shattered, every devil-worshipper who thought they could rebuild what we'd torn down.

They were wrong.

We'd proven that at Lake Cincis when we'd killed their master. We'd proven it in Vienna when we'd burned their first attempt at resurrection. We'd proven it in Budapest when another devil had tried to claim the territory, and we'd ended him before he could establish his hold.

And we'd keep proving it for however long it took.

I leaned forward against Alexi's neck and felt him bank east, toward Prague, toward the next threat, toward whatever came after that. The bond hummed between us, ice and lightning woven so tightly now that I couldn't imagine existing without it. Without him.

We'd lost years to the Devil's lies and separation. But now we had each other, a purpose that mattered, and the absolute certainty that we'd face whatever came next the same way we'd faced everything since the Scholomance.

Side by side. Storm and Frost. Dragon and rider.

Together.

"Let's hunt."

The End

Acknowledgements

To Tony Fuentes, my co-author and partner in crime for over two decades of fabricating fantasy from the dust of dreams—thank you for encouraging me to finally write the dark romantasy I've been thinking about since we finished *House of Cards*. Your enthusiasm for Ilena and Alexi's story kept me going through every revision.

To Finn, our editor, who patiently pointed out every em dash and fragment while helping us find the balance between romantic tension and dragon transformation logistics—you made this book immeasurably better. Thank you for understanding what we were trying to achieve and pushing us to get there.

To the readers who've followed us from epic fantasy into this darker, spicier territory—thank you for trusting us with your time. Writing ice mages and weather magic felt like coming home, but adding dragons and romance? That was new territory, and we hope you enjoyed the journey as much as we did.

To the scholars and storytellers who've preserved Romanian folklore, particularly the legends of the Scholomance and the Devil's school—your work provided the foundation for this dark fantasy world. Any liberties taken with the mythology are entirely our own.

And finally, to everyone who's ever felt like they lost years to someone else's lies, who fought their way back to themselves, who chose love despite every reason not to—this one's for you. May you find your dragon, your rider, your storm and frost.

Side by side.

About the authors

SandDancer Publications

C.S. Kading and Tony Fuentes have been working together and crafting stories for over two decades. Partners in both mischief and memories, this dynamic duo combines real-world experience with formal education, to bring you stories to tickle your imagination and delight your hearts.

SandDancer was born out of the pandemic and a need to stay sane. We could not enjoy the company of others beyond the safety of our bubble, so we came to you the only other way we could - through books and storytelling.

The Authors

C.S. Kading

Literary Titan Gold Award-Winning Author

Charmain is a poet, playwright, and storyteller, whose love for writing began in 3rd grade when she won a district writing contest. Her love for fantastical forces motivates her to create stories of heroes, villains, gods, and monsters that often have a foundation in Old World mythology and legends.

MAED

Member: IASFA, IAN

indie B.R.A.G. Medallion recipient

Tony Fuentes

Literary Titan Gold Award-Winning Author

Tony is Renaissance Man in Geek's clothing; not only an author with a weird imagination, but also a painter, gamer, and part-time occultist. With his writing, he tries to spin humor into the world's grounded reality. At the same, he tries to get the audience to look into the stars and dream further beyond. In all things, he strives to give the weird and the wondrous things a place in the world for all to enjoy.

B.S. COMM

Member: IASFA

indie B.R.A.G. Medallion recipient

Also by

SandDancer Publications

https://sanddancer.pub/
https://sanddancerbooks.myshopify.com/

Sin City Shard Chronicles

House of Cards

The Realm of Gothika

Raise the Dead (a love story)
The Heart of Hanwi
Blood Tithe
End of the Line

www.ingramcontent.com/pod-product-compliance
Lightning Source LLC
LaVergne TN
LVHW091708070526
838199LV00050B/2314